Old Ways and New Days

Michael Embry

Old Ways and New Days

For six months, John had known his departure day was coming, when he first signed termination papers in the personnel office. It was a bittersweet time. At sixty-four, he already knew his days were numbered, so why not go ahead and finalize it? Maybe make the most of it? And he still had six months, which at the time seemed a long way off. And he would hit the Medicare eligibility a few weeks before waving goodbye for the last time. But time flies, whether you're having fun or not. And he wasn't. It was time to move on with his life, even if he no longer had an active career. He knew everything came to an end—the good, the bad, and all things in between—and sometimes the best course was to take the money and run.

The first month or so dragged by, but the countdown to retirement picked up a little momentum as each week passed. Before he knew it, there were only thirty days before he walked out of the newsroom for good. About that time he started gathering his personal belongings, more like mementos, such as newspaper clippings, political campaign buttons, sports memorabilia, and photographs. They were symbolic milestones that seemed miles away. They weren't worth much, at least to anyone else, but a few brought some intangible qualities that only mattered to him. Especially the photographs. They captured the memories of his newspaper career and the people he got to know through the years, even if there were a few faces he couldn't recognize. He could hardly recognize himself, posing with a thick head of dark brown, wavy hair, a bushy beard, thinner and more fit.

What They Are Saying About
Old Ways and New Days

"As a long-time and seasoned journalist, Michael Embry always allowed the story to tell itself. Now, as a novelist, he allows the story to tell itself...and at a riveting pace."

—Steve Flairty, author *of*
Kentucky's Everyday Heroes:
Ordinary People Doing Extraordinary Things
Series and columnist for Ky. Forward
And *Kentucky Monthly* magazine

"In *Old Ways and New Days* Michael Embry masterfully shines a spotlight on retirement and the realities and traumas facing millions of baby boomers. And, like most things lit by the harsh, unfiltered beam of a spotlight, not everything is rosy; just ask John, Embry's main character, as he traverses his first days out from under the world of work. This book is a must-read for anyone who wants to understand the realities facing retirees or who simply want to become immersed in a well-written, engaging novel."

—Bill Noel, author of
Folly Beach Mystery series

"If you are looking for lollipops and sunshine, *Old Ways and New Days* flat out ain't it, friend. Michael Embry's novel of a veteran newsman's retirement years is not filled with slow days on the back porch or vacation cruises. Instead, it's packed with violence and death, cancer and children gone wrong, lost dogs and lost lives. In other words, a hard, honest realistic portrait of life in America today, by a true craftsman of the written word. Read it if you dare!"

—Chris Helvey
Editor of *Trajectory Journal*
Author of *Whose Name I Did Not Know*

Old Ways and New Days

Michael Embry

A Wings ePress, Inc.
Boomer Lit Novel

Wings ePress, Inc.

Edited by: Jeanne Smith
Copy Edited by: Joan C. Powell
Senior Editor: Jeanne Smith
Executive Editor: Marilyn Kapp
Cover Artist: Pat Evans

Wings ePress Books
www.wingsepress.com

Copyright © 2015 by: Michael Embry
ISBN 978-1-61309-763-2

Published In the United States Of America

Wings ePress, Inc.
3000 N. Rock Road
Newton, KS 67114

Dedication

This novel is dedicated to the memory of Patrick Colburn Embry Sr. - 1960-2015.
Son to two, brother to six, father to two, grandfather to six and friend to many.

"To live in hearts we leave behind is not to die."
—Scottish poet Thomas Campbell (1777-1844)

One

"Big day."

John glanced at the doorway to his office where Fred Akers stood holding a cup of steaming coffee in one hand and a book in the other. A crooked smile creased Fred's thin, lined face, one that had aged beyond his years from smoking, too much coffee, lack of sleep, an appetite for junk food and a few alcohol concoctions of the bourbon variety.

"I suppose so," John said softly as he placed a paperweight in a box that contained other personal items on the top corner of his once-cluttered desk top. "It's not every day you get to retire and clean out your office."

"It sure beats the hell out of getting fired and having to go through that routine," said Fred, a long-time copyeditor who was content to work the copy desk and never venture too far from the newsroom except for one of his numerous smoke breaks. "I got the pink slip once, and let me tell you, it wasn't fun to pack up and leave. And it was humiliating."

John let out a small laugh. "I wouldn't know, but I'm sure there are some similarities in packing things up for the final time. My wife Sally would be proud to see I've finally cleaned out my desk. A lot of stuff, which she'd probably label as junk, has accumulated here through the years. She'd probably toss most of it in the trash. I think of them as tangible memories."

"Let me know if you need any help," Fred said, raising his cup slightly. "You know where to find me." If John had to guess, he would probably be behind the building in the designated smoking area, puffing away on a cigarette with a few other diehards.

John opened the middle drawer to keep or throw away an assortment of items ranging from a staple remover to expired membership cards. He was a confessed pack rat, and proud of it. He rediscovered a few things from his early years, such as an official press credential issued by the newspaper. He smiled at the yellowing card that showed him with long sideburns, then dropped it in a waste basket. At the time he had stowed them away, John thought they would bring back pleasant memories. Very few did. As he took them out, he could barely remember why he had kept them, along with an assortment of business cards, neatly stacked and wrapped tightly by a thick rubber band.

After twenty-seven years with *The Post-Chronicle*, he had reached that threshold when he was offered the opportunity to retire with a bonus buyout. So much for being indispensable. He could have opted to stick around a little longer but knew there was the real possibility he would be let go or laid off—a euphemism for getting fired—without the bonus. Everyone knew newspapers were downsizing everywhere, and the best way the corporate suits figured to maximize profits, stay afloat and keep the pencil pushers happy, was to reduce the size of personnel from all departments. Especially a few who commanded top salaries. Not that John was a rich man, but comparatively speaking, he made considerably more than a recent journalism school grad, but far less than one of the company's vice presidents. Corporate didn't seem to give a damn if it was losing institutional history along the way. For the most part, it knew little of the newspaper's history. The profit margin was all that mattered. That wasn't a secret to anyone in the business.

For six months, John had known his departure day was coming, when he first signed termination papers in the personnel office. It was a bittersweet time. At sixty-four, he already knew his days were numbered, so why not go ahead and finalize it? Maybe make the most of it? And he still had six months, which at the time seemed a long way off. And he would hit the Medicare eligibility a few weeks before waving goodbye for the last time. But time flies, whether you're having fun or not. And he wasn't. It was time to move on with his life, even if he no longer had an active career. He knew everything came to an end—the good, the bad, and all things in between—and sometimes the best course was to take the money and run.

The first month or so dragged by, but the countdown to retirement picked up a little momentum as each week passed. Before he knew it, there were only thirty days before he walked out of the newsroom for good. About that time, he started gathering his personal belongings, more like mementos, such as newspaper clippings, political campaign buttons, sports memorabilia, and photographs. They were symbolic milestones that seemed miles away. They weren't worth much, at least to anyone else, but a few brought some intangible qualities that only mattered to him. Especially the photographs. They captured the memories of his newspaper career and the people he got to know through the years, even if there were a few faces he couldn't recognize. He could hardly recognize himself, thinner and more fit, posing with a thick head of dark brown, wavy hair, a bushy beard.

John stepped to the door and surveyed the newsroom for a few seconds. A handful of reporters were typing on stories in their gray, impersonal cubicles, also known as workstations, that were to be kept clean and tidy. So much for individualism. Section editors were gathered in a white-walled room, adorned with gold or silver plaques for numerous awards for various stories, editorials, and community involvements. They were going over the day's budget of news events as well as tentative story and photo placements. They'd reconvene a few more times during the day to finalize the latest edition. He would normally be there, providing an update on the top sports stories. In the past two weeks, he had relinquished that responsibility to Eric Walsh, his assistant for the past four years. John wasn't going to miss those meetings. He admittedly wasn't a meeting kind of guy and didn't hide his feelings about it from others in the newsroom.

He thought these meetings had become so stale, almost scripted, that he could predict with ninety-nine percent accuracy before sitting at the table what would be said and done. They lacked the buzz and excitement from his early days, when the newspaper was flourishing both editorially and financially, and reporters were working their beats and typing their stories on coffee-stained desks to top the competition on breaking news. And truth be told, he had been more enthusiastic and energetic as well. The fire inside his belly now was more like a flickering flame. He didn't have the drive and eagerness in his bones unless it was a really big story. And there weren't many of those coming down the pike. As a pundit told him when he started in the newspaper business, and he had begun to understand a few years ago, "...only the names change while the stories remain the same."

John walked over to the window overlooking a small park across the road. Watching several people meandering along the concrete walk and others chatting on the green aluminum benches, he thought about how the media had changed during his career. News competition wasn't what it used to be either, as radio stations cleared out news staffs and other local personalities and opted for programmed entertainment or syndicated extremist talk shows. Television stations found profitability in doing much the same, relying more on fluff-and-puff feature stories, focusing on sordid domestic crimes, sensationalizing weather forecasts, and cheerleading for local sports teams. The primary competition came from the Internet, where journalists, former journalists, some would-be journalists, and a few with expressed unfounded opinions would rehash the events of the day. John knew it wasn't true competition but wasn't sure if the public was aware of that anymore, as news became more blurred and the boundaries broadened. And those folks in the new media knew how to corral the advertising dollars.

"Everything okay?"

Startled for a moment, John turned and smiled at Eric, who was standing at the doorway. "Just lost in some thought. Going through these things conjure up some memories. Good and bad."

"I can imagine. You've put in a lot of years." Eric, who was young enough to be his son, held a clipboard with a list of upcoming stories from the budget meeting. The ceiling light glistened off the diamond stud in his left ear.

"And it'll be over in a couple hours." John managed a weak smile. "That's enough about me. What's the big story today?"

"Sports or otherwise?"

"Both."

"Uh, the injury to Gomez appears more serious than first suspected. It may be a stress fracture in his foot. As for the news side, the audit of the city's recreation department is expected to be released tomorrow."

"Hot news. Stop the presses!" John knew it sounded sarcastic when the words came out and immediately wished he hadn't said anything.

"You go with what you have," Eric said, raising his eyebrows.

"I know," John said. "Something new each day to keep the paper fresh."

"Well, I need to talk with the layout folks and copyeditors. I'll check back with you in a bit." Eric hurried back to the newsroom to tackle some deadlines, his red ponytail flicking up and down.

That's something John knew he wouldn't have to deal with anymore. At least in the workplace.

John turned around and began removing the plaques and framed photographs from the dull beige wall, leaving lightened spaces of various shapes and sizes. He hadn't realized how much the walls needed a fresh coat of paint. He wished he had taken them down sooner because there were more than he realized. He knew he could always return and get any items he didn't take with him then, but he wasn't sure he wanted to come to the building where he had spent more than a third of his life. And he knew Eric would be anxious to move into the office, since he was his likely successor. At least he hoped Eric would be promoted, something he had recommended to the publisher, executive editor and other powers-that-be in a place where there seemed to be more folks with supervisory titles than people to supervise. But he knew it wasn't a sure thing either, as people had their own ideas on how to fill the vacancy. Such was life in the corporate world of newspapers.

John lifted the heavy box off his desk and set it by the doorway. He took a half-full box on a chair next to the desk and placed wall decorations in it. The three-tiered bookshelf presented another problem. Did he really want to take the books? There were a few reference books, some journalism textbooks from his time as an adjunct professor, and other books that seemed of interest to him when he first received them in the mail for possible reviews or at functions he attended. And there were a few that he had no idea where they came from or what they represented and must have been put on the shelves to keep the clutter down in the office. And no doubt a few from his predecessor and maybe some before him. But John was never one to throw away a book, as he respected the printed word too much.

Staring at the shelves, his hands on his waist for a few seconds, he knew the books would fill some empty spaces in his study at home, and probably never be opened again. Furthermore, they would be too damn heavy to take home. John decided to *donate* them to Eric or the next occupant of his office, knowing they would probably be resentful for taking up the space on the shelves for their own books. He realized some probably should be tossed in the trash, but it wasn't something he'd do. Let someone else do the dirty work.

John sat and leaned back in his worn, black leather swivel chair. His back was a little stiff from all the lifting and stretching. His arms felt some strain as well. He swirled around to see if there was anything he had missed. He closed his eyes for a few seconds.

"Sleeping on the job your last day?"

"Huh?" John sat upright and blinked.

Clay Rawlings, the executive editor, strolled in and sat across from him, placing his feet up on the corner of the desk. His white shirt neatly pressed and in his trademark bow tie, Clay had always been a dapper dresser, usually wearing a dark black or blue suit, as well as a silver Rolex loose enough on his wrist to dangle slightly below the cuff line for others to see. He was tall and there was a presence about him when he swaggered into a room with his confident gait and thick, slicked-back, unnatural black mane. He lifted his right eyebrow and grinned.

"We're going to miss you, John," he said, being a bit too officious for a best friend and colleague. "You've been a damn valuable asset to this newspaper. And don't you forget that."

"Thanks, Clay," John said, placing his hands behind his head. "But I'm sure Eric will fill in ably and perhaps do a better job than I."

"Let's not get carried away or be too self-effacing." Clay planted his feet on the floor, leaned forward and cocked his head in a questioning pose. "You're going to be missed, damn it."

"Cut the crap, Clay." John waggled his head in amusement. "I don't need to hear your official farewell spiel. Save it for one of the suits. Okay? We can do this over beers some evening."

"I'm serious."

"Well, you know as well as I that none of us is indispensable. Things will go on as usual, and within a few weeks or months, hey, maybe a few days, I'll just be a faded memory. As you often say, 'out of sight, out of mind.'"

"Bullshit," Clay said, raising his voice a bit too loudly. He always liked to use profanity for effect, one of his trademarks. Sometimes it worked; other times it could be embarrassing to those around him. The exception would be when women were present and he'd be the charming gent. But, for the most part, Clay didn't seem to care how strong his language was around the guys. That was another charming trait that people either loved or hated about him. As he would often say, "I don't give a rat's ass what others think."

"You know what I mean," John said, dropping his hands to the armrest. "Think back about fifteen years when you were the metro editor. How many folks do you remember from then?"

Clay, running his hands through the sides of his hair, appeared to give it some thought. "Point taken," he said with a quick grin. "But you'll be missed by those who worked with you. They respect you. Hell, I don't know why, but some even like you."

"If you say so." John slowly shook his head and smiled.

"Speaking of that, damn you for not letting us give you a retirement party."

"I want to leave with little or no fanfare."

"Regardless, are you going to have time to have a beer or two after you head out the door?"

"Give me a rain check?"

"Only if you promise you'll honor it. We've been friends for a damn long time. I don't want to see you go off never to be heard from again—out of sight, out of mind." Clay blushed slightly after realizing what he'd said.

"Like others who have gone out to pasture?"

"You don't know if they didn't come back to see their friends."

"I don't know," John said, "but I doubt it. This place isn't exactly a social center. And I'm not going to be one of those who shows up every few days to socialize. This is a workplace. You know, a place where people allegedly work."

"Anyway, I saw Breck Rogers this morning and told him you were retiring. So you'll probably hear from him about the newspaper's alumni group."

"Thanks," John said. "You really didn't have to do that."

"That's what friends are for, buddy," Clay said with a mischievous grin.

"I'll try to return the favor when you retire."

"Seriously, don't be a stranger around here. Drop by for lunch or simply to shoot the shit."

"Like I said, this is a workplace and I'll no longer be working here. Believe it or not, I might be involved in other things in my life. You know people do have lives outside these hallowed sacred walls?"

"Smartass!" Clay stood and crossed his arms. "Maybe so, but regardless, you don't have to be like that. I'll call or send an email and set a time and day for lunch."

"Hey, Clay. Cut the BS. It's not like I'm leaving town and moving across the country. I'll still be around. Maybe we can get back to our tennis matches on a regular basis."

"Yeah, I'd like to get back to whipping your sorry ass in tennis."

"In your dreams."

Clay reached over the desk and they shook hands, then he whispered, "Fuck you."

"Fuck you, too."

"Best of luck, old buddy," Clay said, tapping John on the shoulder as he turned to leave.

"Unfortunately for me, you'll know how to find me."

"And I will."

After Clay left, John set the boxes on a dolly. He glanced around the office one more time to see if he'd missed anything.

"Heading out?" Eric asked at the door.

"About that time."

Eric stepped inside the office and they casually bumped fists.

"John, thanks for everything you've done for me," Eric said with a slight tremor in his voice. "I've learned a lot working with you. I just want you to know I appreciate everything."

"That's nice of you to say," John said warmly. "I've enjoyed working with you. And I've learned a lot from you as well. Don't hesitate to call me if you need any help, although I doubt you'll need to. I'm sure you'll do well."

As John pushed his belongings to the elevator at the other end of the floor, he wished he didn't have to go through almost the entire length of the newsroom. The squeaky dolly didn't help matters as he rolled it down the aisle, drawing more attention to his final departure. He felt many eyes on him. He looked around and acknowledged the wide grins sad smiles, and empty expressions with several saying "see ya" as he slowly wheeled past the desks. It was more difficult than he thought it would be, seeing the solemn expressions on some of their faces.

It seemed to take forever for the elevator to arrive. When the door finally opened, several more colleagues stepped out into the newsroom. Their chatter abruptly ended.

"Time to go," John said lightheartedly. "For the last time."

After several well wishes from the occupants, John backed into the empty elevator and pushed the button that took him down four floors to the employee entrance at the rear of the building.

"Best of luck, Mr. Ross," Arnold, a security guard said as he steered the dolly toward the back ramp. After all these years, and he wasn't sure how many, John only knew him as "Arnold the security guard." He felt a little ashamed about that.

John smiled. "Thanks, Arnold. The same to you."

"Do you need any help with that, sir?"

"I'm fine. Not heavy."

John tugged the dolly across the asphalt parking lot to his car in the warm September air and opened the trunk. Perspiration dotted his forehead. He put the two boxes in and slammed it shut. He returned the dolly to the loading dock and left it where he had picked it up several hours earlier.

"Come back and visit once in a while. Ya hear?"

John looked in the direction of the voice. Fred, along with a handful of other employees from other departments, was standing in the designated smoking area, sucking on their cigarettes.

"I may," John said, waving. "I hope to see you some day in retirement."

"If I make it that far," Fred said before tapping his chest and coughing several times. He took another drag from his cigarette.

John strolled back to his car. An empty feeling suddenly came over him as he opened the door. He stood and looked at the gray building for several seconds, realizing this would be the last time he would be leaving work. Five days after Labor Day.

John sat in the car for a few seconds before turning on the ignition. He felt tears welling in his eyes. That wasn't something he expected. He took a deep breath, pursed his lips, and drove out of the parking lot. He glanced in the rearview mirror for one last view of *The Post-Chronicle* building as an employee.

Tomorrow he would be officially retired.

Two

Driving home, John was amazed that he didn't feel at least some elation or relief about leaving the workforce, something that had been part of his life for fifty years or so, beginning with part-time jobs in high school and college and a two-year stint in the Army. He wasn't sure if it was sadness or just an empty feeling. Maybe it was simply a bittersweet moment.

He would have all this so-called free time on his hands to do practically anything he wanted. Within reason, of course. His wife, as well as some friends and neighbors, had been retired for several years, and they didn't seem to mind not heading off to work five days a week. For John, that meant no twelve-hour days at the office and no calls in the middle of the night on a breaking news story.

A few retiree friends generally laughed and said they worked for themselves. Or, for some of the guys, they were working for their wives. They'd remind him of that infamous, and to some, humorous honey-do list. He figured most women got stuck with the honey-do list the moment they entered into a relationship, in addition to their real jobs.

Some retirees joked that they belong to the "pajama club"—spending most of their days in their pajamas or lounging clothes. John knew a few folks who seemingly spent their entire days in lounging pants. He hoped they restrained themselves from wearing them to supermarkets, department stores and other public places.

But he had seen a few others who seemed lost. They'd linger in their vegetable and flower gardens, tend to their manicured lawns, and do other things without leaving the parameters of their yards. Some seemed to never leave their homes unless to walk to the end of their driveways to pick up mail or newspapers. If they did venture out, it was usually to get a bite to eat at one of the restaurants offering senior specials or to church. Maybe even a senior citizen center. John would sometimes stop and talk to them on his daily walks in the neighborhood and it was like having the same conversation over and over. At first, he would patiently listen to their repeated stories, but after a while, he found himself trying to avoid them. Instead of moving on with their lives, they had stopped in one place as if in a time warp.

There was a woman—her name was Georgina, probably in her seventies—who lived down the street. John had known her for more than twenty years, back when she was a teller for a bank. Every morning when he drove to work, from early spring to late fall, Georgina would be sitting on a small wooden stool, wearing overalls and a bright yellow bonnet, tending to a small patch of flowers with a pair of clippers. Every morning. Same outfit. Same flowers. Doing the same thing. Sometimes she would smile and wave as he slowly passed her house. He was told by a neighbor that she would spend about twenty minutes on her garden, then go back inside for the remainder of the day to care for her physically disabled husband, William. She never had much to say, other than a pleasant "hello," "good morning," or "nice day," regardless of the weather. He wondered if the garden was her escape.

John was tempted to stop off at Bailey's Pub, one of the watering holes he frequented after work, but knew he would run into colleagues and have to explain what his plans were now that he was retired. He wasn't ready for that. And what would Clay think if he happened to drop by and see him after John told him he didn't have time to get a beer after work?

The problem was that he didn't have any plans after retirement. He generalized about having time to travel, write, and perhaps do some volunteer work in the community. But he had never made any commitment to do anything because he was too busy at work. And, as a journalist, he was always concerned about a possible conflict of interest. When he did inquire about volunteer positions, he was told they'd love him to write news releases. Writing was something he wanted to get away from...away from work. For many years, work took precedence over practically everything in his life. Now he had to face reality. He was retired— a new member of the pajama club.

John's plain tri-level house in the Garden Springs neighborhood was dark when he pulled off the crowded street into the driveway. He didn't remember Sally telling him she would be out and about when he got home. Or was he supposed to meet her at a restaurant for a bite to eat? Maybe she was at the grocery store. He eased into the one-car garage and stopped. After pushing the remote to lower the door, he sat with his eyes closed for several seconds with the engine running. He finally turned off the ignition. He glanced at his cell phone to see if he had missed any calls or text messages. Nope.

John left the two boxes from work in the trunk. There wasn't any hurry to bring them inside. Only more clutter. They could probably be stacked on one of the shelves in the garage and wouldn't be missed. Probably forgotten. But he dismissed that idea as well. His arms were beginning to feel tight and sore from the lifting at work.

The kitchen was quiet when he opened the door. When he flipped on the switch, there was an instant shout in unison—"Happy retirement!"

Stunned for a moment, John glanced around the room at all the familiar faces. A banner draped across the wall in the adjoining dining room proclaimed "Happy Retirement, John!" in big red letters. He looked around to locate Sally. She stepped toward him with her arms spread wide and hugged him, then gave him a quick peck on the mouth.

"Did we surprise you, sweetheart?" she whispered in his ear.

"What do you think?" He grinned awkwardly as he looked around the room.

Before John could say anything else, friends and neighbors flocked over and patted him on the shoulders, squeezed his hand, and some of the women kissed him on the cheek. He was at a loss for words. He didn't enjoy being the center of attention. He mentioned to Sally on several occasions that he didn't like surprises, especially on his birthday. Maybe he should have included retirement. Too late now.

He made his way past multi-colored helium balloons strung to chairs and the streamers made from newspapers that dangled from the ceiling in the dining room. In the middle of the table was a large white sheet cake designed to look like a news page with a large "Happy Retirement" in black icing on white across the top like a headline. Brightly wrapped gifts sat on the folding table. Other than accepting the well wishes from the attendees, John didn't know what to say, think, or feel.

"Congratulations, Daddy!" John turned around and his daughter, Chloe, gave him a big hug and kiss on the cheek. A moment later his son, Brody, a half-head taller and thirty pounds heavier, firmly grabbed his hand before giving him a bear hug that felt like air was squeezing from his lungs.

"This *is* a surprise," John said, who could feel some tears coming on. Chloe had flown in from New York City, where she worked for one of the television networks as an assistant producer. Brody, a certified public accountant, was in from Chicago.

"We wouldn't have missed this for anything," Brody said with a beaming smile. "It's not every day a person gets to retire. That officially makes you old."

"Gee, thanks," John said. "I guess that makes you my *old* son."

"Whatever!"

"You deserve this, Daddy." Chloe was teary-eyed, holding his hand. "Now you get to do what you want to do. And, by the way, you're not that old."

"Sometimes I feel that way," said John, slightly rolling his shoulders up and down. "Now I have all the time in the world."

"Or what's left," Brody said.

"Would you stop it, Brody?" Chloe gave him a nudge with her hand.

"Only kidding, sis!"

Before they could say any more, Sally announced to everyone that dinner was ready in the kitchen. On the counter, she had set up two large platters of finger sandwiches, a veggie tray, buffet-style bowls of potato salad, cole slaw, and chips and various dips, along with plates, silverware, and beverages. People began making their way to the food, filling their plates and going to the dining room, living room and den to eat and chat.

John wanted to escape to the bedroom, if only to rest for a few minutes and catch his breath, but he knew that wouldn't be the sociable thing to do at a party given in his honor. He didn't want to appear ungrateful to his family and friends. And he'd never hear the end of it from Sally.

The doorbell rang and Sally hurried to answer it. She returned a few seconds later with Clay Rawlings, who carried a large, wrapped box with a big blue bow on top. Several other newspaper employees followed him including Eric Walsh, sports columnist Dan Easteridge, and metro editor Heidi Snow.

"You're not getting away that easily," Clay said in a booming voice that drew everyone's attention. "Since you wouldn't let us give you a party at the office, we're bringing the party to you!"

"I should have known," John said with a twisted smile. "You seemed too eager for me to leave this afternoon."

"I do hope you have some beer in the refrigerator."

Sally reached into the fridge and handed him a bottle of Bud Light.

"Thanks, Sally," Clay said. "I knew I could count on you. John, not so much."

"I like you, too," John said, grinning.

After everything settled down, John made his way to the food counter although he wasn't hungry. These types of events had a tendency to take away his appetite. But at least it gave him something to do, even if it was nibbling on carrot and celery sticks.

After they had finished eating, Sally called everyone back to the dining room so John could open his gifts. He wasn't excited about that either. But he knew he had to go along with it since it was his party.

John didn't know what to expect when he opened the first gift. He took a watch out of the box, and said, "Thank you, I needed a new watch." Then he looked at it again and realized there were no hands on it.

"It's a retirement watch," said Betty Robinson, a short, buxom widow in her seventies who lived several houses down the street. "You don't have to be governed by time anymore." Everyone laughed as John held it up and passed it around for others to see.

He opened another gift, this one a white coffee cup inscribed with, "Keep Calm. I'm retired."

"You'll get a lot of use for that," said Benny Smith, a thin, short man in his late 50s who lived two doors down. "You can sit around and drink all the coffee you want to from now on."

"Thanks," John said. "I guess that's something to look forward to."

Another gift was a garish T-shirt with a large bass emblazoned on the front with "Retired. I work at fishing now."

"But I don't fish," John said with a light laugh.

"It's something you can do now," said Allen Boatwright, an avid outdoorsman who lived across the street. He had a fishing boat and spent most of his time at a lake about an hour away. "You can join me."

"I may take you up on that," John said, trying to be cordial and lighthearted with his remarks. Fishing would be one of the last things he'd want to do. He didn't even like to eat fish. The only fish product he consumed was a fish oil supplement to help lower the triglycerides in his blood.

Clay handed him the box from the newspaper. Inside was another box, then another, until there was one with an envelope containing five one- thousand-dollar bills.

"We figured you'd need something to tide you over until you get a part-time job at some burger joint," Clay said with a hearty laugh.

"I hope it won't be that bad," John said.

"Oh, we may have a paper route for you."

"Gee, thanks."

After he opened several more gag gifts, Chloe handed him an envelope.

"Now I wonder what this could be," John said, holding it up against the light. "A bill for something?" He glanced at Brody.

He opened it and read the card quietly. It was signed by Chloe and Brody, thanking him for helping them get started on life's journey. It contained a brochure for a twenty-one-day tour of Europe, noting that reservations had been purchased for him and Sally. While seldom showing his emotions, he couldn't help but wipe away tears trickling down his cheeks.

"You didn't have to do this," he said.

"You deserve it, Daddy, for all you and Mom have done for us through the years," Chloe said. "You made lots of sacrifices for us."

"That's right, Dad," Brody said. "It's the least we could do."

"We love you," Chloe said with tears streaming down her cheeks.

"I love you two as well," John said, trying his best to hold back more tears. They came over and he wrapped his arms around their shoulders and pulled them close.

Sally handed him a napkin. He dabbed his eyes for a moment as she kissed him on the cheek.

"I want to thank all of you for this," John said, glancing around the room. "I thank you for the wonderful gifts, but most of all, I thank you for your friendship and support all these years. I guess you'll be seeing more of me now."

"Thanks for the warning," Benny shouted from the back of the room, bringing laughter from everyone.

"Let's cut the cake," Sally said as she picked up a knife on the table. She began slicing the cake into square pieces while Chloe put them on paper plates and handed them to the guests. "There's some freshly brewed coffee on the counter if anyone wants any."

"We need to be going," Clay said. "You know, there's a few of us who still have to work for a living."

"Thanks for taking time out from your busy schedule to be here," John said. "If putting out a newspaper is really working for a living." He tapped Clay on the shoulder with his fist.

"We really just wanted to see if we could get you to return to the crazy house. But it looks like you'll be just fine here."

"I think we'll survive," John said smiling, putting an arm around Sally's waist.

"I believe you will."

A few minutes later, after everyone dispersed from the dining room to eat cake in the living room and den, John moseyed over to Sally and gently put his arm around her shoulders and squeezed. He kissed her on the forehead.

"You didn't have to do this," he said softly. "A quiet evening with you and the kids would have been enough."

"I know, but this is a special day for you," she said. "You've worked hard all these years. This is something the kids wanted for you as well. Now it's time to celebrate and then move on to whatever life holds for us. A new horizon."

"New horizon?"

"Yes, another point in life for us to explore."

"I never thought of it that way, but I suppose that's right. I know I won't be stuck in a rut because you wouldn't let me even if I wanted to."

Before they could say anything else, guests began to return to the dining room to say good night and wish John a happy retirement one more time. Several retired men offered good-hearted condolences on having "honey-do" lists to occupy his time.

After the last of the guests departed, Sally and Chloe began putting items away from the table and kitchen while John and Brody picked up plates and silverware from the den and living room. After Sally put dinnerware in the dishwasher, they went to the den and sat in silence. They all appeared exhausted. Especially John.

John sat in the rocking chair and grinned at Brody and Chloe.

"You guys didn't have to do what you did," he said. "I'm happy you took the time to be here tonight. That means a lot to your mom and me. And believe it or not, we miss not having you guys here once in a while. But the trip to Europe, well..."

"Oh, Daddy, be quiet." Chloe put a forefinger to her mouth and crinkled her nose. "It's paid and done for. Now you and Mom just need to go on the trip and enjoy yourselves."

"I'm sure that money Mr. Rawlings gave you will help," Brody said. "If you don't need it, well, you know who could use it." He wiggled his brows.

"I think we can use it, son," John said. "But thanks for volunteering."

"Anytime, Dad." Brody gave him a thumbs up with both hands.

"As for going to Europe, I don't know when we can do it."

"Mom has already taken care of that," Chloe said. "She gave us the dates when you could go."

John glanced at Sally and raised his eyebrows. "Working behind my back. I can't win."

"You're outnumbered," Sally said. "So don't fight it."

"Yep," John said. "A new horizon."

Three

John was the first one out of bed the following morning. Moments after he walked into the kitchen, the programmable coffee maker clicked on. He ambled to the front porch and picked up the newspaper. It was still dark and only a few lights were on in the houses up and down his shady block. He stared into the clear sky at the twinkling stars and the quarter moon fading in the distance. A new day.

He returned to the house, sat at the kitchen counter and opened the newspaper, waiting for the coffee to brew. There were familiar bylines. The stories were among those he had heard discussed in the newsroom on his final day. It was the last issue in which he had anything to contribute, and it wasn't much. He rose from the stool and poured a large cup of coffee, added a spoonful of powdered creamer, and sat back down. He closed his eyes.

"Good morning, Daddy," Chloe said cheerfully as she entered the kitchen wearing an oversized green robe that belonged to Sally. Her voice startled John for a moment.

"Mornin'. I didn't hear you come in. Pour some coffee and have a seat."

Chloe took a large cup from the cupboard, poured some coffee, and then took out the hazelnut liquid creamer from the refrigerator. Sally always bought hazelnut liquid creamer when Chloe was in town. He should have known something was going on when he saw it before he left for work for the last time. After pouring some in her coffee, she sat next to her father and smiled.

"So are you excited about going to Europe?" She clutched the warm cup in both hands as her elbows rested on the counter.

"You know it. Your mom and I have been thinking about taking that trip for a long time but work or something always seemed to get in the way. You couldn't have given us anything better. But I wish you hadn't gone to all that expense."

"Oh, Daddy," she said, raising her eyebrows and tilting her head. "You and Mom have always been there for us. It's the least we could do. And Brody and I wanted to give you something special for your retirement."

"Well, I'm looking forward to it. I know Mom is, too."

"So what are you going to do now that you have all this free time?" She took another sip of coffee and waited a few seconds for him to answer.

"I hate to say it, but I really don't know what I'm going to do." John took a swallow from his cup and paused for a few more seconds. "I really haven't given it that much thought. I've been working for so long it seems like that's what I should always do. My mind always seemed to be on work, for the most part. I'm glad this is the weekend. At least it will give me some time to think about what I will do on Monday when I'd normally head to the office. That's probably my first official day of retirement."

"I'm sure you'll find lots of things to do," Chloe said, tapping the top of his hand. "And I bet Mom has a few chores for you as well."

"You know it," he said with a chuckle. "We've been putting off some things around the house until I retired. I just didn't think it would be here so quick. I don't have any excuses now."

A few seconds later, Sally came into the kitchen. "Y'all are up early," she said, going to the coffee pot.

"I'm a creature of habit," John said. "You know that. Early bird."

"You don't have to be that way anymore," Sally said.

"We've been talking about what he's going to do with all his free time," Chloe said.

"Oh, don't you worry about that. I've got some things for him to do," Sally said as she sat on the other side of John. "A very long list. He'll keep busy."   .

"I told her that," John said with a sigh. "I just hope you give me a few days to get used to being retired."

"Oh, I can do that," she said, winking at Chloe. "You can start on Monday."

"Gee, thanks," John said. "So it's back to work on Monday. Some retirement."

"You'd better enjoy the weekend while you can," Sally said with a light chuckle.

They heard the shower running.

"I suppose Brody is awake now," Sally said.

"I sure hope it's Brody because if it's not, there's someone else in the house," John said dryly.

"You know what I mean," Sally said. "And don't be such a grump."

"Sorry 'bout that," he said with a quick, toothy smile. He shuffled over to the coffee pot and poured another cup. "Anyone need their coffee warmed up?" Sally and Chloe held up their cups and he poured more.

"It's a shame Sam and Whitney weren't able to make the trip," Sally said. "Whitney is going to grow up before we see her again."

"She is growing like a weed and so active. She's making some friends in daycare now."

"Don't let her grow up too quickly," John said with a smile.

"We'll all visit next spring and spend a few weeks," Chloe said. "I know Whitney is excited about seeing the horses. Sam is trying to get a project finished so we'll see how things work out."

Brody, his long dark hair still stringy and damp from the shower, came in wearing lounging pants and a bath towel draped around his bare shoulders. He sat at the table and grinned at each of them. "So where's the coffee?"

Sally got up and poured him a cup. "Cream and sugar?"

"Both," he said. "Three teaspoons of sugar."

"So what are the plans today?" Chloe asked no one in particular.

"Maybe we can go to the Fayette Mall," Sally said.

"I'm up for that," Chloe said.

"Maybe you and Mom can go to the mall," Brody said. "And maybe Dad and I can stay here and watch some college football on TV. What do you think, Dad?"

"Works for me," John said, giving a thumbs up.

"Maybe we can meet later and get a bit to eat," Sally said.

"You call me when you're ready and we'll be there," John said. "I just want to relax today. Remember, I'm retired." Then he slowly spelled it out.

"We know, honey," Sally said as she padded over to him and playfully planted a kiss on his cheek. "You don't have to remind us. Again."

John glanced at Chloe and Brody and closed his eyes for a few seconds. "Now you see why I didn't retire sooner."

"You know I'm teasing you," Sally said, wrapping her arms around his shoulders.

"I know," John said, winking at the kids. "But I've got to keep you guessing."

"You guys cut it out," Chloe said. "Anyone for breakfast?"

"You fixin'?" Brody asked with a wide grin.

"Sure, but keep it simple."

"Four strips of bacon. Three eggs over easy. Toast, lightly buttered. Grape jelly if it's available."

"Geez," Chloe said, dropping her hands to her waist. "How about orange juice? Pancakes?"

"Orange juice sounds good," Brody said with a wide grin. "I'll pass on the pancakes. You're great, sis."

"I know," Chloe said, then glanced at her parents. "How about you guys?"

"Maybe toast," John said.

"Nothing for me," Sally said. "I'm going to shower and get dressed."

Chloe prepared breakfast for the men, then excused herself to get ready to go to the mall.

"No seconds on coffee?" Brody asked with a wide-eyed expression. "What kind of service is this?"

"You can warm your own cup," Chloe said, sticking out her tongue. "I'm not your babysitter."

"Yeah, but you're my big sister and you used to be."

"You're a big boy now," she said, leaving the kitchen.

~ * ~

John and Brody were watching TV in the den when Sally and Chloe left.

"So how does it feel to be retired?" Brody asked, sitting back with his feet up in the recliner.

"I don't know, Brody," John said from the couch. "It's only my first day and it's Saturday. Ask me in a week or so. Maybe a month. Right now, it seems like any other day."

"I know I could find things to do."

"I'm sure I will as well. Just give me a little time."

"Yeah, I guess," Brody said with raised brows. "You've got all the time in the world. No more punching the time clock, so to speak."

"Yep, no more of that."

"Just answering to Mom."

"Funny."

John dozed off midway through the football game. He was awakened by his cell phone ringing on the coffee table. Sally told him where and when they would meet for dinner.

"That was your mom," John said. "We're meeting at this new Irish pub on Harrodsburg Road at six."

"Sounds like a plan," Brody said.

"I think I'm going to take a shower and get ready," John said as he eased up from the couch. "We've got a few hours so no need to be in a hurry."

After shaving and brushing his teeth, John turned on the water in the shower. He faced the shower as he shampooed his thinning hair. After lathering a cloth and washing all over, he stood with his chin to his chest under the shower head as the steam created a dense fog in the room. He stood there for a couple of minutes, almost as if in a trance, before bending and turning off the faucet. He toweled off and got dressed in the adjoining bedroom. John sat on the end of the bed, staring at himself in the dresser mirror before putting on his socks. He couldn't resist smiling at the reflection of the balding man with speckled gray and thinning hair and white beard and wondering how in the world time had slipped by so quickly.

Brody rapped lightly on the bedroom door, startling John for a moment.

"Everything okay?" Brody asked, peeking inside.

"Oh, everything's fine," John said with a smile as he stood up and buckled his belt. "I was just thinking about some things."

"You sure looked lost in some deep thought."

John chuckled. "I'm not sure how deep it was. Just a few things on my mind."

"Because of retirement?"

"Nah," John said. "Just stuff. Nothing important."

"I'm gonna get dressed now."

"Take your time," John said. "I'll be down in the den."

Brody went to the guest room, took some items from his suitcase and headed to the guest bathroom in the hallway.

John stared at the football game on the TV, but not really watching it. He leaned back on the couch and closed his eyes. He was startled again when Brody tapped him on the knee. "Ready?"

John's eyes flickered several times. "Sure."

"Fall asleep?"

"Resting my eyes."

"Sure, Dad," Brody said with a loud laugh. John turned off the TV with the remote and they proceeded to the garage.

"I almost wish we could stay here," John said.

"Want me to drive?" Brody asked. "Don't want you falling asleep at the wheel."

John hesitated a moment before tossing the keys of his Chevy SUV to him. "Let's hope that won't ever happen, but you can drive. Just observe the speed limits. This isn't Chicago."

John gave him directions to the Shamrock Pub. They arrived before Sally and Chloe, found a place at the bar and each ordered a pint of Guinness.

"I hope the gals being late doesn't hit my wallet too hard," John said with a weary laugh. "That's usually not a good sign."

"One reason I'm still a bachelor," Brody said after taking a big swallow from the mug.

"I suppose that's a good enough reason."

"I've got too many things I want to do without being saddled with a woman."

"So no girlfriend?"

"I've got some girlfriends but nothing serious. Still playing the field."

"No need to rush into anything. Marriage can hold you down."

"You and Mom seemed to do okay."

"She never complained when it came to my career. She was willing to support me because it helped the family. She sacrificed a lot for everyone. Don't ever underestimate what she's done for everyone."

"Not too many like that anymore," Brody said. "They want their own careers, too."

"I don't blame them for that. Times have changed. For the better."

"I think so, too," Brody said. "Just sayin'. That's just a reason I haven't found the right one."

"Takes time."

"Yep."

"Of course, you're not getting any younger. At thirty-seven, you might be getting set in your ways."

"Get real."

"Just kidding, son."

Sally and Chloe entered the front door of the pub, saw them at the bar and waved.

"Sorry we're late," Sally said. "There was an accident on Nicholasville Road near the main entrance to the mall and we were held up in traffic."

A server came over and led them to a booth. She took their drink orders along with an appetizer sampler.

"Buy anything?" John asked Sally. "Or should I ask?"

"We just did some window shopping," Sally said. "I didn't see anything I really wanted."

"That's a first," John said.

"Are you being sarcastic again?" Sally said, squinching her eyes.

"You know I'm joking, sweetheart." John smiled.

"So what did you guys do today?"

"Watched football on TV," Brody said. "Well, I guess I did. Dad took a nap or two. You know, resting his eyes. We've all heard that before."

"Hey, I deserve it," John said. "I am retired, aren't I?"

"Of course you deserve it," Chloe said. "And you should be able to take as many naps as you want to from now on."

"Let's not get carried away," Sally said, grinning. "Don't forget I'm at home as well. I don't take naps, so I don't want some sleepyhead around the house all day."

"Sleepyhead?" John said. "Now when have I ever been a sleepyhead?"

"Just teasing, honey," Sally said, gently nudging her shoulder against his.

"Touché."

Their orders came and they chatted about various things while glancing up occasionally at the TVs mounted on the wall to get game updates.

"Are you going miss covering sports?" Brody asked.

"Not really," John said. "I haven't been to a game in ages. The only thing I was doing was overseeing what sports we covered and offering my input on placement on the pages. You've probably attended more games than I have."

"Maybe we should take in a game or two the next time I'm here," Brody said. "Better yet, the next time you and Mom come up to Chicago."

"Is that an invitation?" Sally asked.

"Let me get my apartment cleaned up first."

"Maybe when you come to New York," Chloe said.

"We'll certainly give that some thought," Sally said. "But I'd much prefer taking in some of the museums and art galleries and maybe a few Broadway shows."

"We can do that, too," Chloe said.

"We can do that after we go to Europe," John said. "First things first."

"That's right," Chloe said. "I don't want you putting that off. There are some great museums in London. And don't forget the West End."

"The West End?" Brody said, creasing his forehead. "A neighborhood?"

"That's London's version of Broadway," Chloe said.

"Oh," Brody said. "I learn something new every time I'm around you."

"Isn't it great having a big sister?" Chloe asked with an exaggerated smile.

"If you say so," Brody said.

"You kids never change," Sally said. "Always needling each other."

"And we probably always will," Chloe said, grinning.

"Yeah," Brody said with a laugh. "That's something we learned from watching you and Dad."

"Okay, okay," Sally said, holding up her hands. "Let's change the subject."

They ate their hamburgers and fries in relative peace. When they returned to the house, John went for a short walk since it was still light and he wanted some time for himself to clear his mind.

John smiled at a few neighbors who were raking leaves or tending to their wilting flower beds. He noticed Bert Reliford near the street in front of his house. He wished he had seen him sooner so he could have turned around and returned to his house. But Bert had seen him and waved.

John reluctantly walked toward him. Although they had known each other for more than twenty years, and been neighbors all that time, John was growing tired of having the same conversation with him. It was something that had been going on for the past two years or so.

Bert was leaning on a rake, taking a short break after moving lawn clippings into a pile a few feet away from the curb. He was wearing baggy shorts, with calf-high white socks and a faded blue University of Kentucky sweatshirt. At least he wasn't wearing lounging pants.

"Evenin', John," Bert said as he took a green John Deere baseball cap off his bald head and wiped his brow with his forearm. He seldom smiled, unless it was after telling one of his jokes or about some event that had happened in his life. Most of the time Bert had a dour expression, and always seemed to be griping about someone or something. He had spent most of his life as a school teacher, and retired more than ten years earlier after putting in the minimum time. He had no intention of ever working again, something he told John many times, because spending twenty-seven years with classrooms of students was like working several lifetimes. It was a story John didn't like to hear—again and again.

"Getting your yard ready for winter?" John asked.

"Yep. I probably should buy a leaf blower, but figure this is good exercise for me. And a rake probably does a better job because you have to use one anyway after putting the clippings in a pile."

"Probably so," John said. "That's the reason I have a mulching mower. I don't have to mess with it."

"I think what I do makes for a better lawn."

"Whatever."

"I saw some cars outside your house last night," Bert said. "Any problems? Sally okay?"

"No problems," John said. "Sally threw a surprise retirement party for me."

"Retirement party?" Bert asked, raising an eyebrow. "Really?"

John wished he hadn't said anything about a party since Bert and his wife Wilma apparently hadn't been invited. Sally seldom saw them anyway, except on her rare walks with John or seeing Wilma at the grocery store.

"A few friends and relatives," John said. "The kids came in as well."

"So no more work?"

"No more work at the newspaper. Twenty-seven years. I'm sure Sally will have some honey-do's for me to take care of." John chuckled. Bert didn't.

"After spending all those years in the classroom, I knew I wasn't going to work again, except around the house. All those years dealing with snotty students, gutless administrators, and clueless parents was like working a lifetime and then some. No more work for me. Never."

John simply grinned, knowing where the conversation was headed.

"I got so tired of being at the school by seven-fifteen in the morning, trying to get the classroom ready, staying around until four or so, then coming home to grade papers. I was putting in sixteen hours a day. You add all that up and it's several lifetimes of work. I don't miss it one iota."

"But at least you got a nice pension and could retire early," John said.

"That's about the only thing," Bert said. "People just don't appreciate teachers and what they do."

"And you've got your health."

"Are you trying to be funny, John?"

John didn't want to argue with him, even discuss retirement with him, because it was a losing proposition. And he had heard it all before, enough to last several lifetimes, even if Bert seemed to forget. John wondered if Bert had any idea how many times he retold these stories, and if they were repeated to others as well.

"I suppose I'd better get moving before it gets too dark," John said.

"Drop by for coffee some morning now that you've got free time. And by the way, give my regards to Brody and Chloe. It would have been nice to see them."

"I'll do that." John felt his neck tighten. He raised his hand as he turned and walked away. "Have a nice evening."

Bert didn't reply as he took a deep breath and began raking more clippings. John picked up the pace on his way to walk several blocks before returning home.

When John returned, Brody was in the den munching on popcorn and watching another football game while Sally and Chloe were at the counter in the kitchen, drinking coffee and talking about the places to see on the European vacation.

"Care for any?" Sally asking, holding up her cup.

"No, thanks. I've already had my three-cup quota for today."

"See anybody on your walk?" Sally asked.

"I had an enlightening talk with Bert about retirement."

"Already worked a lifetime?" Sally asked.

"And more."

"Poor Mr. Reliford," Chloe said with a puckered mouth. "He was a good middle-school science teacher. Very dedicated. I liked him."

"Well, he's a bitter, old, former middle-school science teacher now," John said. "He repeats the same story over and over. I wish I could avoid him but he seems to be on the lookout for me whenever I take a walk."

"Why don't you go in a different direction?" Chloe asked. "Do you go the same way every time?"

"Uh, I suppose I do. I never thought about that."

"You must be getting like Bert," Sally said. "Doing the same thing over and over."

"I don't think that's funny," John said, unable to suppress a grin. "I resemble that remark too much."

"I don't think you'll ever be like Bert," Sally said. "He's always been somewhat of a grump, even when he was your teacher, Chloe. He was never one to bend the rules even slightly for a student."

"Dad, it seems to me that you just need to walk in the opposite direction or find another way to get in your daily exercise."

"Why don't you get a treadmill?" said Brody, who overhead the conversation as he walked over to refrigerator. "I've got some stairsteps and they really help. But they may be too much for you at your age."

"What do you mean by that?" John said. "I'm not exactly using a cane or a walker."

"You know what I mean," Brody said, pumping his legs in step a few times. "They can be rather rigorous. Tough on the knees and calves. With a treadmill, you can adjust the speed and incline."

"I'll consider that," John said. "Thanks for your concern."

"Or you can buy a bicycle," Chloe said. "Maybe bikes for you and Mom, and you could go on rides together."

John looked at Sally without saying a word.

"Sounds like a good idea," Brody said.

"But what if it's cold or raining?" Sally asked.

"Then just get a treadmill," Brody said. "You can both use it."

"I think I'll just continue my daily walks for the time being," John said. "I like the fresh air. I'll just change directions."

"Aren't you worried about hurting Bert's feelings?" Sally asked. "I think he expects to see you on your walks."

"Oh, come on, Sally," John said. "He's a grown man. He can handle it."

"It was just a thought."

"He did ask me about the retirement party," John said.

"Oh, no." The edges of Sally's lips turned downward. "What did you say?"

"I told him you didn't want to have anything to do with him or Wilma and that you were concerned that he'd start talking about his retirement and bore the hell out of the other guests."

"John, you didn't!"

"Only kidding, sweetheart," John said.

"So what did he say?"

"Nothing much, other than wanting to know about what was going on at our house."

"To be honest, I forgot to send them an invitation. I should go visit Wilma and apologize."

"I tried to drop the subject."

"Oh, good," she said. "I hope we didn't hurt his feelings."

"We?"

"Okay, me," Sally said. "So you would have liked me to have invited them?"

"Wilma, maybe?"

"Don't be silly."

"I really wish you hadn't invited anyone," he said. "Except for Brody and Chloe."

"Huh?"

"You know I don't like being the center of attention."

"But you only retire once." Tears began to well in Sally's light blue eyes.

"You know what I mean," John said, somewhat defensively.

"Oh, come on, Daddy," Chloe said. "I thought it was nice of Mom to have a party for you. She went to a lot of trouble."

"Same here," Brody said. "I thought everyone had a great time."

"Okay, okay," John said, raising his hands. "I take everything back. It was a great evening for everyone. We should do it every week."

"It's getting late," Sally said, easing off the stool. "I think I'm going to get ready for bed."

"Now, Sally," John said. "I didn't mean it that way. I was only having fun. It just came out wrong."

Sally looked at him for a moment, walked over and put her cup in the sink, and headed toward the bedroom. "Good night," she said softly.

John looked at Brody and Chloe for support that didn't come.

"Way to go, Dad," Brody said after Sally had closed the bedroom door. "You hurt Mom's feelings."

"Yeah, Daddy, I hope you're satisfied," Chloe said.

"Aw, come on," John said. "It just came out the wrong way. I didn't mean anything by it."

"She put a lot of effort into your party," Chloe said. "And I thought she did a great job."

"Ditto," Brody said.

John and Chloe turned toward Brod and said in unison, "Ditto?"

"Hey, I'm just agreeing with sis," Brody said, his face turning a pale red.

"I need to go to bed, too," Chloe said. "I've got an early flight in the morning. When are you going back to Chicago, Brody?"

"Certainly not early," he said. "Probably later in the morning."

"We'll see you in the morning then," John said. "I think I'm going to stay up a bit longer and watch television. How about you, Brody?"

"I think I'm going over to Drake's sports bar and see if any old buds are there," Brody said. "I shouldn't be out too long."

"Good night," Chloe said before kissing them on their cheeks and going to her old bedroom that had been converted to a study.

"Hey, Dad, could you spare me a twenty?" Brody asked as he got up to leave. "I'm a little short of cash and I left my debit card at my apartment."

"Sure," John said, taking a twenty out of his wallet. "Enough?"

"Well, maybe a ten if you can spare it."

John handed him a ten-dollar bill.

Brody stuffed the cash in his front pants pocket. "See you in the morning."

Four

"Thanks again for coming in," John said to Chloe inside the front entrance of Blue Grass Airport. "You don't know how much we appreciate it. We wish you could stay longer. And thanks for the wonderful gift."

"Ah, Daddy, I wouldn't have missed it for anything," she said, looking up at him with glistening brown eyes. "You deserve a wonderful retirement. You and Mom can do a lot of things now. And start getting ready for your trip to Europe."

"We'll get on that very soon," Sally said, hugging her petite, pixie-haired daughter. "I love you."

"I love you, too," John said, bending down to kiss her cheek. "I hope you have a comfortable flight to the Big Apple."

Tears trickled down Chloe's cheeks. Within seconds, John and Sally were wiping away tears from their eyes as well. Sally removed a tissue from her purse and handed it to Chloe.

"Thanks, Mom," she said, sniffling and gently dabbing away the wet streaks that turned dark from her eyeliner. "I hate goodbyes."

"Me, too," Sally said. "It makes us realize how much we'll miss you. Call us when you get there. And give our best to Sam and hug Whitney for us."

"Tell Brody to drive back safely," Chloe said. "I hope he's home when you get back."

"We will," John said. "I'm a little disappointed in him right now. He knows better."

"Oh, Daddy, it's not a big deal. You know how Brody is. He'll probably call me on his drive back to Chicago."

"I certainly hope so."

Chloe glanced at her watch.

"I need to be going. Love ya," She hugged them both one more time, then picked up her carry-on bag and proceeded to the TSA checkpoint line. She briefly turned and smiled. John and Sally waited until she cleared TSA and waved as she stepped on the escalator. She waved one more time before disappearing as she headed to the boarding area.

"It's hard to believe our kids have grown up so quickly," John said as they walked to the parking lot with their curled fingers clasping. "It seems like only yesterday we were sending them off to college. Now they've got successful careers in big cities."

"I know what you mean," Sally said. "Time really slips away."

"And now I'm old and retired."

"Oh, let's don't go there right now."

"Let me say one thing."

"What"

"I apologize for what I said last night," he said. "I really appreciate all you do…"

"Forgiven."

He leaned over and kissed her on the cheek.

"I have so many mixed feelings right now. I even feel a bit stressed about it."

"I understand."

~ * ~

It was almost noon when they got back to their house in east Lexington. Brody was sitting in the kitchen, still in his lounging pants and hunched over, eating a bowl of cereal and reading the newspaper's sports section.

"Finally decide to come home?" John asked.

"I figured you knew I'd stay at one of my buds'," Brody said without looking up.

"Chloe said to tell you 'bye,'" Sally said as she placed her purse on the counter and sat on a stool.

"Oh, shit," Brody said, popping his hand against his forehead. "She's already left? I completely forgot all about that!"

John, biting his lip, glanced at Sally and headed to the den.

"We just got back from the airport," Sally said.

"I'll call her in a few hours," Brody said. "I can't believe I forgot."

"Are you still going back to Chicago today?"

"Probably around two, after I shower and get packed." He shook his head with a clenched jaw. "I still can't believe I forgot about sis."

Fifteen minutes later, John heard the shower and went to the kitchen.

"So he forgot Chloe was going back this morning?" he said as Sally was wiping off the countertop from Brody's breakfast.

"That's what he said."

"I guess it shouldn't surprise me," he said. "He's always thinking about himself."

"Now, John. Calm down. You'll get your blood pressure up."

"Well, before Chloe went to bed, she did mention about having an early morning flight."

"I guess he wasn't paying attention."

"If you say so."

Twenty minutes later, Brody came bounding into the room, wearing a Bears sweatshirt, faded jeans and loafers, his wet, stringy hair combed back.

"Leaving so soon?" Sally asked. "Can I fix you something to take with you? We have leftovers from the party."

"Nah, I'm good. Better hit the road. Wanna miss some of the weekend traffic along the way."

"Thanks again for everything," John said as he walked over and wrapped an arm around Brody's broad shoulders. "Stay out of trouble."

"And you enjoy retirement," Brody said with a wide grin.

Sally hugged and kissed Brody on the cheek. "Drive back safely. Call when you get back."

John's cell phone rang and it was Eric Walsh from the newspaper. He waved as Brody picked up an overnight bag and headed to the front door with Sally. When he finished talking to Eric, he hurried to the front door only to see Brody pull away in his green Mini Cooper as Sally stood waving goodbye at the curb.

"That boy's a character," Sally said as she entered the front door carrying her pocketbook.

"You've got that right," John said. "I don't know if he'll ever grow up."

"Would you believe he asked me for some money to get back on?"

"Really? How much?"

"I gave him fifty dollars. He said he'd pay me back after he gets back to Chicago."

"Don't hold your breath."

"Now, John," Sally said.

"Hell, he borrowed thirty from me last night. Furthermore, he didn't offer to pay me back."

"Really?" she said with deep furrowed brows. "I didn't know that."

"Really? Now you know."

"What did Eric want?"

"Nothing, really. Just calling to see how I was doing."

"That was nice of him."

"I've only been gone two days."

"It's still nice of him to call."

"If you say so," John said.

"Do you still plan to take a walk?"

"Probably a little later. Do you want to go with me?"

"I have some housekeeping I need to do. The house is still a mess from the party."

"It can't wait?"

"You know me," she said. "I'm sure Brody's room is a mess."

"You can count on that," John said straight-faced.

"Let's not talk about Brody."

"Good."

After going to the den, perusing several magazines and flipping through the cable channels, and even dozing off for an hour, John decided to take a walk. "Just don't forget what we told you," Sally said.

"What's that?"

"Take a different route."

"Oh, yes," John said. "Thanks for the reminder."

John left in the opposite direction from his usual walk. He glanced down the street and didn't see anyone in their yards. Children were inside since there was school the next morning. After walking for nearly forty-five minutes, he returned home since it was turning cooler, and the only illumination was from houses and streetlights and occasional vehicles going in both directions.

"Did you get in a good walk?" Sally asked as he stepped into the kitchen from the garage entrance.

"It was nice," he said. "Especially not having to see Bert."

"You know you can't ignore him all the time."

"Why?"

"Because it wouldn't be the right thing to do. Would you want someone to ignore you all the time?"

"If they didn't want to see me. Sure, why not?"

"You know what I mean."

"I'll try to remember," he said, lowering his shoulders and gazing upward.

"Hungry? We still have some finger sandwiches, chips and a few other things from the other night."

"I don't think so. I think I'll go to the den and read some more before I go to bed."

"If you decide you want something to eat, it's in the refrigerator. I'll have to throw most of it out in a few days."

"It's too bad I'm retired because I could take it to the sports department."

"You can still do that."

"Nah." John grabbed the newspaper on the coffee table and sat in the recliner. He started with the front news and worked his way through features, local, sports, and opinion sections. He wasn't expecting any changes, especially to sports, but knew it would eventually happen as the new people in charge would want to put their stamp on it. He had done the same when he became sports editor, although he couldn't remember specifically what he did.

Finished with the paper, he turned on the television and clicked through the channels, trying to find something worthwhile to watch. He didn't want to invest time in a movie, since he'd be going to bed soon, and wasn't in the mood to listen to political discourse by what he considered know-it-all no-nothings on the cable-news channels. He turned it off and meandered to the bedroom that included a quick stop at the refrigerator for a small pimento cheese sandwich that he stuffed in his mouth.

Sally was lying in bed, resting her head on an oversized pillow against the headboard, reading a book, while John undressed.

"Anything interesting?" John asked.

"One of my romances," she said without looking up.

John went to the bathroom and brushed his teeth. When he returned, Sally had put the book on the nightstand and pulled the covers up to her chin.

"Going to sleep so early?" John asked. "I thought I might read a bit."

"You can read. The light won't bother me."

John slipped in under the sheets. He was pleasantly surprised when he put out his arm and touched her naked body. He gently pulled her closer to him. She didn't offer any resistance.

"I don't feel like reading either," he said softly.

John kissed her gently on the mouth, then wrapped his arms around her. He held her for a few seconds before the kiss turned passionate. He reached down and removed his boxers as he felt himself becoming aroused. He fondled her breasts and planted soft kisses on her neck and shoulders as he gradually moved between her lean legs and entered her. He could feel her fingers caressing his back as he thrust back and forth inside her moist mound. He eased off her after they climaxed. Sally tucked her head under his chin as they cuddled in the warmth of their bodies.

"That was nice," he said, kissing her on the forehead.

"Very," she said quietly.

"Love you."

"Love you, too."

They didn't say another word as they fell asleep in each other's arms.

~ * ~

The next morning John was up at five-thirty. He prepared a pot of coffee and sat at the counter with his head resting in his arms while waiting for it to brew, thinking how nice it was not having to go to work.

"You're up early," Sally said as she came in the kitchen, buttoning up her pink robe. "Don't you know you're allowed to sleep in now? The bed is better than the counter."

"You know I'm an early riser," he said, slowly raising his head.

Sally took out two coffee cups from the cabinet and stood next to the coffeemaker, waiting for it to finish.

"You could've stayed in bed," John said. "Don't feel like you have to get up because of me."

"I don't mind," Sally said as she poured coffee into the cups.

"It's kind of hard to break old habits," John said. "But I actually like getting up early. It's quiet and a good time to think."

"Do you want me to leave?" Sally asked. "I don't want to disturb you."

"I don't mean it that way," he said, giving her a thoughtful look. "You know what I mean. Your head is clear after a good night's sleep and you can think about what you plan to do. Even when you don't have a job to go to and have nothing in the world planned."

"You'll adjust," she said. "Just don't rush it. Think of it as the first day of a vacation."

"I never thought of it that way, but you're right. That's what it seems like right now. Maybe after a week or two I will feel differently about not going back to work."

"In that time, maybe you'll find a few things to occupy your time after you get up."

"It's going to be difficult filling in the eight to ten hours a day I normally spent at work."

"More like ten to twelve hours," Sally said.

"You're right. I guess I need to reinvent myself. Find other things to do. I sure don't want to become like Bert."

"I don't think that'll ever happen. Bert was that way even before he retired. And he's been a sourpuss since we first met him years ago. I don't see how Wilma has put up with him."

John took a sip of coffee and looked at Sally. "I enjoyed last night. You surprised me."

Sally blushed slightly. "You surprised me, too. I wasn't sure if you wanted me anymore."

"Now how can you say that?"

"You seemed like you were upset with me for the retirement party. And you've been a little hurtful with some of your comments."

"I didn't mean to be," he said, reaching over and patting her hand. "I've just had a lot on my mind lately. This retirement stuff is all new to me. It's been weighing on my mind."

"It's new to both of us," she said. "It's going to take some adjustment for me as well. I'm not sure how I'm going to handle having you around here most of the day." She laughed.

"Thanks a lot," he said, grinning. "You don't want me under your feet day and night?"

"Heck no! I've got a life, too."

"Then you just need to pretend I'm on vacation for a couple of weeks as well," John said.

"I have my book club, garden club, volunteer work with Red Cross blood drives and a few other things, so don't think you'll see me here all the time. And I have my girlfriends. You'll see how busy I am."

"I suppose I will," he said. "You always did those things while I was away at work."

"We'll manage fine."

"By the way, did you hear from Brody?"

"No," Sally said. "I'll call him later this morning and see if he got back okay. So how about some breakfast?"

"I'm so used to having coffee and then picking up a pastry at work."

"How about some pancakes and eggs?"

"If it's not too much trouble," John said.

"Nothing's too much trouble when it comes to you." She rose from her stool and leaned over and kissed him on the cheek. "Besides, you're on vacation."

"Does that mean I shouldn't expect this kind of treatment from now on?" John said, inclining his head slightly in a questioning pose.

"We'll see," she said, tapping him gently on the tip of his nose. "But I wouldn't count on it."

~ * ~

After breakfast, John watched from the counter as Sally placed dishes and silverware into the dishwasher.

"So what are your plans today?" she asked with her back to him.

"None at the moment," he said. "I haven't given it much thought. Do you have any?"

"I've got my book club at noon today over at Millie's house."

"What are you reading?"

"*Fifty Shades of Grey.*"

"Are you serious?" John asked, with a crease in his forehead.

Sally laughed. "Why do you say that?"

"It just seems like it wouldn't be a book for old women."

"Old women?" Sally turned around and placed her hands on her waist. "Now what's that supposed to mean?"

"Uh, older women?"

"Explain what you mean."

John regretted the comment. He held up his coffee cup. "Any more left?"

"Yes. But you answer me first."

"I didn't mean anything by it. I just assumed it was for younger women."

"We may be a bit older but that doesn't mean we've lost interest in romance and sex."

"I know that," he said. "I haven't forgotten last night."

Sally took the coffee pot and filled his cup.

"We thought it would be a fun read," she said. "And it was."

"What was it about?"

"If you want to know, you'll have to read it."

"I'll think about it."

"Let me know and I'll let you borrow my copy."

"Gee, thanks," he said. "And maybe we can discuss it?"

"Maybe." Sally blew a kiss and winked.

They both laughed.

"Well, I think I may take a short walk," he said, rising from the stool. "It's nice out there this morning."

"Go ahead," she said. "Take your time."

John went to the refrigerator and took out several sandwiches and celery and carrot sticks.

"What are you doing?"

"I want to put together a little something for Georgina down the street."

"Oh, that's sweet," Sally said. "Go ahead and take your walk and I'll get something together we can take to her later."

"Sounds like a plan."

He ventured out his usual route and regretted it less than a minute later when he saw Bert standing in his driveway, this time holding a shovel.

"Mornin', Bert," John said.

"Enjoying retirement?" Bert asked.

"It's certainly different, but I'm not complaining."

"I wouldn't trade it for anything. Best decision I ever made. By far."

"I'm sure I'll feel that way before long."

"So what have you been doing with all your free time?"

"Nothing much, just trying to get acclimated to it."

"It didn't take me long," Bert said. "I couldn't wait to get out of the classroom."

John took a deep breath. "I can't say I was glad to leave the newsroom, per se. I still enjoyed my work, for the most part. But it was time to move on."

"You would have felt differently if you had been a teacher for twenty-seven years. You would have been running out the door on your last day."

"Maybe so," John said, wanting to change the subject. "So what have you been up to lately?"

"Nothing much," Bert said. "This lawn occupies most of my time. There's always something to do, every season of the year."

"Never a desire to do much else?" John asked.

"Not really. Wilma and I are homebodies. We go out to eat quite a bit so that's our enjoyment. Maybe a movie once in a while. It doesn't take much to please us."

"Doesn't sound like it," John said with a chuckle.

Bert glared at him for a moment. "There's nothing wrong enjoying the simple pleasures of life, John."

"No offense," John said. "Just agreeing with you."

"Like I said, if you'd spent twenty-seven years as a middle-school teacher, you'd understand what I mean."

"I'm sure I would." John smiled, looked at his watch and waved as he took a few steps. "I need to be going. Have a great day."

Bert didn't say a word. John crossed the street and returned to his home.

"You weren't gone long," Sally said when he came through the garage entrance.

"Ran into Bert. Need I say anymore?"

"I understand, honey."

"I think I may go down to the Y and work out a little," he said. "It's been ages since I've done that."

"Just don't overdo it," she said.

"And what is that supposed to mean?"

"Just be careful and don't try to do too much. You don't want to hurt yourself."

"I think I know my limits," he said, puffing out his chest. "And I'm not that old."

"I know how old you are. Just be careful." She gave him a hug and kissed him on the cheek. "Silly old man."

John squeezed her backside, headed to the bedroom and changed into some exercise clothes.

"I shouldn't be gone too long," he said when he returned to the kitchen. "I just want to check out the facility and equipment and maybe lift a few weights and walk on the treadmill."

"Remember what I said."

"What's that, hon?"

"Don't overdo it."

As he was about to leave through the side door, she handed him a sack with items from the retirement party to give Georgina.

"Thanks," he said, kissing her on the cheek. "I'm sure they'll appreciate it."

"Just remember."

"What?"

"Don't overdo it at the Y."

John laughed as he left the house. When he stopped at Georgina's house, she was just finishing up in her flower garden. She seemed surprised by his visit, smiling sweetly and simply saying, "thank you" before going inside.

John made the short drive to the Y, where he was handed a towel and assigned a locker at the front counter. Most of the men in the locker room were about his age, probably retirees in all shapes and sizes, as well as a few younger guys, also in all shapes and sizes. He didn't feel too bad about his body when he headed to the weight room in gym shorts and a gray T-shirt. There was a little bump on his belly he hoped to work off with weights. He tried to remember to suck in his gut.

He walked on the side of the swimming pool, where a group of older adults, mostly women, were doing water aerobics, splashing water in all directions. At the far side, two men were doing laps in the Olympic-size pool. John didn't feel like he looked too out of shape compared to them.

He sat on a bench press in the weight room. He bent down and lifted a twenty-pound weight and did five curls with his right arm, then his left. He could feel the strain on his muscles, and realized he should have used a five- or ten-pound weight. But with others in the room, and self-conscious about thinking they were watching him, he toughed it out and did five reps of five curls with each arm.

John proceeded to the rear of the room where there was a rack of barbells. Rather than put weights on the bar, he grabbed a sixty-pound set. He reached down and attempted to pick it up, but halfway felt like something was ripping apart in his lower back. He slowly put the weights back down. He glanced around the room and saw no one was paying any attention to him.

John left the room, massaging his fingers deep into his lower back, and moved on to a large area with ellipticals, treadmills, Stairmasters and other sorts of equipment. Hip-hop music with heavy bass beats blasted from wall speakers. He stepped on a treadmill, and set the speed at ten miles per hour, nearly flinging off before pushing the five-mph button.

"Better slow down, buddy," a middle-aged man wearing a black headband on a treadmill next to him said. "They can get away from you."

"I see," John said, feeling his face turn red.

After getting into stride, he pushed the three mph and kept at that walking pace for fifteen minutes. He could feel his calves beginning to cramp and decided it was time to leave before there was any more damage to his aching body. He hobbled back to the locker room. John suddenly felt his age as he sat on the bench, rubbing his calves, waiting for the room to clear out before putting on his sweatpants. There was a Jacuzzi in the corner that was tempting, as well as a sauna in an adjacent room but he knew he'd be pushing his luck if he didn't get out of there and go home.

Sally had already left for her book club when he pulled his SUV into the garage. John was glad because he didn't want to hear "I told you so" from her about overdoing it. He already knew he had overdone it. He got out of his clothes and took a long shower that fogged the room with a heavy mist. He slumped over for a few minutes as the massage flow pinged his lower back.

John still felt slightly sore after he toweled off. He turned over on the bed to pull up khaki pants and wriggled on a long-sleeved brown T-shirt before retreating to the den. He eased into the recliner, propped up his legs, and read the newspaper. Before long he dozed off to sleep. Sally awakened him about two hours later, gently tapping his foot.

He groggily opened his eyes and smiled. "How was the book club?"

"We had a good time discussing the book," Sally said.

"Learn anything?"

"Maybe you'll find out one day," she said, puckering her mouth. "And how was your workout? I hope you didn't overdo it."

"It was good," he said, stretching his arms out wide. "I feel great."

"Have you had lunch? I already ate at Millie's."

"I'm not hungry," he said. "You know exercising can sometimes take your appetite away."

"It's still early. Any other plans?"

"I think I'm just going to take it easy," he said. "You?"

"I may go to the grocery a little later. Do you want to go with me?"

"I don't think so," he said. "I think I'll just watch a little TV."

"That's fine. But can you help me move something in the garage a little later?"

"Sure. What is it?"

"I have a box of clothes I'm donating to Goodwill, and I need to put it in the trunk of my car. I can drop it off when I go to the grocery."

"Why don't you just let me take it to Goodwill tomorrow? It'll give me something to do."

"That's fine with me," she said. "It's next to the garage door."

When Sally left the den, John reached down for the lever on the side to lift the recliner to an upright position. He could feel the strain on his arms and legs as he tried to ease out of the chair. "Ooh..."

"Was that you?" Sally asked from the kitchen. "Are you all right?"

"I'm fine," John said, his face contorted from the pain. "I didn't say anything. That was something on the TV."

Before she could check on him, John forced himself to stand straight, though he could feel a creaking in his lower back. He wanted to sit back down but knew he might have trouble getting back up. And he didn't want Sally to notice his problem.

She came to the doorway, staring at him for a moment with furrowed brows. John stood with his hands braced against his back.

"Are you sure you're okay?" she asked, rubbing her chin.

"Why do you say that?"

"You just look like something is the matter. Did you overdo it at the Y?"

"Of course not," he said, flexing the muscles in his arms, keeping his feet planted to the floor. "See?"

"If you say so."

"I'm good. Honest." John took a step to the recliner, bracing himself with a hand against the headrest.

"Well, I'm going to the grocery. I shouldn't be gone for more than an hour. Is there anything you want me to get while I'm out?"

"Nothing, sweetie. I'm good."

Sally picked up the light jacket she had worn to the book club and headed toward the front door. "See ya," she said.

When John heard the door open and close, he toddled to the kitchen with his hands pressed hard against his back.

"Damn," he said quietly. "I should have known better than to overdo it."

Although he wanted to sit again, John knew that would be a mistake so he walked slowly to the garage to load the box with clothes into his SUV. He let out a small sigh when it wasn't a small box. He tried lifting it, but his back wouldn't allow it. He used his hands and feet to push it but it caused too much pain.

John looked around and saw a dolly against the wall with other tools. He pushed the dolly support under the box and slowly pulled it to his vehicle.

After opening the rear hatch, John crouched on his knees and tried to push the box up and into the SUV. He was unsuccessful on three attempts, grimacing in pain each time. He glanced at his watch and knew Sally would be returning from the grocery store in about thirty minutes, if not sooner. He was hoping it would be longer.

He looked out the garage door and saw two teenagers walking in front of his house. He quickly pushed the control button on the wall to open the door and waved them over.

"Can you guys lend me a hand?" he asked.

The boys sauntered up to him with hands in their pockets and saw he was trying to put the box in the trunk. Without hesitation, they removed their backpacks, picked up the box and put it inside the vehicle.

"You don't know how much I appreciate what you've done," John said.

"No problem," one of the boys said.

They looked at him for a few seconds as if in anticipation of a reward. Then they picked up their backpacks and started to walk away.

"Hold on a second, boys," John said as he took out his wallet. He only had a twenty-dollar bill.

He took it out and handed it to one of them. "Can you split it?"

"Gee, thanks," the boy said.

"You boys were a big help," John said. "You don't realize how much."

"Let us know if we can help you with anything else," the other boy said.

John smiled as they walked away.

As the boys were leaving the house, Sally returned, parking in the driveway.

"What did those boys want?" she asked as she opened the trunk to her car.

"Those boys?" John said. "Oh, they're collecting donations for their high school athletic program. I gave them a twenty."

"I need you to help me carry in the groceries," she said.

John looked into the trunk and saw five large bags. He glanced down the street and saw the boys were three houses down.

"Well, come on," Sally said. "We don't have all day."

"I need to check something first," he said as he shuffled to the other side of the front yard. "I'll be right back. Go ahead and I'll be with you in a minute."

Sally reached into the trunk, took out a sack and headed into the house. John hurried back to her car, knelt, wrapped his hands around two sacks and slowly lifted them from the trunk. When she stepped back onto the front porch, John was standing upright.

"Are you sure you're okay?" she asked.

"Feeling great," he said with a crooked smile. "Why do you ask?"

"Never mind." She went to the car, picked up another sack and returned to the house. "We haven't got all day."

John let out a deep breath when she was out of sight.

"Coming, dear."

Five

John lay still in bed with his eyes closed the next morning, waiting until Sally went to the kitchen to prepare breakfast. He drew his lower lip between his teeth and rolled over on his side, then eased up with his left arm for a few seconds to an upright position before putting his feet on the floor. He hobbled to the bathroom, brushed his teeth and washed up before going to the kitchen.

"Good morning." John forced a smile and straightened his posture to hide his discomfort.

Sally turned and carried two cups of coffee to the bar. "Hi," she said with bright eyes. "Ready for some breakfast?"

"Nah. Just coffee."

John eased up on the stool when her back was turned. He forced another smile before taking a sip from the cup as she glanced back at him.

"You had a rough night," she said.

"Why do you say that?"

"You moaned and groaned all night long. You kept waking me up."

"I did?"

"Yes, you did. So what's bothering you?"

"Bothering me? Nothing's bothering me."

"I know there is, John Ross. Did you hurt yourself at the Y yesterday?"

"Uh, a little," he said with a frown. "I think I strained my lower back."

"I told you not to overdo it."

"I know." His shoulders slumped. "I tried to be careful but I guess I lifted a weight that was too heavy."

"Do you want me to get an appointment for you at a chiropractor or masseuse?"

"I'll be okay," John replied with a grimace as he turned slightly on the stool. "I'll just have to work it out. I've been like this before. You know that. It takes a little time."

"I know you have, but that was several years ago. You're not the guy you used to be."

"Gee, thanks a lot," he said with furrowed brows. "You sure know how to make me feel better."

"Honey, you know what I mean. I'm not the woman I was ten or so years ago. Even five years ago. Age has finally caught up with us. We've got to be careful what we do to our bodies."

"I can't argue with that."

"So just take it easy today. Take a hot bath. That might help ease the pain and loosen your muscles up a bit."

"I may do that."

"I'll go to the drug store later and buy a muscle relaxant."

"Okay," he said with a resigned tone.

"Are you sure you don't want any breakfast?"

"Nah. You can warm up my coffee," he said, raising his cup. "Anything going on today?"

"I had planned on going to the Red Cross blood drive over at one of the government buildings," she said. "But I can stay here with you if you want me to. It won't be a problem."

"No, no," he said. "I'll be fine. I'll take your advice and take a hot bath, and then I'll read some."

"Just don't do anything strenuous."

"Thank you, Dr. Sally. I'll be sure and take it easy.".

"Now, don't be a smarty pants. I just don't want you getting any worse."

"Yes ma'am," he said with a lame military salute and agonizing grin.

Sally got dressed and left an hour later. John dawdled to the bathroom and ran a tub of hot water. For good measure, he poured in bubble bath and one of Sally's moisturizers as well as a couple handfuls of Epsom salt. After it cooled to where he could get in without scalding his body, he slowly slid into the tub and leaned back. He could feel his muscles begin to loosen as he relaxed and closed his eyes. He lay there for nearly twenty minutes, nearly dozing off with his head barely above a thin layer of bubbles. When he decided to get out, he had to push himself up on both sides of the tub, bracing himself so he wouldn't slip back in. He breathed heavily and perspiration dotted his forehead as he stepped out on the floor and toweled off. He moved stiff-legged to the dresser and put on a pair of lounging pants and T-shirt.

Although his back felt somewhat better, there was still a little catch in it when he turned in either direction. He was tempted to get in bed but knew he'd fall asleep and probably have trouble getting back up. Maybe even waking up. He returned to the bathroom and swallowed two Ibuprofen, hoping to alleviate some of the pain and tightness before going to the den.

The recliner looked inviting but John decided to sit in the rocking chair. He read the newspaper and found a few magazines he thumbed through before getting back up and going to the kitchen. He poured another cup of coffee but had to put it in the microwave to get it hot. As he was about to sit, the front doorbell rang. He wasn't in the mood for a visit by Jehovah's Witnesses.

Clay Rawlings was on the porch when he opened the door. "How's the old retiree? And don't you look precious. Planning a visit to Wal-Mart later?"

"I wish." John took a deep breath as Clay stepped inside. In all his years at the newspaper, John could probably count on his hand the times that Clay had dropped by his house. They usually met on the tennis court at the park or at a watering hole near the newspaper.

"So what's up?"

"Just taking it easy," John said. "Care for some coffee?"

"Sure," Clay said as he followed John to the kitchen. "You're even moving like an old man," Clay said. "You're walking like there's a cob up your ass. Is that one of the side effects of retirement? Or too much sex?"

"Definitely not sex," John said with a chuckle as he handed the coffee to Clay. "And, no, I don't have a cob up my rear end. I was working out yesterday and did a bit too much."

"I'll try to remember that when I'm old enough to retire," Clay said with a grin.

"You're not that far behind me, buddy!"

"Just giving you a hard time."

"So what's going on?" John asked.

"Nothing much," Clay said. "I was just in the neighborhood and decided to pay a visit to my old friend."

"How are things at the paper?"

"About the same. Nothing much changes there unless someone retires or passes away. Remember Ben Thomas? Worked on the copydesk?"

"Oh, yeah. Retire?"

"Didn't make it that far. Killed in a car accident last weekend. Only fifty-seven years old."

"Damn."

"No shit, Sherlock."

"So what's been up with you?"

"Hell, you know things seldom change for me," Clay said. "All work and no play."

"I started back at the Y," John said.

"Trying to turn back the hands of time?"

"Just trying to slow them down a little."

"I can see how well it's worked for you."

"Yeah, thanks."

"Might be too late for me," Clay said. "Too much of the good life and the bad life."

"Never too late," John said. "I need to get back in shape, at least for my heart, and to lose a few pounds."

"Good idea. Just don't have a heart attack doing it."

"Hey, it gets more difficult to knock off the weight the older you get. It must be the metabolism or something."

"I hear you," Clay said, tapping his belly. "I need to get off my ass and start doing something. I haven't felt that great for the past few weeks. I think I've picked up a bug of some sort."

"Maybe you can meet me at the Y for some workouts, maybe even some basketball."

"Are you fucking kidding me?" Clay's eyes opened wide. "Basketball? I've seen too many old farts like us twisting or breaking their ankles, tearing up their knees or hurting their backs. I've read where a few have dropped dead running up and down the court. That's a young man's game."

"Okay, maybe some walking. They've got a decent oval track."

"That's more like it. Or perhaps back to the old watering hole where we can work our arms lifting the mugs of beer or our jaw muscles chewing the fat."

"Don't you think that's a bit counter-productive?"

"Probably so but it's my kind of workout," Clay said.

"Maybe once in a while after I get back into decent shape."

"I need to be going," Clay said as rose from the stool. "Just wanted to check in and see how things were going."

"Drop by anytime," John said as they walked to the front door. "And give the Y some thought. I need a workout buddy."

"Will do."

"One more thing." John rested a hand on Clay's shoulder.

"What's that?"

"Take care of yourself. If you're not feeling up to par, go to the doctor. Don't let it linger."

"I'll think about it if I don't feel better in a few days."

Six

John and Sally visited Flannery's neighborhood pub when she returned from the blood drive. After they ordered Guinness drafts, John stared out the dark-tinted window as Sally glanced over the menu.

The waitress returned with their pints. John took a big swallow, almost a third of the mug.

"Clay dropped by for a few minutes this morning."

"That must have been a surprise. How's he doing"?

"About the same. Says he hasn't been feeling well."

"He probably hasn't been taking care of himself like he did when he was married."

A smile spread over John's face. "Like you do for me?"

"Yes, like I do for you, sweetheart."

"You don't think I could take care of myself?"

"Probably," she said, "about as well as Clay does."

"Reminds me of the old saying about wives. 'Can't live with 'em, and can't live without 'em,' or something to that effect."

"Now, John, that's not nice." Sally crinkled her nose and turned her head toward the window.

"You know I'm kidding." John gently tapped her shoe with his and puckered his lips. "You take me much too seriously at times."

"I just have to keep you guessing." She batted her lashes.

"And you do it well."

"Maybe I need to get to know you again since I'm going to see a lot more of you now."

"If you do, I hope you like me as much as the first time around."

"Oh, honey, I loved you then, and I love you now."

"Whew," John said, wiping his hand over his forehead. "You had me worried there for a second."

"I'm sure," she said. "You really looked worried."

John took another swallow from his mug, lowered his shoulders and leaned back.

"Is something bothering you?" She reached over and put a hand on top of his. "Other than your back?"

"You know, this retirement thing isn't that easy. I feel kinda useless now."

"Oh, honey, don't feel that way. You put in many years at work. This is your reward."

"But it's just an empty feeling. You get up in the morning with nothing to do. You look at your day and there's nothing there. At least when I got up before, I'd get dressed and head to the paper. I may not have liked it that much in the last year or so but I had something to fill in the hours. Now I don't."

"Don't you think you need to reflect on that a little more?"

"What do you mean?"

"I remember you complaining about work the past few years, about how you felt unappreciated at times and that some of the younger employees didn't show much respect to the older, experienced editors and reporters. You said on many occasions that you couldn't wait until you walked out of that building for the last time."

"I know," he said with a sheepish grin. "I guess I didn't know what to expect on the other side of retirement."

"But it can't be that bad. You've only been retired a few weeks. You've got to give it time."

"I know. I get antsy. You know me."

"Then you need to find something to occupy your time."

"I'm giving it some thought."

"Just relax and enjoy your free time. There's no hurry to do anything. Go at your own pace. Remember what we said about looking at the first few weeks as a vacation?"

"I'll try. But the vacation is about over."

The waitress returned with the appetizers. John ordered another Guinness; Sally had barely touched hers.

"Plans tomorrow?" John asked.

"Right now my slate is clean. Is there something you'd like to do?"

"I can't think of anything," he said, taking a fried zucchini and dipping it in ranch dressing. "You're the idea person."

"Let me think on it."

"Try not to consider any honey-do's around the house."

"Not with your back the way it is. I'm putting everything on hold, so don't think you're off the hook. And the list is growing."

John chuckled. "So considerate."

John moved his back a little to the left and right and felt a tingle of pain. He knew he wasn't ready for anything strenuous, especially if it involved lifting. He thought that might be a positive and smiled to himself.

"What are you smiling about?" Sally asked.

John wiped the smile off his face. "Huh? Oh nothing."

"Something's on your mind."

"Just wondering what to do."

"Why don't we just stay home? You need to slow down and take it easy. That's a reason you hurt yourself. You keep pushing yourself, and there's no need to do that."

John took a quick swallow from his mug. "You're right. There's no reason to be doing something all the time."

"Maybe you should check out the senior citizens center."

His mouth opened wide as he tilted his head back in disbelief. "You've got to be kidding me. Senior citizens center?"

"I am," she said with a grin. "I just wanted to see how you'd react."

"I can't ever see myself in one of those places. In fact, when I see stuff on TV about them, I almost find it demeaning to old folks. They always show them doing stereotypical things like playing cards or Bingo, square dancing and having holiday parties where they stuff themselves at the buffet table. It's like they're treated like children."

"I feel the same way but I understand why they do the things they do. Some of those folks can't do a lot of physical things. And others need to do things to keep their minds sharp. And some of them don't have families spending time with them."

"I really don't feel that old right now," John said, leaning forward. "I know that sounds silly but I'm not ready for any of those kinds of activities. I still like to hike, mow the lawn, travel to different places, things like that. Clay and I were talking about taking up tennis again. My body may be getting older, but I don't feel my mind is that old. I still like to listen to our rock music from the '60s and '70s."

"You've heard the saying that you're only as old as you feel. I guess we both feel younger than our ages. But let me say one thing."

"What's that?"

"Honey, have you ever thought that the music you listen to is forty or fifty years old? It's not new music."

"Uh, I never thought of it that way," he said. "But that music was the best."

"Don't you think every generation feels that way about their music?"

"Hmm, maybe you're right." He twisted his mouth to the side. "I guess I am an old fogey."

"Oh, John, you're not that old!"

"You know you look pretty darn good for your age," John said.

"Oh, you silly man," she said with a light blush.

"Make that silly old man."

The waitress returned and took their orders for hamburgers, coleslaw and fries. John passed on another Guinness, this time opting for ice water with lemon.

"I guess after talking to Clay, it kinda makes you think about things. He mentioned a guy I knew at the paper, only fifty-seven, who died in a car accident," John said. "We've lost friends but it seems to hit a little harder when it's folks you've been around for many years."

"That's something we have to adjust to," she said. "It's a sad fact of life. And death. We're all getting closer to it each day."

"Unfortunately," John said. "I sure hope I go before you."

"Can we change the subject?"

"I'm sorry. I didn't mean to upset you. It's just something on my mind, and you know how I am when I get something on my mind. I talk it to, er, death."

"We're both healthy right now, so let's just be thankful for that. We'll deal with our sicknesses some other time. When we're sick."

"As long as I don't overdo it."

"Right."

"You know, Clay didn't even look that good," John said. "He seemed a bit pale."

"I hope it's nothing that's catching."

"Could be. He said he thought he caught a bug of some sort."

"Let's hope it's nothing serious."

"I told him to see a doctor if he doesn't feel any better."

"I hope he takes your advice."

"Knowing Clay, he won't. He'll tough it out."

"That's his decision."

"Yep."

"Sounds about like someone I know."

Seven

John went into the den and turned on the television while Sally retreated to the bedroom and changed into her nightwear. He sat in the rocker and flipped through the channels, finally settling on a National Geographic special about endangered species in South America. Sally came in carrying several magazines and sat on the couch with her legs curled.

"You know," John said, "I've been thinking about going back to college. They have a program for seniors where you can attend for free. You can audit or take classes for credit."

"I've thought about doing that as well, maybe taking some horticulture classes," she said. "I think it's a wonderful idea. What would you like to study?"

"Maybe history or literature. I was such a mediocre student when I was in college that I wouldn't mind going back and retaking some courses to find out what I missed during my wild and crazy years."

"You were quite the rebel. Remember when you had your hair in a ponytail and wore a peace symbol necklace? And you were oh-so-groovy in those bell bottoms."

"Hey, sweetie, don't forget those tie-dyed T-shirts and granny dresses you wore. You were one groovy chick back then."

They laughed and flashed two-finger peace signs at each other.

"Those were some crazy times. Civil rights. Vietnam War. Feminism."

"It's a shame things haven't changed much since then," John said.

"I know."

"But don't forget the music. The Doors, CCR, Stones, Led Zeppelin, Moody Blues, Chicago, Crosby, Stills and Nash, Aretha…Woodstock."

"And the Beatles."

"Oops, can't believe I left them out."

"And the movies," Sally said. "*MASH, Rosemary's Baby, The Graduate, The Godfather, Goodbye Columbus, Klute, Patton… Butch Cassidy and the Sundance Kid.*"

"I miss those times," John said with a sigh.

"Me, too."

"They went by too quickly. Either that or I was too young to appreciate it."

"Maybe a bit of both." Sally lowered the magazine to her lap and looked up for a few seconds.

"I was more interested in causes than classwork. I was out to change the world. At least I thought I could. I guess I can see the reason for that, but as you get older, you also question why you did it. I guess I wasn't so 'groovy' after all."

"I think the war protests and civil rights marches were worth the effort," she said. "I did them as well, but not to the extent you did."

"And that's why you graduated with honors and I graduated by the skin of my teeth," he said. "We were committed to the same things but to different degrees."

"I think you did all right. You had a good career."

"I guess I don't have too many regrets," he said. "At least that's where we met."

"Seems like ages ago," she said as a soft smile returned to her face.

"It was ages ago," he said. "More than forty years. A lifetime for many folks."

"Sad but true."

"Sometimes I think about some of the people back then who died young."

"I do too, wondering how their lives would have turned out."

"Oh, well, it depresses me to think about it. I had some friends in high school who died in Vietnam. They were only eighteen or nineteen years old. And there were a few who died in car accidents and a couple from cancer. I still remember them after all these years."

John put his head back on the rocker and closed his eyes. She watched him and remained silent until he sat up and opened his eyes.

"So, are you going to call the university?"

"I think I'll just go online and see if there's anything that interests me," he said. "It's several months before the next semester begins."

"Just don't get caught up in any protests this time," she said, picking up the magazine and grinning.

"Don't worry about that. I want to get good grades this time and make you proud of me," he said with a wink. "And don't be concerned about another ponytail." He rubbed his hand through thinning hair. "Not enough up there to do that."

John slowly rose from the rocking chair and stretched out his arms. "I think I'm going to take a quick walk before it gets too dark." He swayed a little, then placed a hand on the armrest to regain his balance.

"Are you okay?"

"Just a little light-headed for a moment." He blinked his eyes several times.

"Don't forget which way to go."

"Thanks for the reminder."

It was early evening and not many people were outside. Two blocks down the street he encountered two boys standing under a tall oak tree.

"Hey, mister," one said. "Need any more help lifting stuff?"

John immediately knew who they were.

"Not at this time," he said. "But if I have anything come up, I'll get in touch with you. Do you have a business card?"

"Business card?" the other boy said. "Are you serious?"

"How am I going to contact you if I don't have any contact information?"

The other boy took a piece of paper from his backpack and wrote down a phone number and his name, Trace.

John glanced at it, then folded it and put it in the pocket of his jacket.

"Thanks, Trace," John said with a smile. "I'll be sure to give you a call. Do you do things other than lift boxes?"

"Sure, mister," he said. "All kinds of stuff."

"I may have some lifting, raking, and cleanup in the next few weeks."

"We can both help."

"Oh, how much do you charge?"

"Twenty dollars."

"I guess that depends on the chore," John said. "Anyway, I'll let you know."

"Thanks," Trace said. "C'mon, Leon. I need to get home before it gets dark."

As the boys scrambled down the street, John took his time going in the opposite direction, trying to avoid any missteps on the sidewalk that could jolt his back. It was dark when he returned home. Sally was in bed, propped up with a pillow against the backboard reading a book.

"You were gone for a while," she said. "Accidentally run into Bert?"

"No," John said as he started getting ready to go to bed. "I was fortunate. Just took it easy. I did run into those two boys who helped me the other day."

"Two boys? What did they help you with?"

"Oh, I forgot to tell you," John said. "It's not a big deal. Anyway, they're going to help me do some work around the house when I feel up to it."

"Now, John, tell me what the boys did."

"After I hurt my back, they helped me load the stuff for Goodwill into the trunk. So when I saw them tonight they asked me if I had anything for them to do around the house."

"Now you tell me."

"It's not that big of a deal."

"I hope they're reliable and trustworthy," she said.

"Honey, they're only kids," John said. "I have the name and phone number of one of the boys. I'd guess them to be around fourteen or fifteen. I suppose they're about as reliable as you can expect any kid that age. And we'll find out if they're trustworthy. They seem like nice boys." He sat on the side of the bed and slipped off his shoes.

"You never know these days," she said, looking over the top of the book. "You get someone to do some work, then they return and steal from you."

"We'll see." John went to the bathroom and brushed his teeth. When he came back, Sally had closed her book and turned off the light on the nightstand.

"You're a sleepyhead tonight," John said as he got in under the covers.

"I'm just a little tired," she said. "You can stay up if you want to. Your light won't bother me."

"I may read for a little while," he said.

"It's funny but I remember when I could pick up a book and read it nonstop from beginning to end, into the wee hours of the morning," Sally said. "I'm lucky to last an hour now."

"Maybe the books aren't as good."

"I don't think that's it," she said. "I think my eyes aren't as good."

"Well, don't fret over it because I can't do it either. Another one of those great things about getting older."

"It could be worse." She covered her mouth as she yawned.

"Yeah, I guess we could be blind."

"Don't forget my uncle had macular degeneration. Remember how he was before he died?"

"I remember. I'd never heard of it before. It was sad to see him that way. I hope it doesn't happen to us."

"Nothing we can do about it."

"You're right," John said as he picked up a book on his nightstand. Within minutes Sally was snoring lightly. He read for about thirty minutes before turning out the light. He moved next to Sally and put his left arm around her. She snuggled closer with her back to him. He gently kissed her on the neck.

A few minutes later, they were sound asleep.

Eight

John crawled out of bed and meandered downstairs to make a pot of coffee as Sally slept in. He stepped outside in the darkness and located the newspaper in the middle of the front yard. He walked in the damp grass to pick it up, looked down the street, then the other way, noticing that nearly all of the houses were dark. About the only light radiated from streetlamps, casting soft shadows through the oak and elm trees beginning to shed their leaves.

After going back inside, he glanced at the clock on the wall. And looked again. Four o'clock.

It was too late to go back to bed since he generally got up at five-fifteen or so. He poured a cup of coffee, sat at the bar and opened the newspaper. War in the Middle East. A mass shooting in a Midwest rural town. Forest fires out west. Hurricane warnings in the Gulf. Government dysfunction. Corruption on Wall Street. He turned to the sports page and the main story was academic fraud at a high-profile university. He wondered why he even read the paper or followed the news on the Internet, television and radio. It was all depressing. And when there was something positive, it just seemed so fabricated, like it was intentionally put there to balance everything rather than being a natural occurrence. Pure fluff.

John closed the paper and poured another cup of coffee. He was tempted to go to the den and turn on the television but didn't want to disturb Sally. The more he thought about it, he realized there was nothing he really wanted to see on TV, certainly not the negativity on the news or the jolly-faced weathermen. Most of his working life had been spent around negative news, because "it sells newspapers," he was reminded in not-so-subtle ways, and he knew he probably said the same thing to those in his department. But he could walk away from it now if he chose to do so.

"You're up early," Sally said as she entered the kitchen in her unbuttoned robe. "Not feeling well?"

"I'm here because I didn't look at the clock before I got out of bed. I didn't realize it was so early until it was too late," he said, shaking his head with a grin.

"You could have come back to bed," she said.

"I didn't want to wake you."

"That's sweet but I wouldn't have minded," Sally poured herself some coffee and sat across from him. She picked up the newspaper for a second, glanced at the front-page headlines, then put it back down.

"Nothing much there," he said.

"I'll look at it later. Any plans today?"

"Not sure," he said. "I may go to the library and check out some books. Maybe read a few magazines. You?"

"I've got a retired teachers' association meeting at noon," she said. "It'll probably last a few hours."

"Sometimes I wonder if I shouldn't have gone into teaching like you," he said. "Graduate from college, work twenty-seven years, and then retire at a relatively young age."

"You could have," she said, "but you wanted to experience the thrill and excitement of being a newspaperman."

"Hah! Very funny. You've been retired for almost fifteen years. I don't see how you did it."

"Did what?"

"You know, stayed focused and occupied with all that free time."

"It wasn't that difficult. I had things I wanted to do, got involved in some others, and that quickly filled things up. And don't forget there are things around the house you seem to take for granted such as laundry, preparing meals, cleaning."

"I think I would've gone stir crazy," he said. "I would've ended up like Bert."

"I doubt that," she said with a soft laugh. "You're too fidgety to just to sit around and do hardly anything."

"You think?"

"I know so. I've lived with you more than forty years."

"I guess you'd know then."

After eating toast and jelly for breakfast, it was only six o'clock. John went ahead and showered, got dressed, and took a short walk while Sally showered and dressed.

He headed in the direction of Bert's house, thinking that at six-thirty it was too early for him to be out working on his yard. Wrong.

"You're out early," Bert said, stepping out from behind a bush where he was laying down mulch. "Don't you usually walk in the late afternoon or early evening?"

"Usually," John said. "A change of routine, I guess, since I retired."

"I've seen you walk down the other way the past few days. Got tired of going in this direction?"

"No, Bert. Just a change of scenery. I try to mix it up. Don't want my walks to get stale."

"I thought maybe you were avoiding me."

"Huh?"

"I kinda thought that."

"You should know better, Bert," John said, forcing a smile and wondering if Bert could read minds.

"Getting used to retirement?"

"Still kinda early, but I think I can get used to it. Sure beats going to work." John raised his brows and smiled.

"It does take a while."

"Sally and I were discussing it this morning over breakfast. She's been retired nearly fifteen years."

"I'm sure she's used to it."

"She's been used to it almost from the get-go," John said. "She said the key is finding things to do."

"She must have had a better time when she was teaching. I think that affects how one feels about retirement."

"Maybe so," John said, wanting to get off the subject because he sensed the direction it was taking. "We all have different work experiences. Even teachers."

"I know I couldn't wait to get out of the classroom. Another day and I don't know what I would have done."

"It was good that it finally came for you." John forced a grin through clenched teeth.

"Retirement was what I needed. After twenty-seven years dealing with those bratty students, I was more than happy to walk away from it all."

John cleared his throat. "It's too bad the experience couldn't have been more enjoyable and rewarding, like it was for Sally."

"It was pure hell, especially the final years."

John took a deep breath. "I can't say it was like that for me. I feel like I left at about the right time."

"You're a lucky man then."

John took another deep breath. "You know, Bert, I really think one of the keys to retirement is not to dwell on the past. We've all had good and bad days in our careers, but there comes a time to move on with your life."

Bert stared, or maybe glared, at John for a few seconds.

The side door opened at Bert's house. Wilma, wearing a bright pink housecoat, looked out and waved. "Oh, good morning, John. Sorry to interrupt."

"Good morning to you, Wilma." John flashed a big smile. "No problem."

"Breakfast is ready, Bert," she said sweetly. "Would you care to join us, John? Maybe some coffee?"

"Oh, no thanks." John felt tension released from his shoulders. "Some other time. I need to finish my walk and get back home. But thanks anyway."

Before Bert could say anything else, John turned and waved as he hurried down the sidewalk. "Have a great day, Bert!"

Bert was still staring at him without saying a word.

When John returned home after thirty minutes, Sally was sitting in the den watching the morning news.

"Did you have a good walk?" she asked as he sat in the recliner and kicked off his shoes.

"Only if you think getting to see Bert along the way to start your day," he said with a laugh.

"I didn't think you were going to go in that direction anymore."

"For some stupid reason I didn't think he'd be out there at this time of the day. I've learned my lesson. He's out at all hours."

"Do you have a nice chat?"

"What do you think? Did you know he had a terrible time as a teacher?"

Sally couldn't suppress a giggle. "I'm sorry," she said with puckered lips.

"It's not your fault. At least Wilma came to the rescue. It was time for their breakfast. Apparently, Bert doesn't miss breakfast."

"You need to keep in mind about what time they eat breakfast."

"A great idea! I'll try to remember around six-thirty."

"I also learned that Bert knows when I go the opposite direction. He thought I was trying to avoid him."

"Oh, that's awful."

"Well, I couldn't lie to him."

"Oh, John. You didn't."

John lowered his head. "Just kidding, but don't think I wasn't tempted."

"You wouldn't do that."

"I know but it's nice to think about. He's such a sourpuss anymore."

"Anymore?"

"Okay, he's always been a sourpuss. The degree has only increased in his bitter old age. Let me know if I ever get that way."

"Don't worry," she said. "I won't put up with it."

"Promise?"

"You can count on it."

John went to the kitchen, poured another cup of coffee and returned to the recliner.

"Anything good on the news?"

"Not that I've seen," Sally said. "Just some chit-chat about a fashion show somewhere. Nothing interesting."

"By the way, my back feels a lot better. It just takes time to get over the strain."

"That's good to hear. Now, just don't overdo it again."

"I think I've learned my lesson."

"Yeah, until the next time!"

"I said it feels better, not that it's completely healed."

"I have some light duty chores on the list."

John cleared his throat. "Well, I think I'll head on over to the library after I finish my coffee. I think it opens at eight."

"Changing the subject?"

"Huh?"

"Never mind," she said. "Take your time. You'll know where I am if I'm not here when you get back."

~ * ~

John waited in the parking lot for ten minutes before the library opened its doors. He found a comfortable chair in the periodical section and skimmed through several magazines and newspapers before someone came up behind him and touched him on the shoulder.

John turned around and looked up. He didn't recognize the man, who was probably around fifty, balding, a bit portly and wearing a tight-fitting blue sweatshirt, baggy jeans and white high-top basketball shoes.

"Aren't you the sports editor at the *Post-Chronicle*?" the man asked with a gap-toothed grin.

"Used to be," John said with a smile. "Retired now."

"Oh, congratulations. You follow the Cats?"

"Not really."

"I was wondering what you thought about the new basketball recruits."

"Really haven't followed it. Sorry." John looked back at the magazine.

"They say this point guard is something else and the power forward is a top twenty recruit."

John glanced up from the magazine. "Like I said, not that familiar with them."

"I figured you guys followed that recruiting and stuff."

"I was the sports editor," John said, forcing a tight smile on his face while trying to be polite. "It wasn't my beat. I read the stories like you do, but my job was assigning people to write stories and editing copy. I must admit I wasn't a fan." He immediately regretted the comment.

"You're not a fan?"

"It was my job to be objective, as well as the rest of the sports staff."

"No wonder things are screwed up."

"Huh?"

"If you can't get behind the Cats, then you shouldn't be trying to knock them down."

"I don't know what you're talking about, sir."

"No wonder the program has problems."

"The newspaper reports the problems. It doesn't make them."

"Sure. You expect me to believe that bullshit?"

"Well, I don't what else to tell you," John said.

"You know what you can do."

"What?"

"Get fucked, asshole!"

Several patrons looked in John's direction as the man stormed off toward the exit. John felt himself getting a little red-faced before turning his attention to the magazine. When he couldn't concentrate, he walked over to the rack where the latest books were located. He found a title about retirement and a biography of President Bill Clinton. He quickly checked them out and left the building.

On the way to his car, John looked around to make sure the overly zealous Cats fan wasn't watching him. He quickly got into his SUV, locked the doors and drove away. If anyone were following, he didn't see them. He had hoped to spend more time at the library. He didn't want to return home but wasn't sure what to do. It was times like these he wished he were sitting at his desk in the newsroom. At least he could get up and walk around, perhaps go to the cafeteria for coffee, or talk to other editors and reporters.

He recalled what Sally had said about taking things as they came and not rushing into anything. This was still the honeymoon period of his retirement, when it seemed more like a vacation. It would soon end and then he would have to face the harsh reality of finding activities that interested him.

John drove past the newspaper building. Since it was a morning paper, most of the folks inside were from the production, advertising, and circulation departments. The publisher would be there as well as a few senior staff editors, laying the blueprint for the next day's paper. Reporters would trickle in throughout the day, writing their stories and conferring with editors.

The more John thought about it, the less he wanted to be back there, even to visit. He missed most of the people he worked with in the sports department, and a few from the other news sections. But there were some folks he didn't miss. Every newspaper had its share of prima donnas, from editors to reporters to copyeditors. He didn't miss them at all. And there were a few who sought to improve their position by kissing a boss's ass instead of improving the newspaper for the reader. He didn't miss them either. And there were some folks that hardly anyone liked, but who had been there for so long it was too late to send them packing. He hoped people didn't think of him that way but realized some probably did. Regardless, he didn't miss those pricks either.

John pulled into the McDonald's parking lot located six blocks from the newspaper building. Sometimes reporters would show up there to shoot the bull before going to the office. But usually it was retired news folks who would sit in the back and talk about old times, why today's newspaper just didn't stack up, and anything else that came to mind. He used to avoid their conversations by saying he was on his way to work, but now he really didn't have an excuse. He was one of them. Old dudes.

John stepped to the front counter and ordered a large coffee. As he stepped away, several men waved at him to come on to the back. John reluctantly proceeded to their tables.

"Hey, Rossy! I heard you finally left the newspaper," said Mel Snider in a loud, distinctive New Jersey accent that commanded attention. "Welcome to the ranks of the retired." Mel was short and practically bald, and had been for years, but had a gregarious attitude and seldom met a stranger. He was a copydesk chief, so that probably accounted for his loudness as he had to get people to move copy.

"Thanks," John said as he sat and removed the top to his steaming coffee. "Twenty-seven years."

"I thought you'd been there longer," said Curtis McKenzie, who had been retired for about fourteen years from the sports staff. John remembered him when he had a thick mane of red hair; now it was fluffy white, as were his bushy eyebrows.

"Just seems that way," John said. "I worked for the wire service for twelve years before joining the sports staff at the paper."

"Pardon the cliché, but time sure flies, doesn't it?" said Curtis, whose soft voice and small, gold, hoop earring belied his hardy six-foot-four frame. Age added to the burliness of the former college lineman who still played a mean game of tennis.

"Faster than I ever expected. So what have you been up to?"

"Now that I'm closing in on seventy-seven, there's not a lot going on with me. I do go to the humane society a couple times a week and walk the dogs, wash out the kennels, or do whatever they need me to do. I also go to the hospital and visit veterans. And some tennis now and then. That's about it."

"Seems like quite a bit," John said.

"I used to do more, but the energy level just isn't what it used to be. And the missus doesn't want me away for too long. She's having some mental issues...they call it early onset Alzheimer's, so I stay around the house as much as I can. One of my daughters comes over and watches her so I can get out and socialize with these wonderful old farts."

"Sorry to hear about your wife," John said. "That must be difficult."

"You learn to adjust," said Howard Brock, who worked on the layout desk for many years. "My wife passed away four years ago. I've had a few friends suffer health-related issues. I even had heart bypass surgery a year after I left the paper. It's all part of the territory." Howard had been overweight when he worked at the newspaper but had transformed into a fit seventy-something who still tried to comb a few long strands of black hair over his balding pate.

"But we're not complaining," Curtis said. "We're glad to be here. We try to make the most of the situation. Remember Barney Wilders?"

"Sure," John said. "He was an editor on the business desk."

"He and his wife are touring the Amazon region. They've been away for nearly two weeks. We're hoping they're not going to get eaten by piranhas."

Mel bellowed a large laugh.

"But it just shows that some of the retired folks are getting around and doing all sorts of things," Curtis said. "Barney and Muff probably spend half the year on the road and their winters in Florida."

"My wife and I plan to go to Europe in a few months," John said. "A gift from our kids."

"That's great," Curtis said. "Worst thing you can do is sit on your ass and do nothing. Even coming down here every day or so sure beats the hell out of doing nothing."

"At least your mind is engaged to some extent," Howard said.

"Not much, but to some extent," Curtis said with a chuckle. "We aren't exactly the brain trust but we can provide all the free opinions you'd ever want. But I doubt we'll ever solve any of the world's problems."

John grinned and took a sip from his coffee. "I'll keep that in mind."

"So you're on cruise control now?" asked Howard, running his hand over the top of his head to keep the few strands of hair in place.

"Pretty much so," John said. "Still making that adjustment. I just came from the library where I got lectured by some reader for not supporting the Cats."

"That's another thing you'll learn," Curtis said. "Don't broadcast that you worked in the media. Folks seem to either love you a little or hate you a lot. You might be better off telling them you're a former politician or used-car salesman. Practically every time I've mentioned being a former newspaperman, I get some kind of opinion about the news. Fortunately, most folks who read my columns are dead or have forgotten about me. That's been a blessing in disguise. I don't need those hassles anymore."

"Not that you won't get opinions here," Mel said. "But at least you know where the bullshit is coming from and you won't get any grief—well, not much grief—about it. We all try to kiss and make up before we leave."

John glanced at his watch. "Guys, I need to be going." The others said the same, and they all rose from their seats.

"Hey, John," Curtis said. "Don't be a stranger. One of us is usually here nearly every morning. We've even been known to get together for poker once in a while."

"Thanks, Curtis. I'll remember that."

~ * ~

Sally had already left for her teachers' meeting when he got home. He went to the kitchen and fixed a bowl of Cheerios with a sliced banana. He grabbed the newspaper and read the editorials while he ate.

Despite the encounter at the library, he thought he was having a good day after seeing some old friends at McDonald's. He wasn't sure if he'd be a regular, at least not at this juncture, but thought it might be a possibility at some point. It sure beats sitting at home.

John put on his walking shoes and headed out the front door. He made a slight turn toward Bert's house, but quickly reversed himself and glided in the opposite direction.

Five blocks down the street, John heard rustling behind a crape myrtle in a vacant lot. He stopped for a moment, then walked slowly to where he heard the sound. There was a soft whine and whimper. He tip-toed around and saw a small dog tied to a clothesline rope entangled in the shrub. The dog barked several times as he approached.

"What's up there, little fella?" John said softly, holding the back side of his hand toward the dog. The canine sniffed hesitantly. John cautiously reached in and gently petted the animal's furry head. When he sensed the dog wasn't afraid, or wasn't going to bite, he untangled the rope to set him free.

There wasn't a collar on the dog. John surmised it had been left there by someone. He looked around and didn't see anyone watching him with the dog. He thought about untying the pup but wasn't sure how it would react. He didn't want the dog running off and getting struck by a car.

John took the rope and led the animal back to the sidewalk. The dog didn't struggle or try to get away from him. He was surprised the little creature obediently followed his lead.

"What am I going to do with you?" John said as the dog followed him back to his house. "I guess I'll have to call the humane society and see if anyone is missing a dog. Maybe they'll take you in until your owner can be located."

The dog looked up at John with his big brown eyes, tilting his head back and forth as if he knew what was being said.

He had long whiskers, a thick brown and black coat and a compact build. He had a confident bounce in his walk with his head held erect. He weighed no more than fifteen pounds.

"Okay, let's go inside and see if we can find something for you to eat," John said as he opened the side door. He looked in the refrigerator to see if there was anything that might satisfy a dog's appetite.

"Hungry?"

The dog licked his mouth.

"Cheese?"

Again, the dog licked his mouth.

John took out a slice of American cheese, broke it up into small squares and put them in a saucer. The dog gobbled them within a few seconds.

"Boy, you are hungry," John said, opening the refrigerator again for more food. He found a packet of lunch meat and took out a slice of ham, tearing it into small pieces. The little dog devoured the bites and licked the saucer clean.

"That should do you for a while," John said as the dog looked attentively at him.

John picked up the phone book and called the humane society. They told him they didn't have any notices about missing dogs but took a description in case someone called. He asked if he should bring it over to them, but they asked if he could keep it because they were overcrowded. John glanced at the dog, which appeared to be smiling at him, and reluctantly agreed to provide a foster home for several days.

After ending the call, John removed the rope from the dog's neck, noticing several raw spots from where he had apparently struggled to break free or where someone may have dragged him to the bushes. The dog was satisfied to stay in place, right at John's side.

"Okay, little whiskers," John said, "let's see if we can find a place for you to rest."

He found a medium-sized cardboard box in the garage and carried it back to the kitchen. He proceeded to the bathroom with the dog following a step behind, took out an oversized beach towel and returned to the kitchen. He neatly folded the towel twice, placed it inside the box and patted it several times.

"How's that for a bed?" John said. "I hope Sally won't mind."

The dog sat on his hind legs with his tongue out.

"Are you telling me you're thirsty?" John took a small plastic cup from the cabinet and filled it with water from the sink. The dog lapped from the cup until it was nearly empty.

"So what do we do now?" John said.

Without hesitation, the dog dashed to the kitchen door and softly tapped a paw against it.

"You want to leave already?"

The dog tapped against the door again.

"Okay, if that's what you want," John said as he opened the door and followed the dog to the side yard. The dog ran to a barberry shrub and lifted his hind leg.

"Oh, so that's what you wanted," John said with a laugh.

"Who are you talking to?" Sally asked from the kitchen door.

Startled for a moment, John turned his head. "Uh, a new friend."

A few seconds later, the dog pranced over to John.

"A dog?"

"Let me explain," John said, who then told her about finding the dog on the vacant lot and calling the humane society to see if anyone was missing one. He told her they would be foster owners until the dog could be placed in a permanent home.

Sally walked over to them, knelt and rubbed the dog on both cheeks. "What's his name?"

"I don't know," John said. "How about Whiskers?"

"That fits him. He does have long whiskers."

They returned to the house and the newly named mutt bounced along behind them.

"Have you fed him?" Sally asked.

"Ham and cheese. That's all I could find in the fridge."

"Why don't you drive over to the store and pick up a couple cans of dog food?" she said.

"I guess I can," John said as he grabbed his car keys on the counter. When he opened the door to leave, Whiskers was at his feet, ready to go with him.

"Maybe I should do it," Sally said. "He already seems attached to you."

John put his keys back down and retreated to the den, followed dutifully by Whiskers. Sally watched as John slowly sat in the rocker and Whiskers lay next to him.

"I'll be back in a few minutes." Whiskers didn't move as she went to her car. A few minutes later, with his head resting in his front paws, he was asleep.

"Busy day for you, little fella," John said.

Sally was back within fifteen minutes with three cans of dog food, dishes for food and water, and a rawhide bone. She scooped a couple spoonsful of food into the dish. Whiskers smelled it for a second before wolfing it down in several bites.

"That should do you for a while," Sally said. "We don't want to overdo it."

She took the rawhide bone off the counter and held it down for Whiskers. Again, he took a couple of whiffs before taking it in his mouth.

"He looks satisfied," John said.

"I hope so. I don't want him chewing on furniture or shoes."

John sat at the counter and watched Whiskers munch on the bone.

"Want some coffee?" Sally asked.

"Do we have any decaffeinated? I've been getting headaches lately and I think it might be from too much caffeine."

"I think we have some instant decaf. I'll go prepare some." Sally made the coffee as John retreated to the den, followed by Whiskers with the rawhide firmly in his mouth. Whiskers didn't budge from his spot next to John.

John's cell phone rang. He looked at it for a second and didn't recognize the number. Then he answered. Sally walked to the doorway.

"I'll be happy to," he said.

Sally mouthed, "Who is it?"

John raised an open hand. "Sure. No problem."

Sally pursed her lips tightly.

"Anytime," John said as he lowered his arm. "I'll see you then." He ended the call.

"Who was that?" Sally asked, walking toward him. "Whiskers' owner?"

"No," he said with a smile. "There's a neighborhood association meeting Thursday night. They're just notifying everybody. That's all."

"I was worried it might be Whiskers' owner."

"It sounds like you're getting a little attached to him as well."

"I guess I am," she said. She knelt on one knee and stroked Whiskers' back. "You can't help but get attached to him. He's a cute little dog."

Sally returned to the kitchen to make the coffee. John picked up the remote on the footstool and turned on the television. He was surfing through the channels when Sally returned and handed him a cup of coffee.

"There's simply nothing on TV anymore," he said. "Amateur singing contests, reality shows that aren't real, so-called news that's anything but objective. You can't even find a good classic movie anymore. It's all crash, bang crap. Trash. Sometimes I think we should just quit taking cable and save a few bucks."

"There's a few programs I like," Sally said. "It's not all bad."

"I'm sure you can find something to watch out of two hundred channels. And that's too damn many as well. It gets too confusing. You need a notebook to keep track of everything. Remember when we had four or five basic channels?"

"Yes, dear," she said with a smile. "Back in simpler times. Or was that the good old days?"

"Okay, okay," he said with a chuckle. "Don't patronize me. I know I'm getting old but my mind hasn't totally deserted me. Not yet."

"You're just getting older," she said. "We change as we grow older. Maybe you're just bored with TV overall. You never watched much TV anyway because you were at work a lot."

"And the TVs at work were on weather, news and sports channels," he said. "None of this other junk. Maybe I'm expecting too much. I didn't realize how bad it was until I got to see what was on the other channels."

"So maybe you should focus on weather, news and sports channels."

"Thanks, but no thanks," he said. "Maybe weather, but the news depresses me, always about terrorism, epidemics, shootings, various and sundry sordid crimes and whatnot. And then you get those wing nuts expressing all kinds of political viewpoints and conspiracies. I don't need to hear that stuff all the time. I can read it in the newspaper. To be honest, even the weather reports are getting out of hand. They seem to want to scare the hell out of people. We used to laugh at one meteorologist who got so worked up it seemed like he was going to have an orgasm every time there was a threat of snow. And I've had my fill of sports, especially after that clown I encountered at the library."

"Clown?"

"A delusional sports' fan apparently recognized me from the newspaper. He chastised me for not being a fan of the Cats. Told me to fuck off, right there in the library." John raised his hands and laughed. "Can you believe it? What's this world coming to?"

"Yes, I can believe it. People always thought you were totally consumed by sports. They didn't realize you had other interests."

"Maybe being away from the newspaper will help change that perception."

"There will always be someone out there who recognizes you."

"Maybe we need to move to another city."

"Are you serious?" she said, raising her brows.

"Not really," he said. "But it would be a solution. Maybe folks will forget about me after a period of time. You know, as Clay has said many times, 'out of sight, out of mind.'"

"Remember that time we took the kids to Disney World in Florida and ran into folks who knew you from the paper?"

"Don't remind me," he said. "You can't get away from the nut jobs."

"Now, that's not being very kind," she said. "They just love their teams."

"That's easy for you to say because you never had to deal with them."

"Let's change the subject," she said. "I don't want you getting your blood pressure up."

"And having a heart attack or stroke?"

"That's not funny, John."

"Sorry." He took a sip of his coffee.

"What do you want to do the rest of the evening?"

"I know I don't want to watch TV," he said, clicking the power off button on the remote. "I wish I had something good to read."

"You didn't find anything at the library?"

"I checked out a bio on President Clinton and a book about retirement but I left them in the car."

"Do you want to play Scrabble or anything?"

"That'd give me a bigger headache."

"You just want to sit in the rocking chair all evening?"

"Maybe just to relax for a while."

"Well, I think I'm going to get ready for bed and read."

"Maybe I'll join you in a bit."

Sally rose from the couch and took John's empty coffee cup to the kitchen. "You'll know where to find me."

John slowly rocked back and forth for a few minutes, occasionally reaching down and rubbing Whiskers between his ears.

"Whatcha think, Whiskers? Should we call it a night?"

Whiskers looked directly at John and tilted his head slightly.

"Okay, let's go on to bed." John got up from the rocking chair, and without any commands, Whiskers followed him to the bedroom. The dog bounded into his makeshift bed and watched John go to the bathroom. When John returned, Whiskers was curled in a semi-ball, eyes closed.

Sally lowered her book to her chest. "You're going to bed as well? It's only eight-fifteen."

"Nothing else to do," he said as he got under the covers. "I'm not going to stay up for the sake of staying up."

"And you used to be such a night owl," she said.

"And you as well."

"We'd put the kids to bed, then stay up past eleven-thirty or so watching the talk shows. I miss Johnny Carson."

"I couldn't tell you who is on the late-night shows now," John said. "I don't remember the last time I was awake at eleven-thirty, unless it was during tournament season."

"Want to stay up and see who's on tonight?"

"We can try but I doubt if I can make it."

Sally picked up the remote on her nightstand and turned on the small television near the foot of the bed. A reality show was on the station. She offered the remote to John. "You want to find something?"

"Nope," he said. "I've already tried it in the den. Maybe you can have better luck."

Sally clicked through several channels before setting the remote next to her on the bed. "I give up. I think I'm going to read some more. Feel free to look again."

John was tempted to pick up the remote but changed his mind. "Not interested."

"How are you going to stay up without doing anything?"

"I'll just look at your pretty face," he said.

Sally blushed. "Quit being silly."

"Hey, I'm serious," John said, easing closer to her and placing a hand on her waist.

Sally put a bookmark in the book, closed it and put it on the nightstand. "Do you want to talk some more?"

"No," John eased his body next to her.

"So what did you have in mind?" She lowered her head and batted her lashes.

"You crazy woman." John slipped his hand under her gown, gently rubbing her soft belly before fondling her breasts. She closed her eyes and turned her head toward him. He lifted his head and kissed her softly on the mouth.

"Mmmm," she whispered.

They continued to touch and kiss before they both reached down to slip off her panties. He eagerly touched the moist softness between her legs before removing his boxers. She turned and pressed her body against him as he caressed her back and hips through deep kisses. She rolled over on her back and John entered her. They both moaned in delight during their lovemaking.

After their climax, they were startled as Whiskers let out a several loud barks. They both laughed.

"It's okay, little fella." John rose on his elbows and looked over at him in the box. "We forgot you were here."

Sally quickly slipped out of the bed and tip-toed nude to the bathroom. She turned on the shower. John followed seconds later and got in the tub with her. He took a washcloth filled with body wash and smoothed over her backside, then she turned around and he did the same to the front of her curvy body. He couldn't resist giving her another lingering kiss under the flow of the showerhead.

She stepped out of the shower to towel herself while John stayed in for a few more minutes. She was already back in bed when he returned to the bedroom. Whiskers appeared to be asleep.

John climbed back into bed, lying on his back and closing his eyes.

"You're not staying up for the late show?" Sally said.

"I think not," he said with a light laugh. "I've already had my late show and this old boy is going to sleep."

"So much for having a bad back," she said.

"That wasn't on the honey-do list?"

"Oh, you silly man."

Sally reached over and turned off the lamp, then curled up in John's waiting arm.

Nine

A week passed and John hadn't received a call about Whiskers. He was getting more attached to the little canine, and every time the phone rang, he would think this would be the one inquiring about a missing dog.

Whiskers was becoming more involved in John's life. In addition to the walks, he was riding in the car with him on short trips. Wherever John journeyed in the house, Whiskers would follow him like a shadow.

"Do you think it's about time to take him to the vet?" Sally asked one morning as they were getting dressed in the bedroom. "He's getting a little shaggy looking and we need to know about his shots."

"That's a good idea," John said. "I'll make an appointment this morning. Maybe we can get him in this week."

"It appears like we're not going to hear from his owner."

"Sure seems that way."

"I think I'm going to run to the grocery and pick up some more food for our little friend," Sally said. "Anything you need?"

"I'm good. Take your time."

John and Whiskers ventured into the garage while Sally was away. He looked at several boxes, books and various tools stored at the rear of the room. He finally picked up a push broom and began sweeping the floor.

"At least it's a start," John said to Whiskers.

"John?"

John flinched at the unexpected sound then saw Preston Miles standing outside the garage, wearing neatly pressed khaki pants, a lavender polo and a light dark brown, button-down sweater wrapped around his shoulders. John pressed the door opener as Preston took a step back in the driveway.

"You startled me for a moment," John said.

"I apologize for that. I probably should have tapped on the glass."

"No problem. What's up?"

"This is more of a personal issue."

"What is it?"

"I've noticed your pet has been relieving himself by the barberry bush between our homes," Preston said.

"Is that a problem?"

"Well, it could develop into a health issue if there is an accumulation of his feces. And I'm concerned that his continued urination could also kill the lovely shrub. And furthermore, and I don't mean to be a difficult neighbor, the smell could become odorous over a period of time."

"I understand your concerns," John said, glancing down at Whiskers. "I hadn't realized he had become such a problem."

"Well, you know, animals can be such a pest at times."

"I don't consider Whiskers a pest."

"Whiskers. What an odd name."

John pursed his mouth and held his breath for a few seconds. "Anything else, Preston?"

"That's it, John. I just wanted to bring it to your attention."

"I'll look into it."

"I need to be going," said Preston. "Margaret and I are attending a matinee performance of *Death of a Salesman* at the university."

Preston smiled curtly and walked away.

"Have a nice time." John turned and returned to sweeping the floor.

Ten seconds later, John reached over and pushed the remote to close the garage door. "And don't let the door hit you in the ass."

John leaned the broom against the wall and stepped back into the house with Whiskers. He could feel his blood pressure rising so he sat at the counter and took several deep breaths.

Sally returned from the store with a sack of groceries and placed it on the counter.

"You look upset," she said. "What's wrong?"

"Oh, that dickhead next door complaining about Whiskers."

"Preston?"

"Is there another dickhead?"

"I'm sorry." She sat next to him. "What did he say?"

"He doesn't like Whiskers relieving himself between our houses."

"Are you serious?"

"He's concerned the shrub may die and that there may be some smelly shit to deal with. What a pretentious ass!"

Sally patted him gently on the forearm.

"Oh, honey, you know how Preston is. He's always had that air of superiority about him, thinking he's so important and intelligent just because he teaches at the university."

"Still pisses me off."

"Did you tell him the barberry is on our property?"

"I was too upset to say much of anything. He kinda caught me off guard."

"I've got something else that may upset you," she said, reaching into the sack. "Do you want to see it now or wait until later?"

"Oh hell, may as well look at it now."

Sally took a flyer she had found posted on the bulletin board at the supermarket and handed it to John. It stated: "Lost Dog. Black and Brown color. Small. Goes by Poncho." It listed a phone number to call.

"Well?"

John let out a long sigh. "Damn."

"Do you want to call?"

"I don't want to but I suppose I should. That's what I'd want if I had lost a dog."

John looked down at Whiskers, who was staring at him with his deep, dark eyes. "Why don't you feed him while I make the call?"

While Sally was scooping food into Whiskers' dish, John meandered to the den holding the flyer with his head down. He picked up his cell phone and punched in the number. He got a voice message and left his name and number.

"Well, let's see if we hear from the person," John said when he returned to the kitchen.

"That's all you can do."

"I wonder how long it's been posted?"

"I have no idea. That's the first time I've seen it."

"I think I'm going for a walk," he said. "After dealing with Preston and seeing this flyer, I need to clear my head."

He put the leash on Whiskers' collar and stepped outside. As he stood on the porch, he watched as Preston and his wife backed out of their driveway and drove down the street.

"Come on," John said to Whiskers, leading the dog to the barberry shrub between the houses.

Whiskers squatted.

John smiled.

Ten

"I have an appointment to get my car serviced this morning. Can you follow me over there so I can drop it off, and bring me back home?"

"Let me check my calendar," John said, taking out his cell phone. "Sure. I don't have any plans or anything going on."

"Aren't we the comedian this morning?"

An hour later they left the house, leaving Whiskers at home since they wouldn't be away long.

When they returned forty-five minutes later, John parked his SUV in the driveway and pushed the remote to open the garage door. They walked to the side of the garage, where John pointed to some rain damage to the foundation before going in the side door.

"Holy shit!" John held up his hand to caution Sally after he took his first step inside the house.

Sally peeked over John's shoulder into the kitchen. "Oh, my god!" She placed her hand over her mouth.

Cabinets and drawers had been emptied on the floor. Plates, cups and glasses were shattered on the floor along with scattered silverware and utensils.

"Stay back," John said, "and call nine-one-one."

He walked cautiously to the den, which had also been ransacked, with books and magazines scattered everywhere. The flat screen TV and Blu-ray player were missing. He proceeded to their bedroom, where the TV had been ripped off the wall. Sally's antique armoire had been turned over, with jewelry strewn about the floor. The mattress on the bed was pushed off, while sheets and pillows had been tossed in every direction. As a slight breeze rippled through the curtain, he noticed the window was open. He looked out and saw a light path on the grass leading to the back corner of the yard.

Moments later a siren wailed in the distance. Sally rushed to the front door to await the arrival of the police. Several neighbors came out and stood in their yards as two cruisers screeched to a stop in front of the house.

"We've been robbed." Sally trembled with her arms crossed as two officers approached the house. "The inside of our home has been destroyed."

John was standing in the living room when they walked in. He put his arm securely around Sally, who was weeping. The officers took out notepads and asked several questions about the break-in before going in different directions to see assess the damage.

"We weren't gone very long," John said, explaining to an officer returning to the living room that they had taken a car to be serviced at a dealership.

"Look here, a little pup," an officer shouted from the den. They dashed in and saw Whiskers lying on his side in the corner, almost lifeless.

"Damn," John said, wide-eyed. "I forgot all about Whiskers."

The officer placed his hand on Whiskers' chest. "He's still alive, but barely."

Sally hurried to the bedroom, stunned for a moment after seeing what had been done to the room, then picked up Whiskers' sleeping box and carried it to the den. John gently cradled the dog and laid him in the box.

"I'm going on to the vet's office," he said to the officer.

Sally walked with him to the SUV and opened the passenger side so he could place the box on the seat. "Call me when you know something," she said, wiping away tears.

John tried not to exceed the speed limit as he drove to the vet's office, but he knew time was of the essence when he glanced at Whiskers, who was breathing faintly. Blood had trickled from his mouth and congealed on his fur. John tapped the accelerator a little harder.

The veterinarian's office immediately admitted Whiskers ahead of others who had animals in the waiting area for care. A tech took the box from John and carried it behind swinging doors to the emergency room. Less than a minute later, a vet came out and John explained to her what had happened to his house, only speculating that Whiskers had been kicked or slammed against the wall.

X-rays were taken of Whiskers, showing some internal bleeding. A breathing tube was inserted in his mouth and he was given injections to stop the bleeding.

"We think we have him stabilized," the veterinarian said in the waiting room after spending more than an hour with him. "He suffered a concussion and subdural hematoma. Fortunately, there are no broken bones. We'll need to keep him here for a couple days for observation in case other issues arise."

John thanked the vet for saving Whiskers' life. He went to the SUV, called Sally and gave her the news before driving home.

The police officers had left when he pulled into the driveway. Sally was in the kitchen, sweeping the mess into a dustpan and dumping the debris in a large black trash bag.

"I'm so thankful Whiskers is alive." Sally took a deep breath, leaned the broom against the wall, sat on a barstool and began to cry.

"Me, too." John walked over to console her. "I was afraid that little bugger would die on the way there. We got him to the vet just in time."

"Thank goodness."

"What did the cops say?"

"Hardly any evidence," she said with a heavy sigh, wiping away tears. "They said there've been several break-ins around here in the past month or so. They say it usually goes this way, with one neighborhood targeted for a few weeks, then moving on to another one."

"Have you checked out the bedroom yet? Any valuables stolen?"

"Not that I could see," she said. "It looks like they were only interested in TVs and electronics. In fact, the policemen said that's what happened in the other homes that were burglarized."

"I suppose our insurance will take care of everything," John said as he surveyed the mess on the floor. "This makes me sick. Why would anybody do this to someone else?"

Sally let loose a heavy sigh. "I know. It feels like we've been personally violated."

"No clues?"

"About the only thing is they believe it was done by someone young because they were more concerned about taking electronics."

"So we'll have to go to the pawn shops or whatever now?"

"They said our belongings won't likely be at pawn shops. They'll probably sell them to friends or others who are in the market for stolen goods."

"Well, let's just be thankful Whiskers wasn't killed," John said.

"Yes, that's something to be thankful for."

Sally returned to cleaning the kitchen, even noticing that the coffeemaker, toaster, and radio were missing from the counter, while John headed to the den to clean up the damage.

"What a mess," he muttered with clenched teeth.

A few minutes later, Sally went in and plopped down on the couch. She took a deep breath, looked around the room and began to sob again. "I still can't believe this happened."

"I know how you feel, sweetheart." John sat next to her and kissed her on the cheek. "We've lived here for more than twenty years and nothing has ever happened. In some weird way, I guess we should feel fortunate it didn't happen sooner."

"Fortunate?" she said. "What in the world are you talking about? Our home has been vandalized and we should feel fortunate? What are you thinking, John?"

"Honey, I'm not making light of it," he said, rubbing her knee. "It's just that people have their homes robbed all the time. We've had neighbors who have had their cars broken into, bicycles stolen from their yards, lawn ornaments destroyed. You name it and it's probably happened."

"You're right," she said. "But I don't have to think we're fortunate. And it doesn't make it any easier. I thought we lived in a good, safe neighborhood. I'm beginning to wonder now."

John took her by the hand. "Come on, let's get things cleaned up in the bedroom."

Sally peeked in the bathroom off the bedroom. "It doesn't look like anything was taken here."

"Probably noticed there wasn't much there to take."

After getting the bedroom back in order, they weren't sure what to do. They wanted to call the vet's office to check on Whiskers, but lost track of time, and the office had already closed for the day.

"I wonder why the burglars harmed Whiskers?" Sally asked.

"My guess is the barking," John said.

"I sure hope that little bugger is doing okay. The house seems empty without him."

"It sure does."

"I'm getting a little hungry but I don't want to go out to eat," Sally said. "I'm afraid they'll come back and do some more damage. I know that sounds crazy but that's the way I feel. I just don't feel safe right now."

"I don't think we'll see them again, if it's more than one person," John said. "But I know what you mean about leaving the house. I think I'll call a home security system company tomorrow."

"What do you want to eat?"

"Call out for pizza?"

"That should be safe."

While John placed a call for a veggie pizza, Sally returned to the den and ran the vacuum cleaner over the carpet.

When the doorbell rang, John expected to see a deliveryman. It was Bert.

"Problems today, John?" Bert asked. "I saw police cruisers down here earlier."

"Robbed and vandalized," John said as he stepped out on the porch. "Doing a little cleanup now."

"This is getting to be a rough neighborhood. That's one reason you see me out front a lot. Just checking on the things at my place and up and down the street."

"Did you see anyone at our house? Anything suspicious?"

"Can't say that I did, unfortunately," Bert said. "Appeared to be a quiet morning. I did see you and Sally leave and come back. Then the cops. Wish I could have seen more."

"No one walking on the street?

"Ah, maybe some neighborhood kids but that's about it. I didn't pay that much attention to them because I see them all the time."

"The police said our neighborhood has been targeted the past month and they believe it was done by youngsters."

"Oh, really?" Bert said, tilting his head. "I should be more attentive."

"I suppose we all should. Maybe get a Neighborhood Watch going."

"Good idea, John. You going to organize?"

"I'll think about it. Give me time."

"I'll support you."

"Thanks, Bert," John said.

John smiled when the pizza delivery arrived, thinking Bert would leave.

"Our dinner tonight," John said after paying for the pizza.

"I like pizza," Bert said.

"Uh, care to join us?"

Bert hesitated a moment. "Sure," and followed John to the dining room.

"We've got company for dinner," John said as they passed the den.

"Company?" Sally asked, raising her voice.

"Bert."

Sally walked into the room, wiping her hands on a dish cloth.

"Oh, hi Bert," she said.

"Heard you had some visitors today," Bert said with a knowing grin.

"I guess you could say that." Sally bit her lower lip, trying not to sound irritated. "What would you like to drink? Water? Soda? Beer?"

"Hmm, a beer would be nice. Domestic or foreign?"

"Bud."

"Okay, Bud then."

"You John?"

"Only domestic?" he said with a wink.

"Yes, dear."

"Bud then."

Bert glanced around the room as they ate. "You know, it's been a long time since I've been in your home."

"Really?" John said. "I'm not sure if I've ever seen the inside of yours."

"Oh." Bert squirmed in his chair.

"How's Wilma?" Sally asked.

"She's doing great," Bert said, apparently glad to change the subject. "I couldn't be more pleased. She's at the grocery now."

After finishing one slice of pizza and drinking half of his beer, Bert suddenly stood. "I need to be going. Wilma will be home soon and I need to help her unload the car. Thanks for inviting me to share your pizza. We'll have to do it more often."

Before John or Sally could say anything, Bert was already making his way to the front door. "I'll see you folks later. Again, so sorry for your misfortune."

After the door closed, John and Sally looked at each other for a moment and then broke out laughing.

"Yeah, we need to do this more often," he said as they tipped their glasses.

~ * ~

"Want to take a quick walk with me?" John asked after they cleared off the table and put three pieces of leftover pizza in the refrigerator.

"Sure, why not?" Sally said. "Let me get my sweater."

Five doors down from their house they were stopped by Hank Summers, who was spraying his driveway with a water hose.

"Heard you guys were vandalized this morning," said Hank as closed the nozzle.

"You heard right," John said.

"Damn. Take much?"

"TVs, small appliances and a few other things. They also trashed a couple of rooms."

"Police have any idea who did it?"

"Nope, and we'll be lucky if they find out."

"That's a damn shame," Hank said, shaking his head excessively for effect. "I bet it was some of those illegals. You know they've been moving in near our neighborhood."

"I'm aware of that," John said. "But I'm not pointing any fingers."

"You know they move around in gangs, too."

"I don't know," John said. "I haven't heard of that here in Lexington. Maybe in California. I know several Hispanics in town and they're nice people."

"I don't think it was a gang," Sally said. "If there was a gang, someone would have noticed them."

"I'd still keep my eyes open, guys," Hank said with furrowed brows. "Ya never know about them illegals and them gangs."

"How's everything with you these days?" John asked. "Are you still at the dairy?

"Yep. Going on seventeen years. They've expanded my territory."

"Congratulations," John said. "Always nice to get a promotion."

Seconds later, Hank's son, Bart, and a friend pulled up in front of the house in a late model red Camaro. Music blared from the radio as they sat in the car with the windows half up.

"Turn that goddamn crap down," Hank shouted.

Bart turned off the ignition and walked over to the driveway. "Sorry about that, Pops." He was wearing tight jeans and a denim shirt flared open at the top. His friend, who was standing several feet away, was decked out in jeans and white dress shirt as well as dark sunglasses that he didn't remove.

"Hi Bart," said Sally, who had been his fifth-grade teacher. "How are you doing?"

Bart, in his early twenties, flashed a big smile. "I'm doing great, Mrs. Ross. I'm taking a break from college this semester but hope to get back in the spring and work on my degree."

"That's wonderful," she said. "What are you studying?"

"I'm still undecided," Bart said

"Hell, it will be wonderful if he ever graduates," Hank said "He's taking the six-year plan to get his degree. Maybe seven. Who knows?"

"Just stick with it," John said to Bart. "You need an education if you want to succeed in today's world."

"Thanks, Mr. Ross," Bart said. "I plan to."

"You wanna foot the bill?" Hank said to John. "This education stuff's expensive."

"We know it," John said. "We had to help put two kids through college."

"Bart, did you hear that the Ross's house was robbed this morning?" Hank asked.

"I didn't know that," Bart said, titling his head at John. "That's awful. Do they know who did it?"

"No idea," John said.

Bart glanced at his friend and took a step toward the house. "We need to be going. It was nice seeing you, Mr. and Mrs. Ross. I'm sorry about what happened at your house. C'mon, Derrick."

After the young men disappeared into the house, Hank said, "I'll sure be glad when that boy graduates so he can get a job. He's breaking the bank."

"Doesn't even work part-time?" John asked.

"Hell, no. He seems to think he's too good for that. He says he wants something in management. Isn't that a hoot?"

Sally let out a light laugh, then covered her mouth. "I'm sorry for that. I've seen some other kids the same way."

"So how does he afford to drive the car and other expenses?" John asked.

"How do you think?" Hank said. "I'm the bank."

"Okay," John said with a smile. "Hey, we need to get walking before it gets too dark."

"You guys take care." Hank opened the nozzle and resumed spraying the driveway.

Several doors down, John looked at Sally. "I guess we didn't do all that bad with Brody."

"Bart sure knows how to lay it on thick," she said. "He was that way in my class. He always thought he could get away with things with that cheesy smile of his."

"He should do well in management."

Eleven

John picked up Whiskers three days later at the animal clinic. While the little dog was weak and had lost two pounds, he bounced into John's waiting arms and licked his face.

"It's good to see you, too, little fella," John said with a chuckle.

"He should be almost as good as new," the vet said as she handed John two vials of pills. "Just don't let him overdo it for a week or so."

"We'll take it easy." John softly stroked his four-legged buddy's back.

Whiskers curled up in the box on the way home, glancing up at John whenever they hit a bump or made a turn in the road. John reached down and petted him on the head to reassure him that everything was going to be fine.

When they got home, Whiskers ambled, rather than scampered, to his favorite backyard spot and did his thing while

John watched from the corner of the house. Moments later, Whiskers returned.

"Our little fella is back home," John announced as they came in from the garage to the kitchen.

"Hi there, Whiskers," Sally said as she knelt on one knee to greet him with open hands. "You feel better now?"

Whiskers licked her fingers for a few seconds, then went over and lapped water from his bowl. Sally put kibble into his other bowl, which Whiskers nibbled on before following John to the den. John placed the box in the corner, and Whiskers stepped in and lay on his side.

"He's going to be a tired doggy for a few days," Sally said. "He's been through a lot."

"The vet said not to overdo his activity," John said. "I don't think we have to worry about that. We'll just let him tell us when he's ready."

"I'm going to a blood drive." Sally slipped on a light sweater and reached down and petted Whiskers. "I shouldn't be gone for more than four hours."

"We'll be here guarding the house," John said.

"Let's hope there are no more intruders."

After Sally left, John picked up the newspaper and sat in the rocking chair. When he finished reading, he reached for the remote before realizing there was no remote or TV. He looked at Whiskers and said, "Will you be okay if I take a little walk?"

Whiskers didn't even look up.

John put on a jacket, locked the front door, and headed down the street. There was a slight chill in the air so he picked up his pace. Bert wasn't anywhere to be seen, but John wondered if he might be lurking behind a pulled-back curtain or from a far corner of his house.

He stopped at the corner and waited for a car to pass before crossing the street. Preston was the driver, going well over the 25 miles per hour speed limit and appearing oblivious to any pedestrian, bicyclist, animal or anything that could possibly get in his path.

"Asshole," John said as he watched Preston pull into his driveway seconds later.

John took in some of the fall colors that were beginning to show on the trees, before returning to his house thirty minutes later. Whiskers was still resting on his cushion but padded into the kitchen for water while John sat at the counter and sorted through the mail.

There was an envelope addressed to him from Riley High School. It contained an announcement for a fiftieth class reunion the next year. A few classmates from his graduating class were already making plans, noting in their letter that it might take several months to locate everybody. It included a list of students they had been unable to find and asked if he knew the whereabouts of any of them. John didn't recognize a single name. It had been a long time since he left high school, and he had never attended any of the class reunions. He even wondered how they had located him this time unless it was another classmate who had given them his home address.

John wasn't sure if he would return a postcard indicating if he would or wouldn't attend the reunion. It had been forty-nine years and he really hadn't stayed in contact with hardly anyone except for a few buddies, and it had been a few years since he had heard from them. He wasn't even sure if they were still alive. He put the reunion materials in a drawer and sorted through the other mail, most of which was bills or junk mail. He placed them in a basket on the counter where Sally kept those kinds of things since she was the designated bill payer in the house.

John's thoughts turned to retirement. He figured the *vacation* was probably over and he needed to get focused on what he was going to do with the rest of his life. Maybe not the rest of his life, but at least the foreseeable future. He relocated to the study, a place where he and Sally used their computers and worked on other interests. It had been spared by the burglars as well, perhaps because a desktop computer would have been too difficult to steal. Even his old stereo system was intact, sitting in the corner of the room. Maybe the burglars hadn't seen it because it would have been partially hidden when they opened the door. Or maybe a component system was too much to handle or worry about since a lot of people used hand-held players with earphones. Sometimes it paid to have old stuff.

John turned on the computer and waited while it fired up and plodded through all its startup programs. He hadn't used the computer since he retired. He hardly ever used social media and didn't have much use for personal email since he had used email when he was at the newspaper. Sally was more adept with computers and new technology, often text messaging the children and close friends, using email to stay in touch with others, and websites for shopping. He was virtually clueless in most of those things and didn't mind because it meant fewer complications in his life.

John clicked on the mailbox icon to see if there was anything of interest. There were probably several hundred items, many of which were in the junk folder. He quickly deleted them without reading the subject lines. He glanced at the others, and didn't see anything of interest, and deleted them as well. He sat staring at the screen for a minute or so after he opened the browser, wondering why he had come into the room.

Whiskers tapped him on the side of the leg, signaling potty time. John took him to the backyard, and within a minute they were back in the house. John gave him some food. This time Whiskers had more of an appetite as he chomped away at the kibble.

"Feeling better, little buddy?" John asked.

They returned to the den...this time Whiskers lay on the floor next to the rocking chair. John picked up several magazines from the holder but they were all Sally's subscriptions to various home and garden, cooking, and celebrity periodicals.

John looked at the space where the TV had once been. He thought about missing something when you don't have it, even when you don't use it that often. He then remembered that he had been in the study using the computer before taking Whiskers outside. But he couldn't think of why he had gone there in the first place. He was about to go back to the study when Sally returned from the blood drive, carrying a sack with sandwiches and chips from a nearby deli.

"I tried to call and text you but you didn't answer," she said, arranging the food on the counter.

"You did?" John said. "When?"

"About thirty minutes ago. I went ahead and picked up a veggie sandwich for you. I hope you haven't eaten lunch."

"Nope," he said. "And I'm hungry."

Sally took out two paper plates from the cabinet and put them on the bar as John sat on a stool with Whiskers at his feet. "Anything to drink?"

"Water is fine," he said. She filled two glasses from the water dispenser, then sat across from him.

"So how's Whiskers?" she asked.

"He had a good lunch a little while ago. I think he's getting his appetite back."

"What did you do while I was gone?"

"Oh, nothing much," he said, taking a bite of his sandwich. "Took a short walk. It's been rather quiet."

"We were busy at the blood drive. We had nearly one hundred donors while I was there. I bet they will probably have another hundred or so before they leave today."

"That's great," John said.

"Oh, by the way, I saw Wilma for a few minutes at the deli."

"And Bert wasn't with her?"

"No. She said he was at home doing some work in their basement."

"I guess that's why I didn't see him, or should I say he didn't see me, when I took my walk."

"But that's not what I want to tell you."

"Okay. What is it?" He took a bite from his sandwich.

"Wilma told me something and swore me not to tell anyone."

"Must be serious stuff," he said with food in his mouth.

"It is," Sally said.

"What is it?"

"It's about Bert."

"Okay. So what about good ol' Bert?"

"You remember how he got up and abruptly left the house?"

"Yep. It was a good laugh."

"He left because he's incontinent."

"Huh?"

"She told me Bert was embarrassed by having to leave the house the way he did."

"Prostate cancer?"

"Bert had his prostate removed a month or so ago. She said he has to wear those adult diapers because he doesn't have control of his bladder yet. He has this fear that he will leak on his pants in front of others. That's why he got up from the table and hurried out without hardly saying a word."

"That's awful," John said. "I wish we had known."

"We do now," Sally said. "And she asked that we don't tell anyone."

"It's mum with me." He crossed his heart.

"You just never know about these things anymore," she said.

"I can understand Bert being that way. I've known a couple guys at work who had that done. One of them even said he couldn't get hard anymore."

"I didn't go into that with Wilma," Sally said with a light laugh.

"I can't imagine them having much of a sex life anyway."

"Now you shouldn't say that. They could have a terrific love life for all you know."

"I guess," he said.

As they finished lunch, there was a pounding noise at the side of the house.

"What in the world can that be?" John said, getting up from the stool

"Sounds like some hammering."

"I'll go check on it."

John stepped out onto the front porch and heard the noise coming from the side of his garage. He walked to the side and saw two workmen putting up an eight-foot-tall privacy fence. Preston was standing close by with his arms crossed over his chest. He glanced sternly at John and didn't speak.

John flashed a smile and returned to the house.

"What is it?" Sally asked as she wiped off the counter.

"Preston is putting up a fence. I suppose he can no longer tolerate the aromatic smells deposited by Whiskers."

"That's his choice."

"And something I like as well."

Twelve

The following morning, a light drizzle greeted John when he opened the front door to fetch the newspaper. He spread the damp paper on the counter and took a sip of coffee. He wondered if the newspaper had cut back on using plastic wrap as another cost-cutting measure.

"You're up early," Sally said as she ambled into the kitchen in her night gown.

"Always the early bird," he said, stirring creamer in his cup. "Sit down and I'll pour a cup for you."

Sally lifted a corner of the limp front page and put it back down when John set the coffee in front of her. "Want me to go get my hair dryer?"

"Nah. I can read it later. Probably nothing much to read anyway."

Seconds later, Whiskers padded into the kitchen. He went to his water bowl, took several laps, and then looked up at Sally.

"I think he knows who feeds him," John said. Sally rose from the stool and opened a can of dog food, taking out several scoops and putting it in the bowl. Whiskers turned his attention to eating.

"You know what I find the most depressing thing about the newspaper anymore?" John said as he glanced down at it.

"Reading about all the terrorism in the world?"

"Nope."

"Gun violence?"

"Nope."

"I give up," she said. "What's so depressing?"

"Obituaries."

"Obituaries?"

"I've looked at them every day for a long time, mainly to see if parents or relatives of friends I know have passed away. I suppose even friends. But now that I'm in my sixties, all I see are people in our age group filling up the page. I don't know everyone, but some of the names are familiar. And then you see a few people who haven't even reached their sixties—you know, in their thirties or forties, and they die of heart attacks, cancer, car accidents. And then the children and babies. You think of the loved ones they left behind. I just find it depressing anymore. Sometimes it even brings me to tears."

"Maybe you shouldn't look at them," Sally said.

"But you have to if you want to keep up with those kinds of things. Unfortunately, death is part of life. The bitter end."

"You've really become a softie as you've grown older."

"I don't know about becoming a softie," John said. "I admit there are a few obits I'm looking forward to reading. If I live long enough."

"John, that's mean."

"I know, but there are some folks I've been around that I'll be glad to see dead and gone forever."

"I admit I know a few as well," Sally said. "But I'm not going to tell you who they are."

"Anyway, reading the obits makes me realize more and more just how fragile life is. Even with poor ol' Bert, I never realized his health issues."

"Maybe it's because you worked for so long and didn't really socialize that much outside the workplace. Maybe you need to get to know the neighborhood."

"You're probably right. We get so wrapped up in our jobs that we sorta lose touch with other things going on in our lives. Things that are more important in many ways."

"Being around others helped me understand what goes on in their lives," Sally said. "In our little book group, we've had several gals with breast cancer. One of our members died from ovarian cancer a couple years ago. Several lost husbands to heart attacks. And when I go to the blood drives, we sit around and talk with others about what is going on in their lives. Maybe it can be a little gossipy at times, but we learn about things happening to people. It helps me connect."

"I may have to get out there and do some things. I was just thinking yesterday about how bored I'm getting with life. And I think reading the obits makes it all the more depressing because I'm not doing much about it. It even gives me headaches."

"So what are you going to do?"

"Maybe I should tag along with you," he said with a laugh.

"You're more than welcome but I doubt if you'd enjoy it that much."

"Just kidding, sweetie. I'll give it more thought."

"I saw the invitation to the class reunion," Sally said.

"Yeah."

"Yeah? Don't you want to go?"

"I'll think about it. It's still a ways off."

"Don't you want to see your old friends from high school?"

"Some. I don't need to have a reunion to do that."

"Okay, suit yourself," Sally said, shaking her head. "Just don't forget to RSVP."

"I'll think about it."

"Anything on your agenda today?" Sally asked with a touch of exasperation.

"I'm not really sure. I thought about going out and shopping for a new TV. Then I think how nice and quiet it is around here without a TV. But I know you have programs you enjoy watching."

"I'm in no hurry to replace the TVs. I've been able to catch up on some reading. And, believe it or not, I really don't miss some of the programs I was watching. They become somewhat addictive, but once you quit watching them, kinda like soap operas, you wonder why you watched them in the first place."

"Well, whenever you're ready, we'll go shopping for one or two."

"Only one. I like not having one in the bedroom."

"You know how I always felt about that. The bedroom should be for sleeping and screwing, er, I mean making love."

"You better say that," she said. "And I agree that it should be for intimacy and sleeping. And maybe reading. Not much else."

"You put it so nicely," he said. "You have such a way with words."

"Quit being sarcastic," she said, crinkling her nose. "You worked in a newsroom too long."

"Yep," he said. "So do you have any plans for right now?"

"What do you mean?"

"Some intimacy plans."

"What do you have in mind?"

John took her hand and led her to the bedroom. Whiskers followed right behind, then hopped into his cushioned box.

"Now you turn your head," John said to Whiskers.

Sally stood next to John at the side of the unmade bed. He lifted her pink gown over her shoulders, then unfastened his lounging pants. They embraced, naked, for several seconds before she slipped onto the bed and he followed, pulling the sheets over their bodies. Sally snuggled into his arms and they kissed softly, then passionately as he fondled her breasts and squeezed her soft buttocks. After a brief pause, she straddled him and began kissing the side of his neck. He slowly entered her as his hands deeply massaged her lower back. She smothered him in long, lingering kisses before he pulled her tightly against him and they climaxed.

Her limp body rested on top of him, as he softly ran his fingers through her short gray hair and down her slender back. They closed their eyes and drifted into a dream-like state lying next to each other before Whiskers began barking and dashed off toward the front door.

"What's up with him?" John got out of the bed and put on his lounging pants and a T-shirt.

Whiskers was still at the front door with a low snarl as John entered the living room. "What's the matter, little fella?"

John opened the front door but didn't see anyone. "Stay, Whiskers," he said and motioned with an open hand at his side while he stepped out on the front porch. He walked about twenty feet into the damp yard and looked both ways. It was quiet and nothing seemed out of order. He returned to the house. Sally, wearing her robe, stood in the hallway leading to the bedroom.

"What was it?" she asked, clutching the top of her robe.

"No idea," he said as he closed the door. "I thought I heard the storm door close."

"Do you think it could have been the burglars coming back?"

"I sure hope not," he said.

"Whiskers was sure alarmed by it,"

John reached down, picked up the dog and petted the top of his head. "Good boy, Whiskers."

"I'm really worried, John," Sally said, her arms folded tightly across her chest.

"I understand. I'll call a home security company this afternoon."

"I can't believe this is happening after all the years we've lived here."

The doorbell rang and Whiskers began barking and trying to wriggle out of John's arms.

"Take Whiskers and I'll answer the door." He handed the dog to Sally and she hurried to the bedroom and closed the door.

John opened the door and Bert was standing a few feet away.

"Good morning, neighbor," he said.

"Hi Bert," John said. "What brings you down this way so early?"

"I saw you standing in your front yard and you seemed a bit concerned about something."

"Whiskers got riled up and started barking."

"Whiskers?"

"Whiskers is a dog we sorta adopted several weeks ago."

"Okay, I wasn't aware of that. Was he in the house the other day when I visited?"

"Nope, he was at the vet."

"Anyways," Bert said, "You seemed concerned so I thought I'd better let you know I was the person at your door."

"You?"

"I can't explain it but a personal emergency came up and I had to run back to my house," Bert said. "I looked back and saw you open the door. I figured you might be alarmed by what happened so I came back."

"I appreciate you letting me know," John said. "Sally and I were concerned, especially coming so soon after the break-in."

"That's what I thought."

"Why did you come down?"

"I just told you," Bert said. "So you wouldn't be alarmed."

"No, Bert, the first time."

"Oh, sorry John, losing track of time. It was about Neighborhood Watch. I thought you might be up eating breakfast since I saw some lights on in the house."

"Okay. Can we discuss it later?"

"Now's not a good time?"

"No, Bert," John said. "Sally is a bit upset by what's happened."

"I understand. I'll get back with you on it."

"Thanks, Bert."

Bert stood on the porch for a few seconds without saying anything.

"Anything else, Bert?" John asked with furrowed brows.

"No, just thinking. I'll get back to you."

"Okay. See ya." John smiled and closed the door. He heard Bert step off the porch, and after several seconds, opened the corner of the curtain to see him next door talking to Preston. They appeared to be looking at the side of the house where the privacy fence had been erected. Preston, wearing a purple robe and house slippers, appeared to admire the new construction, pointing to different areas.

Sally was dressed in black Capri pants and a yellow sweatshirt when she came back to the living room with Whiskers right next to her.

"It was Bert," John said. "He told me he was the person at the door and that he ran from the house."

"I think we know the reason."

"He came down to talk about Neighborhood Watch."

"At this time of the morning?"

"I told him we were getting it on in bed."

"John!" Sally's eyes opened wide.

"You know better than that," he said, kissing the tip of her nose.

"Seriously, I hope you call one of those home security companies today. I know I'll feel better when you do."

"I will," John said. "You don't have to remind me."

"I'm going to the grocery store to pick up a few things," she said. "I shouldn't be gone more than an hour."

"Well, you're dressed for it."

"What do you mean?"

"You remind me of a cute bumble bee."

"You're right. Let me go change my top."

She put on a white blouse, and after getting an approving wink from John, left for the grocery. John and Whiskers sauntered to the study. He sat at the computer, glanced at his emails and read several news stories from websites. Before he knew it, Sally was back home and putting groceries in the cupboard and refrigerator.

"You weren't gone long," he said. "Need some help?"

"I can do it," she said, looking over her shoulder. "What did they have to say?"

"What did who have to say?" he said with a raised brow.

"The home security company?"

"Huh?"

"I thought you were going to call them."

"Oh, I will. Just give me time. I was busy looking up some things on the Internet."

She lowered her head and raised her eyebrows. "John, please, go call them now."

"Okay, okay."

She opened a drawer and took out a telephone book. "You may need this."

John took it without saying a word and retreated to the den. He called a home security company and set up an appointment for them to drop by the next day.

He returned to the kitchen and put the telephone book back in the drawer.

"A home security representative is coming by tomorrow at eleven," John said. "Satisfied?"

"Thank you, honey," she said with a big smile.

Thirteen

"Let's go for a walk," John said to Whiskers. He put on a heavy sweatshirt, connected a leash to Whiskers' collar, and headed to the front door. "We'll be back later."

"Do you want lunch when you get back?" Sally shouted from the kitchen.

"Nah," he said. "Go ahead and eat. I'll find something when I get back."

John turned in the opposite direction of Bert's house and walked at a pace that was comfortable for Whiskers. They had gone about seven blocks when a car suddenly pulled over to the side of the curb. The driver, alone in the vehicle, lowered the passenger-side window.

"Sir, can I ask where you got that dog?"

John walked over to the side of the car. "I found him tangled in some bushes a few weeks ago, several blocks from here."

"My family lost a dog about the same time. We posted some flyers in the neighborhood."

"Yes, I recall seeing one. I even called the number but didn't hear anything back."

"He sure looks a lot like our dog. May I come over and look at him?"

John reluctantly agreed. "Sure."

The bearded young man got out of the car and walked around the rear side. He knelt and held out his hand. "Hey, Poncho."

Whiskers took a few steps toward him, then stopped. He turned his head and looked up at John.

The man edged closer and petted Whiskers and rubbed his chin with his index finger. He showed Whiskers the back of his hand. Whiskers sniffed for a few seconds and looked up at John again.

"How's the dog been for you?" the man asked politely.

"Well, he's been a very good companion. He's been to the vet for shots and we got him cleaned up. He even had a contusion around his neck from the rope that has about cleared up from the antibiotic the vet gave him."

"You've already invested quite a bit." The man petted Whiskers on the head again, then rubbed between his floppy ears.

"Oh, yeah," John said. "We almost lost him a couple weeks ago. Someone broke into our house and hit him. He was in the animal clinic for three days with a bad concussion and some internal bleeding."

John cringed for a moment and immediately wished he hadn't said anything about the break-in.

"He seems to be doing fine now," the man said, a friendly smile crossing his face.

"He's been awfully good to my wife and me," John said. "Kinda like part of the family now."

"Well, listen, mister..."

"It's John Ross."

"Okay, Mr. Ross. If you see a dog that looks a lot like, uh, what's his name?"

"We call him Whiskers. You don't see many dogs with long whiskers, so that's how he got his name."

"If you run across a dog that looks like Whiskers, please give me a call." The man took a business card from his wallet and handed it to John.

John glanced at the card and said, "I'll be happy to do that, Mr. Reagan. Whiskers and I walk every day so if we see another dog like him, I'll let you know. I'll even bring him home with me."

The man smiled and returned to his car. "Thanks again." He waved and slowly drove away.

"What do you think about that, Whiskers?" John said as they continued their walk at a brisk pace. "I think that nice young man just gave you to me."

John suddenly felt a sense of sadness sweep over him like a dark cloud, knowing his gain was someone else's loss. He stopped at a corner, and instead of crossing the street, took his cell phone from his pocket and dialed the number on the business card.

John didn't waste any time identifying himself to the man.

"You know, I think Whiskers may be your dog, Mr. Reagan," John said.

"I think he may be as well. But you seem to be taking very good care of Poncho, er, I mean Whiskers. He appears to be very attached to you. My wife and I have been looking at some other dogs at the humane society since we lost him. Whiskers was a rescue dog, and in a sense, you rescued him after he ran away from our home. You can keep him if you want him."

"I appreciate that very much," John said, feeling a sense of lightness. "And yes, Whiskers and I are very attached."

"I know he has a good home with you."

"Can I pay the adoption fee for your next dog?" John asked. "That's the least I can do."

"That's very kind of you but there's no need to do that. If you want to, simply donate to the humane society."

"I'll do that. And thanks again."

John couldn't help but pick up the pace again after ending the call. Whiskers bounced along with him, ears flopping up and down, as they ventured to a small park for the first time.

John sat on a wood-slatted green park bench facing a large pond populated by swans, geese and ducks. He lifted Whiskers next to him.

"That's a long walk for us," he said. "I bet your little legs are tired, buddy."

They watched the birds on and around the pond and other wildlife scampering about the grounds as well as occasional joggers and walkers on the asphalt path behind the bench. After a few minutes, Whiskers barked to let him know he had to potty. He padded several feet next to a Rose of Sharon behind the bench and returned to John.

"Aren't you going to clean up that shit?"

John looked both ways before realizing there was a person about thirty feet behind him.

"I plan to," John said. "Is there a hurry?"

"Well, some folks seem to believe they can bring their dogs here and let them shit all over the place. It's not a damn animal park. They seem to forget this is a park for people as well and we don't want to step in the shit."

"I'll make sure it's picked up before we leave," John said, forcing a smile.

He watched as the man, using a wooden cane, hobbled away.

"What do you think, Whiskers?"

Whiskers didn't react one way or the other.

"Now I have to find something to pick up your poop. I should have thought of that before we came here."

John could feel someone watching him, and he looked in the direction of the man, now standing on a small knob facing them. He was wearing a blue cap with what appeared to be some sort of military insignia on the front and cluster on the bill. John wondered if the old fart had anything better to do than harass people in the park.

John saw a trash can along one of paths and got up to see if there was anything in it he could use to retrieve Whiskers' poop.

"Hey, where in the hell do you think you're going?" the man shouted as he swirled his cane in the air.

John didn't say anything but pointed at the trash can. As luck would have it, the can was empty.

"Damn," John said softly. "There's only one thing to do."

They returned to the spot where Whiskers had done his thing. There wasn't a lot but John didn't want to touch it. With the man still watching, John and Whiskers returned to the bench. John took off his shoe and sock, then slipped the shoe back on. They returned back to the poop, and John picked it up, using the sock as a mitten.

John held up the poop, almost triumphantly, so the man could see it. He then walked over to the trash container, held it high and plopped it in so the man could hear it make a thud.

"How's that?" John shouted, smiling broadly.

The man waved him off and continued on his walk.

"Let's go home, Whiskers," John said. "I don't want to deal with that old fart again."

Sally was sitting in the den reading the newspaper when they arrived home about forty minutes later.

"We had some excitement today," John said as he unleashed Whiskers, who ran to his water bowl in the kitchen.

"What happened?"

John told her about the man asking about Whiskers and how he thought it may have been his dog.

"And he let you keep him?" Sally asked.

"Very nice young man," John said. "I told him we'd make a donation to the humane society."

And then he recounted the incident in the park. He raised his pant leg to show her his sock-less foot.

"I'll buy some doggie bags the next time I go to the grocery," she said. "I'm surprised you haven't needed them before now."

"Our walks haven't been that long. Whiskers usually goes before or after in our yard, next to Preston's new privacy fence."

"I'm glad you didn't get into much trouble at the park."

"It's done and over with. So what's for lunch?"

"I've already eaten," she said. "I had tomato soup and a grilled-cheese sandwich."

"Why didn't you wait for me?"

"Because you told me to go ahead and eat."

"I did?"

"I'll fix you some lunch. You go sit in the rocker and rest for a bit. And be sure and wash your hands."

After washing off in the half-bath next to the den, John took off his sweatshirt, tossed it on the couch, grabbed the newspaper and sat on the rocker. He glanced at the front page, then instinctively turned to the obituaries.

"Ah, no sad news today," he said quietly.

"What's that?" Sally asked from the kitchen.

"Oh, nothing. Just looking at the paper."

Several minutes later, Sally carried a tray with the sandwich and soup to him. "How's that?"

"Could I have some milk?"

Sally smiled and returned with a small glass of milk.

"Here you go," she said, placing the glass on the tray. "Anything else, sir?"

"Thanks," he said. "I'm good. Too bad we don't have any cookies."

"Yes, it's too bad." Sally sat back down on the couch and looked at him. "Are you feeling okay?"

"Sure," he said. "My back doesn't bother me anymore. Maybe a headache from the episode at the park."

"Just checking."

"Are you sure we don't have any Oreos or chocolate-chip cookies?"

"Yes, dear," she said. "I'll try to pick up some the next time I'm at the grocery. And when did you start liking cookies and milk?"

"Dunno. Just sounded good when you brought the glass of milk."

"Okay."

Sally sighed as she went to the couch.

John smiled, then continued eating. Whiskers padded into the den and lay next to the rocker. "Whiskers is doing good, too, although he's probably a little tired from our long walk."

"Do you want to go out later?" she asked.

"For what?"

"I thought we might look at the televisions and some dinnerware," she said.

"If you'd like," he said. "But can it wait until tomorrow?"

"You have other plans?"

"No, just a little tired from the walk. I thought I'd take a little nap after I finish this."

"We can do that," she said.

"Why don't you go on by yourself?"

"I could but I thought you'd like some say in the TV."

"I don't really care," he said, taking the last bite from the sandwich. "I trust your judgment. You're the one who watches most of the TV anyway. Get whatever you like. Whatever makes you happy makes me happy."

He looked at her and smiled.

"There's no hurry, honey," she said. "Really, we can do it tomorrow, or the next day, or the weekend. It doesn't make any difference to me."

"Just make sure it's at least a fifty-inch screen with high definition. We want a smart TV, too. Maybe even 3D if it's a good price."

"I definitely think you need to go with me then," Sally said. "For someone who doesn't seem to care what to get, you seem to know what you want."

"Okay, okay," John said with an impish grin.

John got up, stumbled slightly and carried the tray to the kitchen counter. Sally followed and took the bowl and glass and placed them in the sink.

He lowered his head slightly and blinked his eyes several times.

"Is something wrong?" Sally asked.

"Just a little light-headedness. I'm okay."

"Since you don't want to go shopping, how about letting me lie down with you for a nap?" She kissed him on the cheek.

"If you want to."

John removed his shoes and pants, then pulled back the sheets and got into bed. Sally went to the other side, removing her house shoes, and lay next to him. She pulled up the covers and cuddled next to his back.

"I love you," she whispered.

"Love you, too."

Before long, they were sound asleep.

Fourteen

"Honey, is something the matter?" Sally asked at breakfast. "Are you feeling okay?"

"I'm fine." John lifted an eyebrow and paused for a moment. "Why do you ask? Am I acting weird or something?"

"You just seem forgetful and kinda edgy."

"Maybe a little tired and bored at times, but I think I'm adjusting to this new life now that the so-called vacation is over."

"Are you depressed about anything?"

"Let me assure you I'm fine." He smiled and took a sip of coffee. "Don't worry about me."

Sally took a swallow from her cup. "I have my book club today over at Dot's house."

"What are you reading now?"

"*The Great Gatsby*. You'd be surprised how many of the gals haven't read it. They've seen the movies but never picked up the book. It should be an interesting discussion."

"I should say so. One of my favorites."

"So it should be a quiet afternoon for you and Whiskers."

"I just have to remember to take some doggy bags with me in case Whiskers has to do his thing while we're out for our walk. I think I'll take along a plastic grocery bag. I certainly don't want to get chastised again by that grumpy old fart or anyone else."

"I'll try to remember to buy a box of doggy bags while I'm out."

"I think I'll go read the newspaper in the den," John said.

"Nothing else for breakfast? Cereal? Oatmeal? Pancakes?"

"No thanks. I'm good."

As John took several steps, he swayed a little and placed his hand against the wall to keep his balance.

"Are you okay?" Sally hurried over to him and put her hands on his shoulders.

"I'm okay. Just got a little dizzy. I probably got up too quickly."

"Honey, I think you need to go see the doctor. Let me make an appointment."

"No," he said, raising his voice slightly. "Don't you ever get light-headed?"

"Well, yes...."

"So that's what happened. It's not a big deal." He forced a smile and headed to the den, then picked up the newspaper and slowly sat in the rocking chair. Sally furtively watched him from the kitchen but didn't say anything.

Whiskers sauntered down the hallway from the bedroom.

"Hey, sleepyhead," Sally said. "You finally decided to get up?"

Whiskers padded to the door, and without any prompting, Sally let him out. Whiskers returned in less than a minute and headed to his water and food bowls Sally had already prepared.

John read quietly in the den. He was relieved when he didn't recognize any names on the obituary page. He glanced through the sports pages and didn't discern any notable changes since he left the newspaper. He wasn't surprised because he knew it would be gradual, since newspapers don't move at a fast pace, even when they should.

Sally ate a bowl of oatmeal and drank another cup of coffee at the counter while keeping an eye on John. Whiskers finished his kibble and plopped down at his usual spot next to John. He rolled over on his back, prompting John to reach down and rub his belly for a few seconds.

"Boy, you are spoiled," John said with a laugh. "You've got the life of Riley."

"Another cup?" Sally asked at the doorway.

"I think so. I'll be there in a minute. Let me finish reading this story about the investigation of that stupid councilman."

"The one who took those bribes?"

"Can you believe he took money from a group that's trying to build a new library branch?"

"Nothing surprises me anymore. Here or anywhere."

John got up from the rocker and Whiskers stood as well, both of them stretching lightly before going to the kitchen. A couple of steps from the bar stool, John slumped over and lost his balance again. Sally rushed over and supported him as he leaned against the wall.

"Honey, I'm calling nine-one-one," she said.

John's eyes glazed over as he swayed his head groggily. She picked up her cell phone from the counter and dialed the emergency number. She explained to the dispatcher what had happened. Within five minutes a siren could be heard in the distance and getting louder the closer it approached their house.

She opened the door for the emergency medical techs carrying a gurney to enter the house. She led them to John, sitting with his back against the wall and head bowed. Whiskers barked a few times at the techs until Sally shushed him to be quiet. The techs checked John's vitals and called in their findings to the hospital. After strapping John on the gurney, they whisked him outside and put him in the back of the red-and-white ambulance. Sally was about to lock the front door when she noticed Bert standing in the driveway.

"What's up, Sally?" he asked.

"I'm not sure," she said. "John nearly passed out."

"I'll keep an eye on your house while you're away."

Sally tossed the keys to him, and got into the back of the ambulance, sitting next to John, who was lying with his eyes closed. A paramedic was on the phone to the hospital, providing information about John's condition.

~ * ~

Bert walked into the house and looked around for a few seconds before noticing Whiskers crouched under the dining room table.

"Come here, pooch," he said, bending down on one knee and opening his hands. Whiskers cautiously crawled up to him. Bert softly petted him on the head, then picked him up. Whiskers seemed to sense something was wrong and didn't put up any resistance.

"Everything's going to be all right," Bert said quietly. "Let's go for a little walk to my house."

Bert checked to make sure the side door to the garage was locked before locking the front door and stepping out on the front porch with Whiskers in his arms.

"What's going on?" asked Allen, who had walked across the street to John's front yard.

"Not sure," Bert said. "Sally said John apparently had a fainting spell. I told her I'd watch her house."

"I'll do the same," Allen said. "Let me know if you hear anything."

"Will do," Bert said as he continued on to his house holding Whiskers.

~ * ~

Within a few minutes, the ambulance pulled into the emergency entrance at the rear of the hospital. The techs removed John from the vehicle and wheeled him into the emergency area, where two nurses and a doctor led them to a curtained-off bed in a large room.

Sally explained to the doctor what had happened and her concern that John may have had a heart attack or stroke. The nurses connected him to several machines to monitor his heart and other functions. Sally was told to go sit in the waiting room. She sat there with others, several of them sobbing and others in quiet conversations. She kept her eyes focused on John's room.

Finally, a nurse came over and led her to the hallway that connected the waiting room and emergency area. She told Sally that John was resting and it appeared he hadn't had a heart attack. They would know more about a stroke after other tests and an MRI were completed.

Sally returned to the waiting room, this time for only twenty minutes when she was summoned back by the nurse. A doctor came out from behind the curtain. Sally saw Dr. Marvin Gallanet on his nametag.

"Mrs. Ross," said Dr. Gallanet. "We don't believe your husband had a stroke. It looks more like a transient ischemic attack, or TIA. It has some similarities to a stroke but can be treated. Has your husband been under a lot of stress lately?"

Sally told about John's recent retirement and their house being vandalized. "He has seemed somewhat depressed but isn't that normal under those circumstances?"

"I'd say so."

"Doctor, I've been concerned the past few days because of his memory. He's been forgetful and that's not normally like him. He's even complained of headaches and lightheadedness."

"Does he take any medication for high blood pressure?"

"Every day he takes a pill for it. He's been doing it for several years."

"His blood pressure was one-ninety over ninety-five. Is there a chance he hasn't been taking the pills?"

"He takes them before going to bed," she said. "I really haven't paid much attention because he's always been good about it."

"We'll have to ask him after he wakes up," the doctor said. "We've got him on a nitro drip to lower his blood pressure. I have a couple other patients to see but I'll be back soon."

The nurse led Sally to John's room, where she sat next to his bed. John's eyes were closed but several minutes later he partially opened them.

"Where am I?" he mumbled.

"At the hospital, honey," Sally said. "You passed out."

"I did?"

"Honey, I need to ask you something. Have you been taking your blood pressure pills?"

"Uh, no. I didn't think I'd need them anymore after I retired. You know I hate taking them."

"You shouldn't have done that without talking to the doctor," she said with a stern look. "I can't believe you did that."

Sally glanced over at the nurse, who heard what John had said. "That may explain his dizziness and fainting," the nurse said. "I'll let the doctor know."

The doctor came in ten minutes later. "Mr. Ross, you need to take your medication," he said. "You're fortunate because this situation could have been a lot worse. We've got you stabilized. You need to start taking your pills, beginning when you return home. And I want you to set up an appointment with your primary physician and tell him everything that's happened." He glanced at Sally and she nodded in agreement.

"I'm sorry." John said meekly. "I just thought that getting out of a stressful job and retiring would mean I wouldn't have to take them, that my blood pressure would return to normal."

"I wish that would be the case but it's not," the doctor said. "Now, go home, take your pills and get some rest. And like I said, see your primary physician."

"Thank you, Dr. Gallanet," Sally said, shaking his hand. "I'll be sure he does."

John eased off the bed, holding Sally's hand for support, and slowly got dressed. Sally took her cell phone from her purse and called for a taxi to take them home.

"I'm so embarrassed," John said as they waited in the lobby for their ride.

"Honey, I'm just glad you're okay," she said, holding his hand.

"Where's Whiskers?"

"With Bert."

"Bert? What's he doing with Whiskers?"

"He noticed the ambulance and came down to the house."

"That's nice of him to take care of Whiskers."

The taxi arrived and they were back in their house in ten minutes. A note was posted on the door from the home security representative, saying he had been there for a consultation.

"I forgot all about that," John said as Sally led him into the house.

"Not much you could have done about it," Sally said. "Now where are your blood pressure pills?"

"I think in the medicine cabinet."

"How long has it been since you had one?"

"Since my first day of retirement."

Sally shook her head in disbelief. "John Ross, I can't believe you! You know better than that."

The doorbell rang and John was about to get up to answer it. "You stay put," Sally said. "I'll get it."

When she opened the door, Bert was there holding Whiskers. Bert even smiled.

"Thank you so much," she said as she took Whiskers from him.

"How's John?"

"Much better. It appears he had a TIA."

"A transient ischemic attack."

"Yes. How did you know that?"

"I just keep up with things like that," Bert said matter-of-factly. "At a certain age you start learning about TIA, heart attacks, strokes, enlarged prostate, cancer. It comes with the territory of being older." Another smile cracked his face.

"Again, thanks for watching the house and taking care of Whiskers."

"Let me know if I can be of further assistance," he said. "Oh, by the way, Allen kept an eye on your house as well. Tell John I hope he starts feeling better soon."

"I will." Sally closed the door and returned to the kitchen. When she didn't see John at the counter, she put Whiskers down and watched him dash to the bedroom. She followed and found John lying on the bed, his eyes closed and his head propped up on a pillow.

"You frightened me for a moment," she said.

"I just wanted to lie down for a bit. I've got a slight headache. Since Whiskers is here, that must have been Bert at the door. Did you thank him?"

"Yes, I did," Sally said. "Allen also watched the house. It's nice to have good neighbors."

"Even when they're a little weird like Bert?"

"Speaking of weird, let me go get your blood pressure pill so you won't be acting so weird."

Fifteen

On his doctor's advice, John stayed around the house for several days since he was concerned about another fainting or dizzy spell. Although getting a bit stir crazy, John didn't argue the point, especially since Sally was enforcing it. But after a week of taking his blood pressure medicine, it appeared his condition had stabilized and he was given the go-ahead by Sally to resume his normal activities. Since his activities had never been strenuous, especially after giving up tennis several years earlier, he could do practically anything within reason. He hoped it temporarily excluded him from Sally's honey-do list as well.

"We're going for a walk," John said to Sally as he put the leash on Whiskers for his first venture farther than the front yard to get the newspaper. "Probably to the park so we'll be gone an hour or so."

"Be sure and take a doggy bag with you."

"I've got one stashed in my pocket."

"And your cell."

"Will do, sweetie."

"And don't hesitate to call if you feel the least bit dizzy."

"Will do, sweetie. Bye."

A mild chill enveloped the mid-October morning air as they began their trek to the park. Whiskers took his time along the way, sniffing and lifting his leg at every available post and tree.

"We'll never get to the park at this rate," John said. He had learned to go at Whiskers' pace and simply try to enjoy the moment. Returning to his blood pressure med had also helped his disposition and attitude as well as memory. At least he thought so. And Sally hadn't complained so he must be getting better.

They passed Georgina working on her tiny garden patch. Bart was washing his car in the driveway and waved. Allen drove by in his truck and beeped his horn, apparently on his way to the lake.

They found an unoccupied bench when they reached the park. It faced the pond so they could watch the various waterfowl. "We should have brought some breadcrumbs," John said to Whiskers.

"I hope you brought something to clean up after your dog."

John turned around, and standing on the pathway was the old guy wearing the blue military cap who had scolded him a few weeks before.

"I beg your pardon?" John said.

"I hope you have something to clean up after your dog."

"I do." John turned back around and faced the pond.

The man continued to stand on the path, about ten yards away, staring in John's direction and apparently waiting for Whiskers to do his thing. Whiskers seemed to sense it as well and didn't oblige the cranky onlooker.

"Ready to go home, little fella?" John said after several minutes. "We came here to relax but that doesn't seem possible now."

Whiskers bounded up to him at the bench, waiting for him to get up and start walking again. They maneuvered around the man, who didn't step to the side for them, standing there as if at attention.

"Have a nice day." John said gleefully.

When they were out of sight, Whiskers squatted next to an old maple tree. John was tempted not to pick it up, leaving it for the self-designated poop patroller, but took out the doggy bag, grabbed the poo, and dropped it in the trash receptacle at the park's entrance.

"That should make the old fart happy," John said as he looked back to see if he was being watched. And he was, as the man stood in the distance, arms folded across his chest and a scowl on his pudgy face.

A half block from his house, John noticed Trace and Leon walking up to Preston's house. He saw the door open and the boys step inside. He wondered what kind of chores Preston had for them and if he paid them twenty dollars.

When John opened the front door to his house, Bert was sitting on the couch in the living room, chatting with Sally. He rose when John entered the room.

"I'm here about the Neighborhood Watch program," Bert said. "I just got here so you haven't missed a thing. I saw you go on your walk in the other direction and figured you'd return about this time. It seems to take you about forty-five minutes or so."

"Really?" John said as he removed the leash from Whiskers. "I've never timed myself."

Sally, taking the leash from John and with her back to Bert, rolled her eyes. Whiskers went over to Bert for a few seconds, who petted him on the head, then scampered back to John.

"You know now," Bert said. "But getting back to why I'm paying you this visit, you know, Neighborhood Watch."

"That's good, Bert," John sat on an armless accent chair. "So what's up?"

"There was another break-in last night, this time at the Solomons' house three doors down from me. They had some electronics and jewelry taken."

"Where were they when it happened?" John asked, leaning forward.

"The Solomons?"

"Yes, Bert, the Solomons."

"Phil and Edna had just returned from a weeklong Caribbean cruise when they discovered it. Needless to say, they're very distraught about it. I am as well. In fact, we all should be."

"So the burglary may have occurred earlier than that?"

"Yes, that's very possible," Bert said matter of factly. "I talked to them this morning and they indicated a strong interest in forming a Neighborhood Watch program. So I told them that you have been leading the effort."

"You did?" John said, raising a brow. "Thanks, Bert."

"You're welcome. I've spoken to several other homeowners and they all seem interested. Especially the older folks like us, John. Sometimes they feel a little defenseless."

"They could always get a home security system like Sally and I had installed a few days ago. That provides some peace of mind."

"But it's not the same as neighbors looking out for their neighbors. Remember how Allen and I watched your house when you had that little fainting episode?"

"Yes, I do," John said.

"And some folks simply can't afford security systems like the one you have. They're on fixed incomes and just barely get by."

"In our neighborhood?"

"Yes, John," Bert said. "You don't realize how some unforeseen medical issues can zap savings. Social Security only goes so far. Some folks don't have supplemental pensions. It can be a rough world out there."

"I guess I never gave that much thought. I'm sorry."

"That's okay, John. Most folks don't think about it unless it happens to them. I learned from my prostate cancer. How about Georgina and her invalid husband? And did you know Bertha

Williams, Bill's widow, may need back surgery after falling in her backyard last month."

"I wasn't aware of that."

"Is there something I can do for her?" asked Sally, standing at the doorway to the kitchen. "She's such a sweet woman."

"Her children are looking after her," Bert said. "But thanks for asking. It's things like that that can drain savings."

"Okay, Bert, I see your point," John said. "I'll give the police a call today and see what we can do to set up a Neighborhood Watch."

"It would be much appreciated," Bert said as he rose from the couch. "I'll let others know what you're doing. It will provide them with some hope. That's something we all need."

"Are you running for office?"

"Huh?"

"Never mind, Bert."

"I'm looking forward to getting things in motion."

"You'll be the first to know once I hear something from the police."

"So you'll be calling them today?"

"Today?"

"We need to get moving on this, John," Bert said. "Who knows whose house will be vandalized next. Maybe yours again." He raised his brows.

"Good point, Bert." John took a deep breath. "I'll call them after lunch."

"Good deal." Bert smiled sharply, shook John's hand and tipped his head to Sally as he stepped to the door.

"While you're here, let me ask you something," John said. "You seem to know what's going on in our block."

"I try to keep an eye on things," Bert said. "What do you want to know?"

"I noticed some boys go into Preston's house. Have you noticed that lately?"

"Not that often, but occasionally," Bert said. "Something wrong?"

"Oh, no, just curious."

"I figure he may be doing some tutoring or helping with college entrance exams because of his background at the university. He's a learned man."

"Without a doubt," John said.

"I spoke briefly with him the other day. He showed me the privacy fence between your houses."

"And?"

"I thought they did a nice job. I may consider one across the back of my yard."

"Discuss anything else?"

"That's all. Why do you ask? Having problems with Preston?"

"No, nothing like that. Just curious."

"Good enough. He's a solid citizen. Good people."

"I'd appreciate it if you don't mention to him that I asked about it."

"My lips are sealed," Bert said, running two fingers across his mouth. "I need to be going now."

"Thanks again, Bert," John said.

Bert opened the door and left without another word.

"Any coffee left in the pot?" John asked. "I'd like something stronger but it's too early in the day. Bert's sure a persistent guy."

Sally laughed. "Bert has always been that way. Very business-like and little humor. But he's a good person."

"Or as Bert would probably say, 'good people.'"

"But he has good intentions."

"I know that," John said. "I'm just surprised that he doesn't form a Neighborhood Watch program since he's so damn gung-ho about it. Why me?"

"Probably because you mentioned it first. And another reason is that Bert, with all his good intentions, knows he would have difficulty getting people involved in it. He'd probably run it as some para-police operation."

"I'm sure he turns a lot of people off with his stiff demeanor," John said. "I don't find him that endearing myself, but he's not a bad person to have as a neighbor. Certainly not a person I want to drink beer with at the pub."

Sally poured him a cup of coffee as they sat at the kitchen bar. Whiskers had already lapped some water from his bowl and shuffled to his bed for a nap.

"So, busy lady, what's on your agenda today?" John asked.

"I think I'm going to stay home and clean out one of the closets. I have some clothes I should give to Goodwill or the Salvation Army."

"If you see any of my stuff that needs to be tossed, go ahead and do it. No questions asked."

"And what are your plans?"

"As if you didn't know?" John said with wide eyes. "Neighborhood Watch. I'm sure I'll hear from Bert tomorrow about the call, even though I promised him he'd be the first to know."

"You may hear from him this evening."

"You've got that right, so I'd better hop to it," John said.

"Anything else?"

"Maybe we can go shopping for a new TV."

"That sounds like fun," she said.

"I'm sure it will be."

"Are you sure you're up to it?"

"I think so," he said. "There's a good football game on this weekend."

Sally playfully tapped her forehead with an open hand. "That figures. I knew there had to be a reason."

~ * ~

Later in the morning, John called the police department and spoke to the person in charge of Neighborhood Watch. He was given brief details of the program and told they would need to have an organizational meeting as well as a presentation from the police about how it works.

"That seems simple enough," John said to Sally after he got off the phone. "I'm going down to Bert's house and tell him before he gets the opportunity to come here and ask me. Unless you want the company."

"I think you'd better go down there."

He was surprised that Bert and Wilma weren't home when he got there. He heard some movement inside and peeked in the front window. He saw a dark figure picking up something in the corner. John tapped hard on the window. The person dropped the item, which crashed to the floor, and ran out the back door of the house. John rattled the front door, then hurried around to the backyard, but whoever was in the house had already vanished from sight.

John quickly dialed nine-one-one and gave the dispatcher Bert's address and what he had just witnessed. Within three minutes a police cruiser pulled up in front of the house. As John was giving them details, Bert and Wilma pulled into their driveway, as well as another cruiser.

Bert walked up to the police officer and asked what was going on. Wilma was told not to go inside while two other policemen were gathering what information and evidence they could about the burglary.

"I wished we had had Neighborhood Watch," Bert said without looking at John. "Maybe this wouldn't have happened."

"In a sense you did," the officer said. "It was your neighbor who called nine-one-one when he saw something suspicious." He pointed toward John.

"Oh," Bert said. "Thank you, John."

After the police completed their investigation, Wilma ventured into the house while Bert sat on the porch swing and John stood on the steps. She began picking up the pieces of a broken lamp.

"Again, I'm sorry for what I said," Bert said. "It was totally uncalled for."

"That's okay, Bert. Under the circumstances, I can understand you being upset. But the reason I came down here was to tell you that I had talked to the person in charge of Neighborhood Watch. She said we need to schedule a meeting for a presentation."

"How about the Methodist church a few blocks over? I know the minister there. I can give him a call and ask if we can use their community room for a meeting."

"Sounds like a plan," John said. "Let me know when it's available and we'll set up a date and time."

John returned to his house. Sally was busy cleaning out the bedroom closet, with clothes, shoes and other items strewn on the floor. Whiskers appeared half-asleep, occasionally glancing at her, then dozing back off.

"You wouldn't believe what happened," John said.

"Bert wants to have a meeting tonight?"

"Close. I caught someone burglarizing their house."

"You've got to be kidding," Sally said, holding several clothes on hangers.

"Bert and Wilma weren't at home. I heard something inside and called nine-one-one."

"You didn't see who it was?"

"Well, I ran around to their backyard but whoever did it was long gone."

"My goodness. What's this neighborhood coming to?"

"Bert's going to check with the Methodist church a few blocks over to see if we can use it for a meeting."

"You and Bert already got the ball rolling."

"Thanks," he said. "We're a crime-busting team."

"He may end up being a best bud."

"Oh, almost forgot," John said. "If we can't get the Methodist church, Bert asked if we could have the meeting at our house. I told him it wouldn't be a problem."

"John, you didn't!"
"Nah, just keeping you on your toes."
Sally picked up a shoe and tossed it in his direction.
"Now that's not funny!"

Sixteen

John pulled into McDonald's for coffee. His old buddies were sitting in the back as usual, occupying about eight seats, and jabbering away about all sorts of things.

"Come and join us, Rossy," Mel said as John walked toward them. "We're still trying to solve the world's problems."

"I can't think of a more august group to do that," John said as he sat across from Mel.

"So what's up with you these days?" Curtis asked. "Keeping the missus happy with all the honey-dos?"

"I'd say it's been rather eventful," John said, mentioning the break-in at his home, his medical scare, and the beginnings of a Neighborhood Watch.

"Everyone here has some sort of medical issue," Howard said. "It comes with growing older. You live long enough to start enjoying some things in life, then your body breaks down and you die. What a joy!"

"Yeah, they tell you to exercise and eat right so you'll live longer," Mel said. "I'm not so sure living longer is better."

Everyone laughed.

"So you had a TIA?" Howard asked. "I had one as well a few years back. Scared the hell out of me. Made me think of Jess Oglethorpe and the stroke he had. He seldom gets out of the house anymore except for physical therapy. He looks pitiful with his drawn face and lame arm, being pushed around in a wheelchair. I sure in hell don't want anything like that. That's a reason I gave up smoking, if that does any good. At least I was told it does."

"I didn't know that about Jess," John said. "I thought he was still working on the business desk."

"Happened about six weeks ago," Howard said. "He was vacationing in Florida with his wife. Out on the golf course when he collapsed. Lucky they got him to the hospital in time."

"If you call that lucky," Mel said.

"Shit," said Randy Willis, who had worked in the composing room. "I don't think anything helps. If your number's up, then you die. No matter whatcha do, if it's your time, then it's your time. Ya know what I'm sayin'?"

"I'm not sure if I agree with that," John said with a smile. "We all know that smoking causes cancer and other health-related issues."

Randy curled the corner of his upper lip. "Yeah, maybe. But I know folks who've smoked all their lives and they're as healthy as can be. Hell, I know people in their seventies and eighties and they smoke all the time. Like I said, when it's your time, there's nothing you can do 'bout it. God's got your number."

"They should count their lucky stars," Mel said. "I think they're rolling the dice."

Randall gave him a dismissive glare. "Whatever."

"Okay, guys, let's talk about something important," Curtis said. "How about them Cats? Looks like they could go unbeaten this season."

"Sure looks that way," Howard said. "They're loaded. What do you think, John?"

"I haven't really followed them that closely, but I know they've had some very good recruiting classes so I'm not surprised they're ranked number one."

"They have so much size under the basket," Curtis said. "And that shooting guard is something else. If they lose, it'll be because they shot themselves in the foot. Or crappy-ass coaching."

"Could be," John said. "But in all my years covering sports, I know it doesn't take much to change things, be it an injury, dissension, disciplinary action. Or simply an off night when the other team is hot. Sometimes you have to give the other team credit."

"That's one thing the fans refuse to accept," Curtis said. "Nobody beats the Cats; the Cats beat themselves."

"You've got that right," Mel said.

"I don't think there'll be any players benched for breaking rules," Howard said. "If so, that stuff will come after the season's over. Winning basketball games is too important with these so-called elite programs."

"Winning seems to be the bottom line in college sports anymore," John said.

"Been back to the newspaper, Rossy?" Mel asked.

"No, I haven't." John took a sip from his cup. "I can't think of a reason to unless the personnel office needs something for me to sign. I'm content to observe from a distance. I spent my time there, now it's time for others to run things. And I enjoy my *me* time."

"I can see that," said Curtis, tugging the sagging skin under his chin. "I've gone back a few times for retirement parties. It's kinda nice seeing those folks again. But no desire to stay. When the party's over, I'm outta there. And really, there aren't many of the people I worked with there anymore."

"I'm still trying to get used to this retirement stuff. This may sound crazy but it's almost like work trying to find things to do," John said.

"Hey, Rossy," Mel said. "Let it come to you. Don't go looking for it. That's my free advice for the day."

"Thanks," John said. "I may just have to follow it."

"You'll probably hear from Breck Rogers about joining the alumni group," Curtis said. "He can be a persistent cuss. Nice guy and everything, but I think it's a second calling for him to be a social director."

"I've already been warned," John said with a chuckle. "But like I said, I'm more concerned with what to do with my life now. The other stuff can come later, if ever."

"Hey, John," Howard said, "it takes some getting used to. But I think it's important to find something to occupy some of your time at the beginning."

"I think this Neighborhood Watch program is going to take up some of that time," John said. "We've had several burglaries in my neighborhood the past few months. Yesterday, I caught someone breaking into one of my neighbors' homes."

"Hell, tell your folks to be like me," said Dan Wilson, a former city reporter. "I keep a few weapons in my home. If anyone unannounced shows up at my place, they might get their frickin' head blown off."

John looked around at the others. "Really?"

"I'm not going to put up with any lowlifes breaking into my home," Dan said, his voice rising a bit. "I've got every right to defend myself from intruders. I saw too much crap going on when I was on the police beat years ago. Too many innocent folks getting robbed, and some of them killed by deadbeats and thugs."

"I can see your concern," John said. "But I'm not sure I would want to go to that extreme. Have you ever had to use a gun?"

"Only once," Dan said. "I fired at a guy but missed. But I'm sure I scared the shit out of him because the frickin' punk never returned. I think the word gets around these gangs about which houses and businesses to hit."

"Never thought about it like that, but you could be right," Curtis said. "Makes some sense."

"I got a home security system," John said. "That may deter anyone from doing anything. At least it will alert the police if someone is trying to break into my house."

"I just hope those home security folks notify police to get to your place in time if something does happen," Dan said. "Those lights and alarms may cause some punk to start shooting in all directions."

"I'll take my chances," John said. "Anyway, most of the folks who've been burglarized weren't home when it happened. That's why we want to have people watching out for others."

"Good luck," Dan said with a smug expression. He glanced at his watch. "I need to be going. Believe it or not, but I'm going to the shooting range. Gotta keep my aim sharp for any punks." He winked.

"Don't shoot yourself in the foot," Mel said with a chuckle.

"You're real funny, Mel."

"I'm just kidding. Don't take it so seriously."

After Dan left through the rear exit, Mel looked around and raised his arms. "How in the world did we get on that subject?"

"I mentioned Neighborhood Watch." John said. "Sorry about that."

"You've got to be careful what you say when Dan's around," Mel said. "He's kind of an extremist when it comes to those things."

"Has he always been that way?" John asked.

"Seriously, I think he got that way covering crime at the paper," Mel said. "After he retired, he became rather paranoid about things. Then when his wife died a couple years ago from ovarian cancer, he really got carried away. I don't know but I wouldn't be surprised if he has a small arsenal at his house. He comes across as a survivalist at times."

"Scary," John said. "I'd be afraid someone would use the guns on me."

"You talk about scary," Mel said, "then you should see his son. He's a squirrelly guy with a shaved head, wears camouflaged clothes, those earrings you could throw marbles through, and has tattoos up and down his arms. Even one on his neck."

"And the funny thing about it," Curtis said with a chuckle, "is that he seems like a nice kid but wonders why he can't find a decent job."

"I hope Dan keeps his guns under lock and key," John said.

"I'm sure he does," Mel said. "He seems somewhat responsible about it. He knows that if any gang members hear about it, they're gonna to try to steal them from him."

"Dan isn't the most intimidating person you'd meet." Curtis said with a playful grin. "John, you do know what we call him, don't you?"

"No clue."

"Dan Nuts. Kinda like Don Knotts. Remember Barney Fife on that *Andy Griffith Show* on TV?"

All the men chuckled except for Randy.

"You guys can laugh all you want, but Dan ain't no damn fool." Randy was red-faced and his eyes narrowed. "There's something going on in this country with the government doing all kinds of illegal stuff like drones, wire-tapping, and shit like that. It ain't safe no more."

"Hey, Randy, we're not poking fun at Dan," Mel said.

"Well, it sure fuckin' sounds like it." Dan clenched his fists on the table. "Libtards are screwing us every which way. This country is sinking in the sewers."

"Okay, that's enough. Just calm down." Curtis pushed his hands downward. "You know one of the unwritten rules is that we don't discuss politics and religion here. Let's just have a friendly conversation and try to show some respect."

"Sure." Randy unclenched his fists and picked up his cup of coffee. "Just sayin'."

"Well, guys, I need to be going as well," John said as he took a deep breath, abruptly stood and stepped toward the aisle.

"Going to the gun range, too?" Mel said with an impish grin.

"Now cut it out, Melvin," Curtis said, shaking his index finger at him.

"Sally is going to start wondering where I am," John said. "Or worse yet, if I'm wandering from place to place."

Except for Randy, the others got up to leave. They'd be congregating again there in a day or so, with some of the same guys and some others who dropped by occasionally. John didn't plan to be one of them, at least for a while. Dan and Randy's outbursts were a bit unnerving.

John stopped by the library on the way home, checking out a couple books on neighborhood security since he wanted to be somewhat informed about Neighborhood Watch before he met with the police.

"Where have you been so long?" Sally asked when he came in the front door. "I was beginning to get worried about you." Whiskers was also there to greet him, standing up on his hind legs. He reached down and stroked Whiskers' back for a few seconds.

"Solving the world's problems at McDonald's," he said with a faint laugh.

"Learn anything knew?"

"I learned never to go to Dan's house when he hasn't invited you or doesn't expect you and to steer away from politics around Randy."

"Why's that?"

"Dan's liable to blow your brains out. His solution for a safe home is shooting someone. And Randy is totally against liberals, or should I say libtards, who are ruining our country."

"My goodness," Sally said as they retreated to the den and sat on the couch. "I don't want a gun and go to that extreme. At least I hope we don't have to."

"Me, either. We'll just stick with our home security system and Neighborhood Watch to keep us safe. And remain independent in politics. Or keep it to ourselves."

John handed her the two books he got from the library about keeping neighborhoods safe.

"I thought it'd be nice to know something about safe neighborhoods before our meeting," he said.

"Are you ready to go back out again?" she asked.

"Are you serious? I just got home."

"I'm ready for a new TV."

"Forgot all about that," he said. "How about letting me take a quick nap first?"

"That's fine," she said. "I want to go through the closet in the front foyer and see if there is anything else of yours we can donate to charity."

"Mine?"

"Gotcha."

John and Whiskers headed to the bedroom, with John lying on the bed and Whiskers curling up in his cushioned box. John was asleep within minutes.

Sally finished her chores, went to the bathroom, undressed and got into the shower. A minute later, John opened the curtain and stepped in next to her, causing her to jump back and let out a shrill "Eek!" as she was washing her hair.

"Don't do that!" she said, wiping shampoo from her eyes. "You scared me. You want me to have a heart attack?"

"You were expecting someone else?" he said as he lathered a washcloth with body soap.

"George Clooney, Brad Pitt or Antonio Banderas?"

"Sorry to disappoint you." He lowered his head and pushed out his lower lip. "Looks like you're stuck with reliable, old John Ross."

"Oh, I guess you'll do." She pecked him on the mouth.

"You want someone to wash your back?"

"Well, if you insist," she said.

"But only if I get to wash your front," John said.

"You'd think that after all these years you'd be tired of doing it," Sally said. "Especially now that I'm old. I'm not my perky self." She turned around and lifted her breasts in her hands for a moment. "See?"

"I see, sweetheart, but you're not that old," he said as he gently scrubbed her back. "Only older. And you've aged beautifully. Boobs, butt, belly and all."

Sally turned around, with the shower spray to her back, and rinsed her hair while John slowly cleansed her chest, breasts and tummy with the soapy cloth. "How does that feel?" he asked. "Cleaner?"

Sally pressed her body next to his and kissed him squarely on the mouth. John could feel himself getting aroused from the closeness.

"Mmmm, that makes me so very hot." she said melodramatically.

"If I were fifteen years younger, I'd pick you and make love to you right here," he said as he softly kissed her neck.

"And I'd let you do it," she said.

"But if I tried to do it now, my back would probably go out and we'd both tumble to the floor," he said with light laugh.

"Let's save it for some other time," she said.

"Like after we get back from shopping?"

"We'll see," she said with an exaggerated wink.

"I hope I'll still be up for it."

Sally looked down at his midsection and wiggled her brows. "Me, too."

Seventeen

A sixty-inch flat screen TV adorned the wall in the den.

"It looks a lot different in here now," John said, standing back from the TV after connecting the cables to the cable box and Blu-ray. "It kinda fills the wall. In fact, it is the wall."

"I know," Sally said. "I hope we can keep this one for a while."

"No reason why we shouldn't since we have a home security system and a Neighborhood Watch program about to get off the ground. We'll be safe and secure. Now doesn't that make you feel better?"

"You're so full of it." Sally exhaled deeply and looked up to the ceiling.

"All I have to do now is go out and buy a handgun for us to shoot any intruders."

"I think we can wait on that," she said. "If someone wants that TV bad enough, or anything else for that matter, they can have it."

"I'm inclined to agree with you, but I'm certainly not ready to tell folks we have stuff for the taking."

"You know what I mean," Sally said. "And quit being sarcastic."

"Truth is, it would be difficult to carry it out of the house without being noticed," John said.

"I would certainly hope so."

John picked up the remote and turned on the TV. He quickly surfed through the channels to see if everything was like it had been on the other set.

"New TV, same old crap," he said. "Anything you want to watch?"

"Well, not really," she said. "I'm kinda getting used to not watching TV."

"Then why did we buy it? To fill the space on the wall?"

"Just because there's nothing I want to watch at this very moment doesn't mean I don't ever plan to use it," she said. "And the same goes for you. You've been known to watch an occasional football and basketball game or some kind of nature documentary."

"You're right." He turned off the TV and placed the remote on an end table next to the couch. "I think it's time for Whiskers and me to take a walk. Care to join us?"

"Thanks, but I'm going to work on another closet," she said.

"When you set your mind to doing something, you go full bore."

"That's the only way things get done, Mr. Procrastinator."

"Is there any reason you're doing this stuff now?"

"Mother may come and visit us for Christmas so I want to be ready if she does."

"When did you hear from her?"

"It's been a while, but I know it's about time for her to leave her cozy place in Arizona and spend a few weeks here."

"Get back to work then, and thanks for the warning." John snickered and put the leash on Whiskers. The dog was full of energy after being in the house for most of the day, bouncing along at a faster pace than usual.

"Hey, slow down, little fella," John said, picking up his stride. "You want me to have a heart attack?"

Two young men were standing on the opposite corner as they were about to cross the street. Whiskers started barking and darted toward them, but was yanked back by John shortening the leash. "What's the matter with you, Whiskers?"

The men stared at them for a moment, then hurried down the street without looking back. Within a few seconds they had turned another corner and were out of sight. John thought for a moment that it was Bart Summers and his friend, but why would they run away?

"Look at what you did," John said, pointing his finger at Whiskers. "You're a bad boy. You scared those guys. They didn't do anything to you."

After Whiskers settled down, John bent over and stroked his furry withers. "Are you going to be okay now?"

They resumed their walk to the park, finding their favorite bench by the pond. Several young families were there with small children, tossing breadcrumbs to the waterfowl. Whiskers seemed content to lie on the ground.

John thought back to the encounter with the men on the street. It was so unlike Whiskers to behave that way. He hoped there wasn't something changing with the dog's disposition.

After thirty minutes, John rose from the bench and stretched his arms. Whiskers jumped up and seemed ready to go back home. He was detoured by a big oak tree, where he lifted his leg. He then took a couple steps and squatted.

John reached in his jacket pocket for a doggy bag, but it was empty. He looked around for a trash receptacle, and then his eyes locked on the self-anointed doggy policeman. The man glared at John, watching his every move.

John looked at the poo, then looked at the man. And did it again. Without hesitation, he quickly picked up Whiskers' dirty deed and put it in his coat pocket.

As they left the park, John spotted a trash can and took the poo from his pocket and got rid of it. He wanted to wash his hands but there was nothing he could do other than to hurry home.

"I hope you're satisfied," he said to Whiskers, who seemed to have a "who me?" expression as he looked up at John. "The things I do for you."

When they got home, Sally was sitting on the rocker in the den, watching a home improvement program on the new TV. After taking the leash off Whiskers, John hurried to the bathroom and scrubbed his hands. He took off his jacket and stuffed it in the hamper.

"How was your walk?" Sally asked when he came into the den.

"It wasn't the best of walks. First, Whiskers got all riled up at two men on the street. Then, at the park, he did the number two and I didn't have a doggy bag on me. It wasn't his fault, but I had to pick it up with my bare hand because the doggy cop was spying on me. One of these days I'm going to tell him to stuff it."

Sally laughed. "Maybe you need to put the box of doggy bags next to Whiskers' leash."

"Not a bad idea," John said. "I'm going to do that now before I forget. What would I do without you?"

Sally gave a cockeyed grin. "Sometimes I wonder."

He went to the kitchen, took the small box of doggy bags from a kitchen drawer and placed it next to the leash in the living room. Someone knocked at the door as he was about to go back to the kitchen.

"Now who in the world can that be?" he said softly. Bert was on the porch when he opened the door.

Bert, holding a clipboard, stepped inside. "Did you have a nice walk, John?" he asked.

"Yes, I did," John said. "Thanks for asking."

Bert sat on the couch and glanced at the clipboard. "I've talked to the minister at the Methodist church and he said their community room is available on Mondays, Tuesdays and Thursdays at six-thirty. I took the liberty of scheduling our Neighborhood Watch a week from Tuesday. I hope that's okay with you."

"Well, I guess, Bert, but I need to check my schedule or see if Sally has anything planned. I also need to get back with the person at the police department who runs Neighborhood Watch and see if that date works for her. That's the important thing. But off the top of my head, I can't think of anything."

"I figured that Monday wouldn't be a good day because that's when most of the folks go back to work. And for retirees, some folks might be out of town for the weekend and not return until Monday. So Tuesday should be a good day."

"I guess that logic makes sense," John said.

"So you need to schedule that person you spoke with at the police department to come and give the presentation."

"Like I said, I hope they're not busy with another presentation that evening."

"My goodness, I never thought about that," Bert said with a tight grimace.

"I'll let you know as soon as I talk to her."

"Please stress to her that a week from Tuesday would be the very best day for it."

"I'll see what I can do. Anything else?"

"Well, I've prepared a draft of a flyer I'd like to pass out to every home in the neighborhood." Bert removed it from the clipboard and handed it to John. "I figure this would be the most efficient way to let people know about the meeting since we don't have everyone's email address and mailing this would be prohibitively expensive."

"I guess that would work as well," John said as he quickly perused the flyer.

"What do you think about the flyer? Do you like the Neighborhood Watch image I used?"

"It looks very good," John said. "Just wait until we get things finalized before you print it."

Bert grimaced again.

"What's the matter?"

"I printed three hundred copies."

"Oh," John said, pursing his lips. "Too bad."

"At least we won't have problems getting them delivered."

"How do you propose that?"

"I figured that since you and your dog take daily walks, you could go from door-to-door and hand them out. Wilma and I might be able to assist you with that."

"Really?" John said, tilting his head. "Do you think we could enlist some more help? I don't go by all the houses in the neighborhood."

"I'll think about it," Bert said with a tight smile. "I figured that if you and me take care of it, we know the job will get done. You know how some folks are. They say they're going to do it, and then they forget, and it never gets done."

"Yeah," John said wearily. "I know exactly what you mean. Anything else?"

Bert quickly stood. "No, John, that should take care of things for the moment. I'll keep you posted on how things progress."

"I'd appreciate that," John said as he walked Bert to the door.

"One more thing, John."

"What's that?"

"I just want to thank you for taking care of this. I'm sure the neighbors will appreciate it too once we have Neighborhood Watch up and running."

"I hope so."

Sally came into the living room after John closed the front door. She couldn't help but laugh.

"What's so funny?" John asked, unable to suppress a little irritation as his mouth tightened shut.

"I heard the conversation. It looks like you have something to occupy some of your time now."

"I never dreamed it'd be something like this."

She took his hand and led the way to the kitchen. "What do you want for dinner?"

"How about a stiff drink?" John said.

"Oh, it's not that bad. After what we've gone through, and now Bert and Wilma, I think it's good idea for neighbors to look out for each other."

"I think it's good, too. I just didn't think I'd be the organizer and Bert the ringleader."

"You know I'll be behind you every step of the way."

"I know you will," John said with a grin. "Once I start handing out flyers door-to-door, you'll be with me and Whiskers every single step of the way."

"Can I buy some new walking shoes?"

"Whatever," John said.

Whiskers padded into the kitchen, going directly to his water bowl. Sally got a small scoop of his dry dog food and put it in his food bowl.

"How about pizza tonight?" she asked.

"That works," John said. "You paying?"

"I'll call and you pay."

"I guess that seems fair."

Eighteen

A cold, rainy morning convinced John to stay in bed, but the melodious Moody Blues tune on his cell phone drew him out of a semi-dream state of mind. At this time of the morning, he didn't feel like a singer in a rock and roll band. He came close to rejecting the call, but noticed through his heavy and bleary eyes that the caller was Brody.

"What's up, son?" John said softly, hoping not to awaken Sally, but who had already turned over and faced him with her head on the pillow.

"I'm in a bind, Dad. I could use a little cash."

"What's the problem?"

"I was involved in a fender bender and need to pay the other driver to avoid calling my insurance company."

"Any damage to your car? Are you okay?"

"I'm fine. My car had very little damage. You can hardly tell it was even in an accident."

"How much do you need to repair the other person's car?"

"Hmm...about two thousand dollars. I think that would do it."

"Are you serious? That sounds like more than a fender bender to me."

"It might be more but the guy says he'd take two thou for the damage. He drives a fancy BMW."

"Hold on a second, Brody."

John put his hand over the receiver and looked at Sally. "It's your son. Believe it or not, he needs some money."

"He was involved in an accident?" she asked.

"So he says. He'd like two thousand dollars."

"Two thousand dollars?" Her head rose from the pillow.

"Yes, dear. Only two thousand."

"Let me talk to him."

Sally cleared her throat as John handed her the phone. He dropped his head back on the pillow and closed his eyes. He wished this were simply a bad dream.

"Brody, Dad told me you were in an accident," she said sweetly. "And you're okay?"

"Yes, Mom. It's just a fender bender."

"And you need some money?"

"Yeah," Brody said. "Two thousand dollars."

"And you can't report it to the insurance company and police?"

"Listen, Mom, the guy says we can avoid all that hassle if I give him two thousand dollars by this afternoon."

"I wish we could see the car or have some repair estimates."

"Mom, please, I really need the money."

"When did the accident happen?"

"About forty-five minutes ago."

"It's awfully early to be out."

"I was at a friend's house watching football last night and I was on my way home."

"Oh, Brody..."

"Listen, Mom, if you don't want to send me the money, that's fine," he said angrily. "I'll find someone here who can loan me the cash. I don't want to put you and Dad out."

"Now, Brody…"

Brody ended the call.

Sally handed the phone to John. "So what did you decide?" John asked.

"Can you believe he hung up on me?"

"Uh, yes." John said as he placed the phone back on the night table.

"So what do we do?"

"Nothing."

"Nothing?"

"Sally, he's pulled this stunt before," John said as he bunched up his pillow. "I've lost count of the number of times he's asked us for money. He needs to grow up and be accountable for his actions. And do you really believe he was involved in an accident? Seriously."

"I don't know," Sally said. "I know what you mean, but what if he was in an accident?"

"Then let him go to one of the loan places and get the money. He doesn't need to be hitting us up every time something happens to him. He doesn't have any friends who could help him? Hell, he's thirty-seven years old. He's not a child anymore."

"He's our child."

"An adult child who refuses to grow up and be accountable for his actions."

Sally let out an exasperated breath and looked both ways. "I don't believe you, John Ross."

"Now don't put the blame on me."

Sally put her head back on the pillow, looking up at the ceiling. "I'm sorry. I just don't know what to think anymore. Perhaps it's the maternal instinct. I worry about him getting hurt or in trouble."

"He said he was okay."

"But he could still be in some kind of trouble."

"Honey, I feel the same way but there comes a time when he has to grow up. This stuff has to stop."

"I'd feel better if he were growing up here rather than three hundred and fifty miles away. It's just the unknown that scares me."

"Chloe seems to be doing fine seven hundred miles away," John said.

"But she's always been grown up and mature."

"Maybe she doesn't tell us everything like Brody does. Maybe she takes care of personal matters in other ways. Like an adult."

"She's always been responsible since she was a child."

"What time is it?"

"Almost six."

"So much for sleeping in this morning," John said as he slowly lifted his legs out of the bed.

"You getting up?"

"How can you sleep after talking to Brody?"

"I'm going to stay here a little bit longer."

"Take your time." John slipped his feet into his house shoes and picked up the cell phone in case Brody called again. "I'll make a pot of coffee." Whiskers was at his feet and followed him to the kitchen.

"Sorry we woke you up, buddy," John said to his furry friend. John took care of the coffee, then got some soft dog food from the refrigerator and put it in Whiskers' bowl. "There you go."

Instead of eating, Whiskers padded to the door and tapped on it.

"Oops, forgot about that, little fella," John said. "You do your thing while I get the newspaper."

John stepped off the porch in the light drizzle to pick up the newspaper on the edge of the walk while Whiskers scampered to his favorite spot at the side of the house. As he waited for Whiskers to return, he glanced up the street and saw a flickering light in a car parked in a driveway. He noticed the lights in the house were out.

"Come here, Whiskers," he said quietly. The dog came up to him and they hurried back into the house. John picked up the phone and called the neighbor, Rufus Martin, who groggily answered the phone. John told him what he had seen.

John stepped out on his front porch and heard Rufus shout, "Hey you!" Moments later, a car door slammed and the two men dashed down the street on the wet pavement. He hurried over to see Rufus, who was looking inside the Camry.

"It looks like they tried to take my stereo system," Rufus said. "I'll have to go through the glove compartment and see if anything is missing."

"Anything important in there?" John said.

Rufus sighed. "Uh-huh, a handgun."

"Oh, my goodness," John said. "Don't touch anything. Call the police."

Rufus scurried back inside his home and notified the police. A few minutes later, he returned, accompanied by his wife, Tanya, her arms wrapped around her chest in the chilly, damp darkness. "The police will be here as soon as they can," he said.

"I wished I had called the police when I first saw someone in your car," John said, "but I wasn't sure who it was. I thought maybe it was you."

"That's understandable," Rufus said, pursing his lips and placing an arm around his wife's quivering shoulders.

"We appreciate that you called us," Tanya said. "I've heard about some other break-ins. I'm not sure if I feel safe here anymore."

As they waited for the police to arrive, Bert suddenly appeared in the driveway. "Problem?"

"My car was vandalized," Rufus said.

Bert walked over and looked inside the front window. "You know my house was recently burglarized?"

"I heard about that," Rufus said as he took a cigarette out of his pocket. "Take much?"

"Thankfully, John saw the person in the act before he could take anything."

"John saw this as well," Tanya said.

"And don't forget that my home was vandalized several weeks ago," John said.

"You know we're organizing a Neighborhood Watch program," Bert said to the couple as a siren grew louder. "Our first meeting is next Tuesday evening at the Methodist church. Six-thirty sharp."

"We'll definitely be there," Tanya said, glancing up at her husband.

"If you can spread the word, especially to the Black residents, that would really help," Bert said.

John looked at Bert in disbelief. "Bert!"

"Sure, Bert, I'll be glad to do that." Rufus took a deep breath with a faint smile. "Okay if I tell some white folks as well?"

"Certainly. The more the better."

"Whatever you can do," John said. "It'd be appreciated."

The police arrived and examined the vehicle before asking questions.

"To be honest with you," the officer said, "I doubt if we'll locate those who did this. It's such a common crime anymore. The only thing you can do is call your insurance company and see if they can repair some of the damage to your car. I'm not sure it was wise for you to have had a gun inside. Was it registered?"

"I bought it several years ago at a gun shop on the other side of town," Rufus said. "I've got the papers inside the house if you need to see them."

"Yes, I do," the officer said. "It might help us track down the perpetrators."

Tanya returned to the house to get the registration. She came back several minutes later and handed it to the officer, who recorded the serial number and other pertinent information.

After the policeman left, John and Bert started walking back to their homes.

"Did I say something wrong?" Bert asked timidly in front of John's house.

"Let me ask you something."

"What?"

"If the tables were turned, do you think Rufus would ask you to tell white residents about the Neighborhood Watch meeting?"

"No," Bert said with a baffled expression. "So?"

"Think about it."

The rain began to come down harder and they parted ways without any more discussion.

Sally sat at the kitchen bar drinking coffee when John came back. He explained the break-in at the Martins' to her.

"And you wouldn't believe what happened while you were down the street," she said, holding up her cup before taking a sip.

"Not Brody again," he said.

"Close. Chloe called."

John looked perplexed. "She wants money as well?"

"No, of course not," Sally said with a grimace. "She called to say Brody asked her for money after he talked to us."

"You've got to be kidding."

"Furthermore, he only asked her for a thousand dollars."

"Seriously," John said. "Is she going to give it to him?"

"She hasn't decided. That's why she called us."

"And what did you say?"

"I told her I wanted to talk to you first."

"So what do we do?"

"Let's talk about it some more," she said. "More coffee?"

After quickly thumbing through the newspaper, John looked at Sally and laughed.

"So it's a thousand dollar accident for Chloe and two thousand for us?"

"I guess."

"I hate to do this but tell Chloe to send him the money and we'll send her the amount so she won't be out any. I can't believe he called her."

"Who knows if this hasn't happened in the past?"

"Maybe you should ask her," John said.

"I'm not sure if she would tell me. They're close."

"I guess we'll have to find out and see."

Nineteen

The Methodist church's fellowship room could seat one-hundred fifty but it turned into a standing-room-only crowd for the Neighborhood Watch presentation.

"I didn't realize we had this many people in the neighborhood," John said to Sally as they stood off to the side of the lectern before the start of the meeting.

"I guess we did a good job delivering the flyers to all the homes," Sally said with a grin.

"Looks that way," John said. "It was fun, especially the day it rained."

"Oh, yes, on my new walking shoes."

Bert strutted up the center aisle and stood next to John.

"It looks like we did it," he said with an expression of self-satisfaction. "We're going to make this a safer neighborhood, by gosh."

"I certainly hope so," John said. The program was scheduled to begin in five minutes. He breathed a sigh of relief when Officer

Kate Washington, resplendent in her sharply pressed black uniform, appeared in the back of the room.

She noticed John and waved as she made her way through the crowd. Once they saw the uniform, people stepped aside to let her through. She firmly shook John's hand, then he introduced her to Sally and Bert.

"What a great turnout." Officer Washington held a small box of pamphlets. "Can we get someone to hand these out before I get started?"

Bert took the box. "I'll take care of it." He immediately recruited a few people in the audience to help him distribute the literature. When he returned, Officer Washington and John stepped to the front of the room. John motioned for Bert to join them, and he reluctantly stood with them.

"I want to thank everyone for being here tonight," John said at the lectern. "I'm sure that most, if not all of you, are aware of the increase in crime in our neighborhood the past few months. I've been a victim as well. I'm not sure if it's a crime wave but it's something that should concern each and every one of us. After talking to several neighbors, it was decided to invite the Lexington Police Department to provide us with information on the Neighborhood Watch program. At this time, I'd like to introduce Officer Kate Washington, who will tell you about the program."

Although Officer Washington was only about five-foot-five and of slender build, her voice boomed over the crowd. She reviewed the program step by step, stressing to them that it wasn't designed to spy on neighbors, but to keep an eye out for suspicious activity. Her presentation lasted about twenty minutes, then she took questions for another fifteen minutes, ranging from setting up security cameras to arming themselves with guns.

"While we support your Second Amendment right to own firearms, we don't believe you should purchase one without proper training," she said. "We see too many instances of innocent people getting shot by family members and friends. I can give you names of certified instructors if you choose to go that route.”

After the presentation was over, the crowd was about to disperse when Bert stepped up to the lectern.

“As Officer Washington said, we need to have a board of officers to oversee the program,” he said. “I’d like to nominate John Ross as president of the organization.”

John shook his head “no” but he was named president by a voice vote. Rufus Martin was selected vice president, Bert as treasurer, and Dorothy Gonzalez as secretary.

After the meeting adjourned, Bert made a point of thanking Rufus for the “excellent turnout by our Black residents.” Rufus glanced over at John and groaned. John turned his palms up and half-smiled.

John and Sally walked to the near empty parking lot in the chilly night air.

“I should have stayed at home,” John said wearily. “I don’t want to be president.”

“You organized it, so you should have expected it.” Sally lightly elbowed him in his side. “But I just know you’ll make a wonderful president.”

“I guess that makes you first lady then,” he said with a chuckle. “And that involves duties as well, deemed by yours truly, so don’t think you’ll be sitting on the sidelines, sweetheart. I’ll be making my own honey-do list.”

“I’ll be honored.”

“I sure hope Bert didn’t say anything to Dorothy,” John said after they got into the car.

“Why’s that?”

“About the Hispanic residents.”

“Oh,” she said with a cringe.

When they got home, Whiskers was at the door to the garage, waiting to be let outside. Sally went to the bedroom to change clothes while John followed Whiskers to the back yard.

John heard music filtering through the fence from Preston's home. It sounded like new popular music but he wasn't sure what it was because he always listened to classic rock. To him, all the new music sounded the same.

"Feel like partying?" John said when he returned to the house.

"What are you talking about?" Sally asked.

"There's some kind of hip-hop or dance music coming from Preston's house tonight."

"Gee, and we weren't invited." Sally pushed out her lower lip.

"Yeah, I feel the same way."

"Oh well, have you taken out the garbage? Pickup is tomorrow morning."

John put on a jacket and walked to the side of the house. The music had stopped as he began wheeling the large red receptacle to the curb. He heard some voices coming from Preston's unlighted front porch, then noticed two people leaving.

When John returned, Sally was sitting on the side of the bed talking to Chloe on the phone. They chatted for nearly twenty-five minutes while he got out of his clothes and into lounging pants and T-shirt.

"Was it about Brody?" John asked when she put down the phone.

"Of course," she said with a long sigh. "She sent him the money."

"I'll send her a check in the morning to reimburse her."

"She said that even if it wasn't a car accident, it was probably something urgent he needed it for."

"Always something urgent with him," John said as he slipped on his house shoes. "I suppose we need to oblige him as well?"

"I have mixed feelings," Sally said. "There's something going on we don't know about."

"You know, looking back, how in the world did he contribute to the retirement vacation?"

"I wouldn't be surprised if Chloe paid for the whole thing and simply put his name on it. Maybe he promised to pay her back later."

"Really?" John said. "Maybe he was going to borrow from us to pay her. You know, sometimes ignorance can be bliss."

"It can be unless it turns out to be something really terrible."

"You didn't have to say that. Maybe he's just short on rent or a car payment."

"I hope so," she said. "Let's talk about something else."

"Deal," he said.

"What did you think about the meeting?"

"It exceeded my expectations," he said. "Officer Washington sure knows her stuff. I hope we can get things moving."

"I'm sure you will with Bert at your side," Sally said with a grin.

"Did you have to mention him?"

"At least he's not talking about retirement and his horrible years as a schoolteacher."

"Good point. Now let's change the subject again."

"Sure," she said. "What do you want to talk about now?"

"Well, I guess it has something to do with Neighborhood Watch."

"And?"

"After what Officer Washington said, would you be interested in owning a gun for protection? We could take lessons."

"I still don't think so," she said. "We've lived this long without having one so I don't see any reason for buying one now. I don't think I'd feel any safer. Besides, you heard what Officer Washington said about shooting family members and friends. That's what scares me. I might shoot you!" She pointed her forefinger at him. "Bang!"

"I'm inclined to agree with you," John said. "Not that you might shoot me, mind you. At least I hope not. I just thought you'd want something for protection when I'm not around."

"I can call nine-one-one," she said. "And if that doesn't work, I'll scream at the top of my lungs."

"That would sure in hell scare someone away."

"Besides, you're home more than I am," Sally said. "Maybe if you were still working long hours I'd consider it. But, like I said, not now. I feel safe with you being here most of the time."

She looked down at Whiskers. "And we have our canine protection as well."

"I'm not sure how much he'll protect us because his bark is bigger than his bite."

"I read in one of my magazines that small dogs can often deter intruders because of their barking."

"I suppose Whiskers is doing his job then."

"I'm hungry," she said, getting up from the bed. "Let's go see if there's anything to snack on in the kitchen."

"And maybe watch TV?"

As they were about to go, John's cell phone rang. He noticed it was Brody and took a deep breath before answering the call.

"Thanks a lot, Dad," Brody said with a tone that bordered on sarcasm. "I thought I could count on you."

"You know, two thousand dollars is a lot since I'm retired now," he said. "Believe it or not, your mom and I are on a fixed income. We're not a money tree."

Brody hesitated for a moment. "Then do you think you could spare a thousand? Is that asking too much?"

John clenched his teeth for a second. "How come you only need half now?"

"I came up with another thousand from a good friend. He said I could pay him back in thirty days."

"That was nice of him," John said, rolling his eyes. "So you need the money now?"

"It's too late today, of course, but if you could wire it to me in the morning, that would be great," Brody said, his voice sounding more enthusiastic and upbeat.

"Okay, son, but the well is about to run dry. And I hope you pay back your friend as you said you would. And I expect to be repaid as well for my loan as well. I'm keeping a tab."

"You're the best, Dad."

"Sure, Brody. Anything else?"

"No, that should do it," he said. "Tell Mom I love her."

"Will do."

John went to the kitchen and sat on a bar stool. Sally had chicken wings and onion rings in the oven. She poured two glasses of Coke and set them on the bar with a bottle of ketchup.

"How's our son?" she asked.

"First of all, before I forget, he sends his love to you."

"That's nice." Sally said. "That was a short call."

"Oh, would you believe a friend loaned him a thousand dollars so he only needs a thousand from us? And furthermore, the friend is a he, and Brody has thirty days to pay him back."

"What did you tell him?"

"You had to ask," John said. "I'm going to send him a thousand dollars in the morning."

"So you kinda side with me?"

"A little. I also figured I saved a thousand dollars since the first demand was for two thousand."

Sally laughed. "Perhaps if we had waited it would have dropped it to five hundred."

"I wouldn't count on that," John said. "On top of it all, he tried to lay a guilt trip on me for not getting the money to him sooner."

"He's done that before so you shouldn't be surprised."

"We're still out two thousand since we've got to repay Chloe. I guess Brody stuck it to us indirectly. We can't win for losing with him."

"We'll survive." Sally said. "I'm glad we're in a position to help our children."

John took a drink from his glass. "You know, since I'm retired now, I should make a visit to Chicago."

"That's something to think about," she said. "Especially if he's in some kind financial bind."

The oven beeped and Sally took the tray out.

"I'll think about taking a little trip." John dipped an onion ring into ketchup. "I'd like to get to the bottom of this."

"You might find out some things you didn't want to know."

"Thanks for the warning."

"But it's better knowing than not knowing."

"Yep, I don't like being kept in the dark," he said. "Especially when it hits my bank account."

"I hope that's not the main reason."

"A bit," John said. "With Brody, it seems to go hand in hand."

"Unfortunately."

After eating, they retreated to the den. Sally clicked on the TV while John picked up the newspaper and carried it with him to the rocking chair.

"Another one," he said to himself.

"Another what?" Sally said from the couch.

"Reggie Bottoms, a guy who worked on the regional desk for many years, died two days ago. He only retired three years ago. He apparently had a heart attack."

"So sad."

"Yes, it is," John said, folding the newspaper and laying it on the floor. "A damn shame. He was one of the good guys at the paper."

"Anything you want to watch?" Sally asked.

"Not really. I think I'm just going to sit here and try to relax. It's been a busy day."

Sally looked at him with pursed lips. "Tomorrow will be better."

"I sure hope so. Maybe I should just stay in this rocking chair. It feels comfortable all the time. Isn't that what retirees do?"

"You could go next door and party with Preston."

"Party's over," John said. "It ended as I was taking out the garbage."

"Must not have been any fun."

"Who knows? I saw two people leave, so it apparently wasn't much of one."

Twenty

John wired one thousand dollars to Brody and mailed the same amount to Chloe the next morning. Although wanting to be helpful to his children, he knew that giving in to Brody's every whim wasn't always the best thing to do. He remembered when he and Sally got married and how they struggled for several years to make ends meet. They learned to sacrifice by living in tiny apartments, driving mile-tested used cars, and eating Ramen noodles several nights a week. Somehow that didn't rub off on Brody, or he simply was oblivious to what was going on.

It was different with Chloe. She had her wishes and dreams but was willing to wait or put things aside. Whenever Chloe asked for something, and John couldn't recall the last time she did after she graduated from college, he and Sally realized it wouldn't be for anything frivolous. There was always a reason for an action. He wondered how they could raise two children who had turned out so differently. He thought that since Chloe was close to Sally, perhaps she had picked up those positive traits from her. And because he wasn't the best role model since he worked crazy hours, perhaps that was the reason Brody turned out the way he did. Who in the hell knew the answer?

After leaving the bank, John stopped by McDonald's to see if any of his old and new buds were sitting in the back. He purchased a large coffee and egg sandwich and meandered toward the rear where they were talking and laughing like they owned the place.

As John neared the table, a heavy-set young man walking down the middle of the aisle brushed against him, causing him to spill coffee on his pants. The man strutted on his way, head held high, seemingly unaware he had bumped into somebody. John regained his footing, turned and stared at him making his way to the front counter, then frowned in disbelief. John felt the contact and he knew the man had to as well.

"Excuse me?" John said as the man continued to walk toward the front. He turned to his friends and said, "Did you see that?"

"Yep," Curtis said. "Young folks have little or no manners anymore. I see it all time. And they have little or no respect for their elders."

"I was nearly run off the street coming over here," Mel said. "Some kids swerving in my lane and cutting in front of me. Then when I blew my horn, some punk in the back seat turned around and gave me the finger—with both hands!"

"What did you do?" Howard asked.

"Hell, I gave him one right back," Mel said, popping up his middle finger high and grinning. "I ain't going to take that crap from anyone."

"I don't understand it at times," John said as he stirred his coffee. "I got along with most of the young folks at the newspaper, but things haven't been the same since I retired."

"You were working with some college-educated kids who respected you," Curtis said. "And you had a position of authority there. Now that you're no longer with the paper, you're just an old man hanging out with other old men. Kinda invisible in a way. Welcome to the old dude's club."

"Damn, Curtis," John said. "That's depressing."

"I hate to break the news to you, Rossy, but life's a lot different out here in the real world," Mel said. "When I was growing up, my parents taught me to respect my elders. And my elders may have been only forty years old, but they seemed old to a ten-year-old. And really old folks, like my grandparents, were to be honored and respected. And if I didn't, they spanked my little ass or washed my mouth out with soap. And that's how my kids were raised. No mouthing back to me or anyone else."

"Are your grandkids raised the same way?" Curtis asked.

Mel frowned. "Uh, not really."

"When was the last time a kid said 'yes, sir,' or 'no, sir' to you?" Curtis asked, raising his bushy brows.

"I don't remember," John said. "It's been a while."

"Hell, kids seldom even say 'thank you' when you purchase something at a store they're working at," Curtis said. "About the only time you hear it is when they want something. And the next time you see them they'll flip you the fuckin' bird and tell you to shove it up your ass."

"And their parents back them up on everything," Mel said, raising his voice loud enough that others sitting at adjoining tables turned their heads at him. "They always feel their kids have been done wrong, if that makes any sense. They don't teach their kids to behave, and then defend them when they misbehave. Pisses me off to no end."

"Calm down, Melvin," Curtis said with a light laugh.

"My son's a teacher and he puts up with all kinds of grief from parents," Howard said. "Like you said, it's never the kids' fault. It's the system's fault. Teachers are more like professional babysitters nowadays."

"By the way, how are your kids, John?" Curtis asked.

"I think they're respectful of others," he said. "I really can't complain." John couldn't help thinking about Brody but it wasn't something he cared to share with others about his son.

"Grandkids?"

"I have a granddaughter. Her name is Whitney. I haven't seen her in a while but I'm sure she's not a problem. She's a toddler. A real sweetie."

"It's too bad they can't stay toddlers a little longer," Mel said with a boisterous laugh. "That's a cute age. Even the so-called terrible twos."

"Oh, they stay cute until they become know-it-all teenagers," Curtis said. "That's when you've got to watch out."

"I guess it's a stage most of us go through," John said. "I'm sure we did a few things back in the day."

"Yeah, but not what these kids do today," Mel said. "I used to think it was because they had too many temptations, but after giving it some thought, I believe it's because there's not enough things to do. They all seem to be wrapped up in those video games or listening to music with earplugs. They're in their own little worlds."

"I know what you mean," Curtis said. "My grandsons and their friends play video games day and night."

"Back when we were kids, we had camping trips, baseball, basketball, school activities and all sorts of things to keep us busy and out of trouble," Mel said. "Seems like all today's kids are into are video games and drugs. That's a crappy environment to grow up in."

"Now there are some good kids out there," John said. "Not all kids are that way."

"You're right," Mel said. "Just most of 'em."

"Now, Melvin, don't be so harsh," Curtis said in a calming voice. "There's a lot of good kids out there. Don't write most of them off."

"One problem is that so many of these kids are from single-parent homes nowadays," Howard said. "And if they're from two-parent homes, it seems like both parents work so they don't get much discipline and supervision. I think they used to call them latch-key kids. They're out on their own."

"Good point," John said. "My wife knows quite a few families where the kids were placed in day care at a very early age, then a few were involved in some after-school programs until the parents came home from work. She said some of these kids only saw their parents a couple hours each day during the week. And then the parents tried to cram a lot of stuff in during the weekends instead of some quality one-on-one time."

"I know my daughter and her husband went through that," Howard said. "My wife and I got tired of seeing it, so we ended up with the kids when they got out of school. I'm not complaining or anything, because we love our grands very much, but it was almost like raising children a second time. It's very time consuming. Sometimes we had to ask our children to watch the grands so we could take a short trip or break. Isn't that crazy?"

"So is it any surprise that some kids are the way they are today?" John said.

"It's really sad," Howard said. "No wonder we read about kids taking guns to schools and shooting people. Even those kids who are bullies are probably victims of neglectful and uncaring parents. That's why they join gangs or do whatever they do to get in trouble."

"I really hate to see what future generations of kids are gonna be like," Mel said. "If these kids are gonna be parents someday, heaven help us. This country of ours is gonna go down the tubes."

"That's painting a scary picture," Curtis said.

"It's too bad Dan and Randy aren't here to set us straight," Howard said, grinning.

"Oh, yeah," Curtis said. "I'm sure they've got some answers."

"Well, guys, I need to be going," John said. "This discussion has really brightened my day."

"Hey, Rossy," Mel said. "We told you we try solving the world's problems here. I'm surprised we haven't heard from the governor or president,—hell anyone seeking our sage advice."

"No doubt the world would be a better place if people would listen to this bunch of old geezers," Curtis said with a chuckle.

John stood and picked up his tray to return it to the trash receptacle. Before he took a step from the table, the man who had brushed against him came sauntering down the aisle with his head still held high and belly bulging, heading toward the rear exit. Curtis eased his knee out from the table, tripping the bearded bully, causing him to tumble to the floor, spilling a large soft drink that splashed on the tiles.

"Oh, excuse me, sir," Curtis said as pulled his knee back under the table. "I didn't see you coming this way."

"Fuck you, old man!" He bounced back up from the floor, wiped his hands and turned toward Curtis.

Curtis eased up from his chair and stared down at the man. "I beg your pardon?"

The man noticed old Curtis was several inches taller and probably more fit, even if he was nearly sixty years older.

"Asshole," he said under his breath as he headed out the rear exit.

"What did you say?" Curtis asked, his hands firmly on his waist and chest puffed out. He didn't get a response. The man huffed and darted out the rear door.

Curtis laughed.

"Time to go on that," John said, as he waved his hand and left the restaurant.

~ * ~

Parking in the driveway, John noticed Preston standing in his front yard talking on the phone. He got out of the SUV and was about to wave when Preston suddenly turned his back to him and walked away.

Whiskers greeted him at the front door and John followed him to the side of the house. On the other side of the fence, he could hear Preston, apparently still on the cell phone since he didn't hear anyone else.

"So what time can you come over?" Preston asked.

After a pause, Preston said, "Wednesday at eight p.m. will be fine." Pause. "See you then."

Whiskers let out a bark. John remained quiet and put his fingers to his mouth to shush him.

"Damn dog," Preston said. A moment later, John could hear him walking away, and then the back door open and close.

"Let's go back inside," John said, motioning with his hand for Whiskers to follow him.

"So did you get everything taken care of?" Sally asked when came into the house.

"It's on the way," John said as he sat on a stool. "Our son is a thousand dollars richer; we're two thousand dollars poorer."

"I wouldn't say poorer," Sally said. "We're not poor. And I'm thankful we can provide for our children, even if we have doubts about it."

"Yeah, things could be a lot worse."

"Oh, I thought you'd want to know that Brody called about an hour ago to remind us about it."

"You've got to be kidding," John said. "He thinks we're that forgetful?"

"No. I think he was worried we'd change our minds."

"Perhaps we should have."

"We'll get to the bottom of it one of these days," Sally said.

"Let me ask you something?"

"What, dear? You want to borrow money as well?" she said with a laugh.

"I wish," he said. "Do you think of me as being old?"

"What? Why do you keep asking me that?"

"I don't know," John said. "Well, maybe it's because some of the guys at McDonald's do seem kinda old to me. We were talking about how the young folks don't have much respect for older folks. To be honest, I never thought of myself as being real old, if you know what I mean."

"You don't seem that old to me," she said, tapping the top of his hand. "I've seen some of my friend's husbands who are about the same age, and some who are younger, and they look older and act older than you."

"I don't want to sound vain or anything but I've always tried to stay in somewhat good shape and keep up with the times."

"Honey, I don't want to hurt your feelings but you harp on it too much," she said. "You're insecure about it."

"I am?"

"Very much so. You sound like some of the gals I talk to at the blood drives."

"Really?"

"You look very healthy." She rose and kissed him on the forehead. "Now just be yourself. Does that make you feel better?"

"Of course, sweetheart," he said with a light blush. "You always make me feel better."

"And something else," she said.

"What's that?"

"Don't forget to take your meds. They keep you younger. Physically and mentally."

"I've been diligent about that. Anything else?"

"I'm not ready to trade you in."

"Gee, thanks. I plan on keeping you for a while, too." He leaned over and kissed her on the cheek.

Whiskers tapped his food bowl several times, signaling to them that he was hungry. John got up from the stool and put some dry food in it.

"Afternoon plans?" she asked.

"Nothing other than my daily walk with Whiskers. You?"

"I've got another closet to declutter and organize."

"Maybe we can do something later on."

"Such as?"

"Some cozy time in bed."

"Oh."

He gave her a quick kiss, then put the leash on Whiskers and opened the door.

"Don't forget a doggy bag," Sally said.

"I almost forgot."

Seconds later John stashed two bags in his back pocket and he and Whiskers were off to the park. Several neighbors were raking leaves, something John knew he should be doing but yard work wasn't one of his favorite chores. He thought perhaps he should contact Trace and his friend and see if they wanted to earn some money. Maybe even another twenty dollars.

John removed Whiskers' leash when they reached the park bench. He sat and watched as Whiskers as sniffed around nearby bushes and trees. It was unusually quiet. There weren't any parents with their children next to the pond, tossing bread crumbs to the ducks. There were only a few walkers and joggers in the distance, on the other side of the pond.

All of the sudden Whiskers began barking at something behind an evergreen shrub. "Get back here," John said. "There's nothing there for you."

But Whiskers continued to bark intermittently, glancing at John and then behind the bush.

"Okay, little fella, what is it?" John said as he walked toward him. Getting closer, he saw the pant legs of a person sticking out from under the bush. He moved around to the other side and noticed blood trickling from the man's nose and ears and a deep gash on the side of his head.

John pressed the man's carotid artery and felt a slight pulse. He quickly took out his cell phone and dialed nine-one-one. A police cruiser pulled up next to the park entrance within three minutes, and less than five minutes later, an EMT ambulance arrived with its red lights flashing and siren blaring as it crossed the park grounds to where John and the officer were standing.

A paramedic checked the victim's vitals. "He's apparently taken quite a beating," he said to the policeman. The EMTs took a gurney from the vehicle and lay the man on it. They scrambled to the vehicle and were on their way to the hospital as the siren boomed again and lights pulsated on the top of the red-and-white vehicle.

After attaching the leash to Whiskers, John was questioned by the police officer. As they were talking, he noticed the officer was holding a black ball cap.

"May I see the cap?" John asked.

The officer handed it to him. "We found it over there," he said, motioning to the right. The cap had military insignia and cluster.

"I don't know the man's name but I see him here all the time, if that's his cap," John said as he handed it back to the officer. "We seldom speak but he seems to be here every time I walk my dog."

The officer gave John a card and asked him to call if he remembered anything else about the man.

When he got home, Sally was in the den watching a garden show on TV.

"You were gone longer than I expected," she said from the couch. Whiskers ran to his water bowl as John sat next to her and told her what he had seen at the park.

"I'm not sure if the park is safe anymore after seeing what happened to that old man," he said. "If it hadn't been for Whiskers, he could have died there. He was barely alive when the ambulance arrived. I wouldn't be surprised if he's dead now."

John called the officer's number on his cell phone, identifying himself as the person who found the man in the park.

"I apologize for calling but I was wondering if you've heard anything else about the man's condition," John asked.

"I don't have much other than he's in critical condition in the intensive care unit at the hospital," the officer said. "That's all I can tell you."

After ending the call, John told Sally about the victim's status. "Maybe I should go over to the hospital?"

"Why don't you wait until we know something more about his condition?" she said.

"You're right. They don't need a stranger interfering in what they're doing."

"I was wondering if Neighborhood Watch would include the park," Sally said.

"Since it's a neighborhood park, I would assume so. But I can't see having people monitoring the park unless they do what I do when taking walks there."

"I don't know what to think anymore," she said. "This used to be such a peaceful, quiet neighborhood. Now we have all kinds of bad things happening."

"Hopefully, that will change."

"By the way, I heard from Brody while you were away. He said thanks for the money. He said he was in a real bind or he wouldn't have asked."

"That's good to hear," John said. "Oh well, I wonder how many more binds he's going to get into."

"We'll see." Sally rose, turned off the TV and walked to the kitchen without saying anything to John.

"Where are you going?"

"I'm going to see if I can find us something to eat. I haven't been to the grocery in a while so the possibilities are very limited."

"For a moment I thought I had bad breath or body odor."

"Honey, I'd tell you that. I wouldn't just get up and walk away."

John followed her. "Why don't we go out and get a quick bite to eat. After what I witnessed in the park, I think I'd like to go someplace where I could have a beer or two."

"I'm not going to argue with you. Let me go and change my top and I'll be right back. You go ahead and feed our little hero."

John fed Whiskers, then moseyed to the bedroom and changed his shirt before going out to dinner.

They visited their usual neighborhood Mexican restaurant. John ordered a Corona while Sally got a margarita. They were not that hungry so decided to split an order of nachos.

"I wonder if some of this stuff going on was going on while I was working and I just didn't notice," he said. "You know, I was spending ten to twelve hours at work, coming home, and not doing much else. Maybe I'm just more aware of what's happening now."

"It's hard to say," Sally said. "Maybe because things have happened to us and some of our neighbors. You know, it's hitting closer to home."

"Could be." John took a big swallow from the glass. "But it's not something we can ignore."

"At least you're going to do something about it."

"I really have mixed feelings about that."

"Why?" she said with a puzzled look.

"I respect privacy and things that go with it. I've always been somewhat private. I just don't want people spying on each other or sticking their noses into places they don't belong. That's not what all this is about. It's neighbor looking out for neighbor."

"Then that's what you need to stress to everyone. I thought Officer Washington made that point very clear."

"I guess what I'm really worried about is someone being overzealous about it. You know, taking the law into their own hands. I'm concerned that some of the folks who own guns may kill someone."

"That's kinda scary."

"I guess we can't control everything," he said. "We'll just have to take things as they come."

"That's all you can do. People are going to do what they want to do."

When the nachos arrived, John ordered another Corona. Sally still nursed her margarita. As they ate, the news about the man assaulted at the park came on one of the large-screen televisions attached near the ceiling. The report showed a photograph, more like a mug shot since it was probably taken from a personal identification card, and gave his name as Bernard Shipley and age as seventy-eight. His condition had been upgraded to serious. The police said they didn't have any suspects in the crime.

"That's the guy I would see at the park who made sure I cleaned up after Whiskers did his business," John said, pointing at the screen. "This sounds mean but I wonder if he told someone to clean up after their dog, and that person turned on him."

"Who knows?" Sally said. "At least I hope not."

"Some people can really get ticked off about things, kinda like road rage. Things they should ignore."

They finished their meals and returned home. Seconds after John pulled into the driveway, Bert was standing in their front yard, almost as if had materialized before their eyes.

"Thought you might want to know about a guy who was brutally beaten at the park today," he said.

"I already know about it," John said as Sally waved at Bert and escaped to the house. John wished he could have done the same thing.

"You do? See it on TV?"

"I reported it to the cops," John said.

"That's good to hear. That sends a message out to everyone that our Neighborhood Watch chief is on top of things. That should put people at ease."

"I don't know about that. I doubt if anyone knows I called the police. If anything, people need to be on the lookout for anything suspicious. I was fortunate to have Whiskers with me."

"Whiskers?"

"Whiskers located the man. I just followed him."

"I don't think we need to broadcast that," Bert said as the corner of his lips turned downward.

"I think you're getting carried away with it. Let's just go one step at a time and get the program up and running. All we've had so far is a presentation from Officer Washington. We still need to have an organizational meeting and educate folks before we start tooting our horn."

"Okay," Bert said. "Just let me know when you want to get the ball rolling and I'll schedule the church's fellowship room again."

"I'll get with you in a day or so," John said.

"Sounds like a plan then." Bert turned and returned to his home without saying another word.

John looked over at Preston's house and noticed Trace and a young girl going in the front door. He thought about trying to get Trace's attention about raking leaves but decided against it, hoping he'd see him when he left the house.

John made sure the doors were locked on his SUV, then returned to the house.

"What did Bert want?" Sally asked as she closed a book when John came into the den and sat in the rocking chair.

"He's ready to roll on Neighborhood Watch."

"I hope the others will be as enthusiastic."

"We'll see but I sincerely doubt anyone can be as enthusiastic as Bert," John said as he reached down and petted Whiskers for a few seconds. "There's only one Bert, thank goodness."

He turned on the TV, and flicked through the channels, trying to find something interesting to watch. After a couple of minutes, he glanced at Sally on the couch. "You want the remote?" She declined so he clicked the off button.

"I think tomorrow I'm going to go over to the hospital and check on Mr. Shipley," he said. "Maybe he doesn't have family or anyone with him. And if he has a wife or children, I can see if I can provide them some comfort."

"Maybe he'll be conscious and tell the police or someone about what happened," Sally said.

"Yeah, I'd like to know what happened, especially since Whiskers and I go there quite a bit. We sure don't want to get mugged."

"Maybe you shouldn't go back to the park until the police make an arrest or something. Maybe they plan to have more patrols in the area."

"I don't want to overreact," John said. "It may have been an isolated incident. I've never heard of anything like that happening there."

"Let's hope it doesn't happen again," Sally said.

"Well, I'm ready for bed," John said, rising from the rocking chair and stretching out his arms. "How about you?"

"I'll be up in a few minutes. I have a few more pages to finish this chapter."

Whiskers followed John to the bedroom and hopped into his bed in the corner. John was already in bed when Sally came into the room. She put on her nightgown and snuggled up next to him.

"Good night, sexy," he said, kissing her on the mouth.

"You, too, handsome."

They were asleep in a matter of minutes.

Twenty-one

"Mrs. Shipley?" John asked as he stepped into the light blue waiting room.

She turned around. Her fuzzy gray hair was askew from sleeping in a chair. Her puffy green eyes were accentuated by a lack of sleep and more than a few tears. From what he understood from living with Sally for so many years, he knew Mrs. Shipley probably would never want to be seen in public this way unless it was under extenuating circumstances. And this was the case.

"Yes," she said softly, glancing up at him from the cushioned, brown plastic chair.

John walked up to her and lightly touched her hand. "I'm John Ross. I found your husband in the park yesterday. I just dropped by to see how he's doing."

"He's slowly improving." She rose from the chair with the assistance of John holding her hand. "They have him on some painkillers. He's been semi-conscious but that doesn't bother the doctors. They say it's normal for a person who has suffered a traumatic head injury."

"That's good to hear. I take my dog for a walk in the park several times a week and I've seen your husband there on occasion. Actually, it was my dog that discovered him under some bushes."

"I'm very thankful you found him. We live across the street from the park. I'm sure you don't know this, but he's been diagnosed with early onset dementia. I keep an eye on him as much as possible. He seems to enjoy going to the park and seeing the ducks at the pond. I've had some people tell me that he's the unofficial park police because he keeps an eye on everyone and everything that goes on there."

"I can see that," John said, biting his tongue.

"I'm afraid that may have gotten him into trouble yesterday. He may have said something to the wrong person that angered them. Bernie retired from the Army quite a few years ago and can still be kind of gruff. He's really gotten bad about it the past year or so."

"I certainly hope he makes a quick recovery. Please let me know if I can be of any assistance to you and him." John took an old business card from his wallet, scratched out the work phone with a pen, wrote down his personal cell phone number, and handed it to her.

"I appreciate it, Mr. Ross," she said. "Again, thank you so very much for coming by and checking on Bernie. I know he'll appreciate it when I tell him."

As John walked past the hospital cafeteria, he heard someone call his name. He stopped and looked around, then saw Mel Snider waving at him from one of the tables.

"What are you doing here?" Mel asked. "I hope there's nothing wrong with Sally." John walked to the table and sat.

"Did you see the story on news about the guy who got beat up at the park yesterday? I dropped by to see him."

"A friend of yours?"

"Not really. More of an acquaintance. I came down to check on his condition. So what brings you here?"

"My grandson, Johnny. He was involved in an accident on his bike. Broke his arm in two places."

"Wow. How's he doing?"

"They had to use a screw on one of the bones so it was a pretty serious break. But he's a tough little bugger. Only eleven years old but not afraid of anything."

"Sounds like he's going to be a handful for his parents later on."

"Damn, he's a handful now. He broke a leg a couple years ago doing some of that skateboarding stuff. A few months ago, he knocked out a tooth playing baseball. He's all boy."

"Certainly sounds like it," John said with a smile.

Mel's wife came to the entrance of the cafeteria and motioned with her hand for him to come over to her. "Looks like the boss is calling. I'll see you at Mickey D's." He got up and followed her down the hall like a dutiful child.

Enjoying the quiet in the near-empty cafeteria, John went to the beverage counter and poured a large cup of coffee. He sat at a table near the corner. On the next table was a newspaper that had been left by a customer. He reached over and picked it up.

On the front page was a short piece about Bernard "Bernie" Shipley being assaulted at the park. As usual, he turned to the obituary page and glanced over the names and ages. He didn't recognize any names. He turned to the sports pages and for a quick look over before laying the paper on the table. He wondered if people spent as little time with the newspaper as he did.

Less than a minute later, a young man came over to his table. "Sir, are you finished with the paper?"

"Sure, go ahead and take it," John said. "It was here when I sat down."

The man smiled, took the paper and sat three tables away, where he had an overloaded tray of two coffees, two orange juices, and two plates of eggs and bacon, and toast. A few minutes later, Mrs. Shipley walked in and sat next to him. The man removed the food from the tray and placed it in front of her. John figured it was probably her son.

As John rose from the table to leave, Mrs. Shipley looked at him with a sad smile. He thought for a second about going back and saying something to her but decided against it and headed outside to the parking lot. He knew they had enough on their minds.

~ * ~

Decked out in jeans and a large, maroon Eastern Kentucky University sweatshirt, Sally was busy clearing out another closet, this time in their purported office study. Whiskers was in the bedroom, napping in his bed.

"How was your visit?" she asked as he leaned against the door frame to take a short break.

"Mr. Shipley seems to be improving," John said. "I spoke with his wife for a few minutes. He's semi-conscious but that's supposed to be normal for what he endured."

"I read the story about him in the newspaper," she said.

"I also learned he's got early onset dementia," John said. "He's retired military. That may explain some of his aggressive behavior. Makes me wonder if he was a drill sergeant. He certainly liked to bark orders. Wouldn't it be funny if he was my drill sergeant in basic training? Those guys were tough SOBs. I told her to call if she needs any assistance."

Sally sat in the chair by the desk. "I should have let you do this. Most of the stuff in here belongs to you. Did you know you're a packrat?"

"Really?" he said with a chuckle. "I don't know why you'd say something as preposterous as that."

"I've found junk, I mean stuff, that's more than twenty years old, maybe even thirty. Key chains, trinkets, cups, pens, caps."

"Valuable collectors' items," he said.

"You wish."

"I'll go through it this weekend," John said. "A few items could be thrown away."

"A few? I can't believe you're saying that. If I had started tossing things, you would have been very upset with me. You'd said there were some important items in there. Sometimes I think you keep things because you think they belong in a museum."

"Oh, please, give me a break," John said, crossing his arms. "You have to admit you've run across several valuable artifacts that are probably museum worthy today."

Sally stared blankly at him, then picked up a paperweight with a company logo inscribed on it. "Such as this?" Then she pointed to four plastic cups on the desk with various baseball team logos. "And these?" She opened a small box filled with pens of various shapes, sizes and colors. "And these as well?" She laughed. "The ink has dried up in most of them."

"Okay, okay, I get your point," he said, raising his hands. "It's still personal memorabilia that brings back some nice memories."

"Of work?"

"Work wasn't all that bad," he said. "The newspaper was once a great place to work until the corporate folks took over. You know that."

"I'm just teasing you," she said. "I know there were some good times for you. But you have to admit the best times were with the people you worked with and got to know."

"Probably so," he said. "But they're all retired, moved away, or dead."

"Do you have to be so negative? How about those guys you see at McDonald's?"

"Maybe so. Things have just changed a lot in the past couple of years."

"Honey, life changes all the time. You know that."

"Yeah, but you don't have to like all the changes. Just like what happened to Mr. Shipley at the park, and the things that have been happening in the neighborhood. Then there's Brody's irresponsibility. I don't have to like any of it."

"I don't like it either," Sally said, "but I've learned to live with it. We've had other bad things happen through the years but we get over them and go on. Your parents getting killed in a car accident. My sister drowning. My father's death. We'll do the same with this. It's just a matter of time. And there will be more good times, too."

"I sure hope so," John said with a frown. "These things really weigh me down."

Whiskers padded into the room and gently tapped John's leg.

"Now isn't Whiskers a good thing?" Sally asked with a smile.

"I forgot about Whiskers," John said as he reached down and picked him up. "You've been a great thing," he said to Whiskers, cuddling him close to his chest. "Ready for a walk?"

Whiskers licked John's chin several times.

"I guess I can take that as a yes," John said with a bright smile. "So we're going for a quick walk."

"I'll have lunch ready when you return, so don't be gone too long."

John attached the leash to Whiskers and they were on their way. They passed Bert's home but he was nowhere to be seen. Along the way he noticed several "For Sale by Owner" signs in the front yards. He wondered if the recent crime was driving people away or if it was just a coincidence. The more he thought about it, it was probably a bit of both.

Several teenaged boys and girls wearing droopy, baggy pants and oversized sweatshirts were milling about in front of a house several doors down from Bert's. Some puffed on cigarettes. They were talking, then suddenly stopped and glanced at John and Whiskers as they walked by. John looked at them for a moment and continued on his way for another six blocks. He couldn't imagine why their parents allowed them to dress that way unless they didn't care or had just given up. And why would they want their daughters hanging out with boys like that? It's no wonder kids got in trouble. He thought about the conversation with his friends at McDonald's and realized he was beginning to sound like them.

John crossed the street and began walking back to his house. He saw some trash littered along the way, mostly empty soda and beer cans that had apparently been tossed from cars. There were some bags and cups from fast-food restaurants that he was tempted to pick up but didn't have any place to put them.

Preston stepped out on his front porch as John got closer to his home. He gave a sly glance and went back inside before John could say anything. What a great neighbor.

When John reached his house, there was an empty beer can by the curb. He picked it up and put it in his trash can for recyclable items.

"Hey, John. Got a second?"

Hank Summers raised his hand as he hurried up the sidewalk toward John's house.

"Sure," John said. "What's up?"

"I heard about the old man getting beat up at the park. Bert told me you found him," Hank said, slightly out of breath.

"Yep. Visited his wife this morning and he's slowly improving."

"That's great. Have you given any thought to what I told you about crime in the neighborhood?"

"Immigrants?"

"No, the fucking illegals. I've seen some of them near the park when I come home from my daily deliveries."

"Maybe you need to notify the police."

"I thought that Neighborhood Watch of yours did that."

"It's not my Neighborhood Watch," John said. "It's for everyone who lives in the neighborhood."

"You think I should call the cops about it?"

"That's your decision, Hank. If you've seen a crime, or something suspicious, let them know. But be careful about it."

"What do ya mean?"

"Everybody has the right to use that park."

"Yeah, I guess you're right." Hank tightened his mouth.

"Why don't you come to our organizational meeting? Bert is getting it arranged."

"Maybe, if I can find the time."

"You might learn something."

Hank turned around. "I'll think about it. Just wanted to let you know about them illegals." He began walking toward his house.

John scratched his head and led Whiskers to the side of the house. He didn't know what to think about Hank's comments

"How was your walk?" Sally said from the kitchen when he came in the front door.

"You don't want to know."

"I hope you didn't find another body."

"Nah, just a bunch of litter everywhere," he said. "Don't people have pride anymore in where they live? We even had a beer can out front. And then I had to listen to Hank rant about 'illegals' at the park. Of course, he wants me to report it to the police since he's too busy. Gimme a break."

"Now don't get your blood pressure up again," she said with a caring look. "Just try to relax."

"Easier said than done."

"I know it is, honey," she said, walking over and giving him a hug. "Let's just have a peaceful and quiet lunch."

"I'll try."

Sally had veggie paninis and broccoli and cheese soup on the counter. They sat and ate without saying a word for a few minutes.

John cleared his throat. "I've been thinking."

"Uh, oh. What is it this time?"

"You know, maybe we should consider selling the house and moving."

"I like it here."

"I don't know," John said. "It just seems the neighborhood has changed too much. It's just not the same."

"I agree but it's still a good neighborhood."

"That may be a good reason to put the house on the market."

"Let's wait and see how things are in a few months. Okay?"

"Sure but it's still something to think about," John said. "Maybe get away from Lexington and move to some smaller town, like Winchester, Georgetown, Paris, Versailles or Frankfort."

"I like Frankfort," she said. "Lots of history."

"Yeah, but lots of politics as well."

"We can think about it. There's no hurry."

"I hope that's the case."

"Almost forgot," she said as she opened a cabinet, took out a package of chocolate chip cookies and placed them in front of John.

"I hope we have some milk."

Sally opened the refrigerator and no milk was to be found. "Sorry," she with pressed lips.

John took one cookie from the container. "Gee, you got my hopes up," he said with a chuckle.

He retreated to the den and turned on the TV while Sally cleared off the counter. He had just dozed off when the phone rang. Sally answered, and after a minute, walked in the den and handed the phone to John. "It's Clay."

"Doing anything?" Clay asked.

"Not at the moment," John said, lying back in the recliner.

"Feel like a few brewskies?"

~ * ~

Fifteen minutes later John was driving to Bailey's with a reminder from Sally to pick up some milk before he came home.

Clay was already seated at the bar with a pitcher and two mugs in front of him. A few of the regulars were there but the popular spot wouldn't start filling up until after people got off from work and stopped in for happy hour.

"What's the occasion?" John asked.

"Occasion?" Clay said as he poured beer into John's mug. "Does it have to be anything special when friends get together?"

"Nope." John took a swig from the frothy mug then wiped the foam from his upper lip.

"So have you been up to much?"

John told him about Neighborhood Watch and the incident at the park involving Bernie Shipley. "It's been somewhat interesting. How about you?"

"Nothing much. You just have to look at the newspaper to see what I've been up to."

John almost felt like telling him it couldn't be much, judging by the contents of the paper the past month or so. No sense in hurting someone's feelings, especially when it's a best friend.

"Still thinking about early retirement?" John asked.

"If that golden parachute comes along."

"Remember years ago when we talked about traveling to different parts of the world?"

"Seems like only yesterday," Clay said, taking a sip from his mug. "All those big plans, but life always seemed to get in the way."

"I think that happens to most folks. The poor can't afford it and the rich are too busy chasing the almighty dollar."

"And then we have family obligations and responsibilities we have to take care of. The next thing you know, you're a sixty-something like us and wonder where the fuck time went."

John picked up the pitcher and refilled their mugs. One of the patrons went to the jukebox, and within a few seconds, "All My Exes Live in Texas" filled the air.

"I haven't heard that song in ages," John said.

"You were always a straight arrow, or at least you seemed to be," Clay said. "Have you ever had any dalliances?"

"Can't say I did."

"Ever tempted?"

"Hard to say. I always tried to steer away from those situations. You?"

"I've had a few," Clay said, looking straight ahead. "Nothing I'm proud of but nothing I can erase. Shit happens."

"You're right."

"I don't know if I ever told you this but my parents divorced when I was a teen. I didn't know why until one day I got home early from school and found one of the neighbors in bed with my mom. My dad was a heavy drinker and, looking back, I think that's the reason mom cheated on him. He could be very abusive when he had too much to drink. He'd smack all of us."

"Sorry to hear that."

"And I think that affected my life and how I got along with women," he said. "I always felt if it was casual and no strings attached, things would be all right."

"And?"

"I suppose I got too careless," he said. "Most of my one-night stands happened at conferences. I never fucked any of the gals at the newspaper although I had my opportunities. That's where I'd draw the line."

"Good policy." John chuckled and took a swallow from the mug. "The old conflict of interest."

"You got that right," Clay said. "Screwed a few gals in town, but that's another story."

"You got around, my friend."

"I did," Clay said with a wicked grin. "That is until Marge found out."

"I guess that would put a damper on things."

"Funny thing is that I asked Marge to forgive me and told her I'd never do it again."

"And?"

"She wasn't that forgiving. That's why she's an ex."

"I guess that's understandable."

"I apologize for telling you this," Clay said. "Just wanted to get it off my chest. I've never told anyone about my infidelities, or even about my worthless Dad."

"No problem. I understand."

"You're a great listener, John. And if you're judgmental, you sure don't show it."

"I think that's what friendship is all about."

"It's more than just friendship. I like the Aussie word *mate* because it means so much more—a close bond that goes beyond friendship. Friends for life, through thick and thin."

"I feel the same, Clay. If ever you need me for anything, or simply to talk things out, you know where to find me."

Clay raised his mug in a toast and John tapped his mug against it.

"Thanks, mate."

Twenty-two

Sally was sound asleep when John slipped out of bed the next morning. Whiskers hopped out of his padded box and followed him to the front door. After a quick trip outside, Whiskers returned to the kitchen, where John filled his bowl with kibble. Sally had set the automatic timer on the coffee pot before going to bed so the coffee was ready to pour.

A minute later, John shuffled out to the front yard to get the newspaper in the middle of the frost-covered grass. He looked up and down the street, and with the exception of two or three houses and the streetlights, all was quiet and dark in the neighborhood.

But out of the corner of his eye he noticed someone leaving Betty Robinson's house under the cloak of the pre-dawn sky. He tip-toed to the edge of his driveway and stood behind a large evergreen that separated his property from Preston's yard. He peeked through the limbs.

Seconds later, he saw Allen Boatwright scampering across the street to his home, apparently oblivious that he was being watched. John covered his mouth to suppress a laugh and returned to the house. Whiskers had already finished his breakfast and was back in his bed.

John picked up his cup and sat on the bar stool. He opened the newspaper, then nearly dropped his cup. A headline below the fold read "Park Victim Dies From Beating." The story stated that Shipley had suffered a stroke, apparently several hours after John had visited the hospital. Police were quoted as saying the crime had turned from an assault and battery to murder. He sat in disbelief, slapping the paper down on the counter hard enough to elicit a bark from Whiskers in the bedroom.

The news struck him hard in the gut since he hadn't been expecting it. He picked up the paper again, almost afraid to turn to the obituaries for fear that other names of people he knew would be there. They were anonymous names but still painful notices to family, friends and acquaintances of those who knew them. He didn't look at the sports section. It all seemed so irrelevant this morning.

John crept back to the bedroom and grabbed the pants and shirt he had worn the previous day. Not wanting to awaken Sally, he carried them to the den and put them on. He slipped on his shoes at the front door and left the house. He briskly walked down the street in the cold morning air, going directly to the park. When he reached his destination, there was no one to be seen or heard. He sat on the park bench as the morning light was beginning to filter through the trees. Only two days earlier, he had found Bernard Shipley several yards away.

He was startled for a moment when someone came up behind him. "Mister, may I ask what you're doing here at this hour?"

"Apparently, I'm sitting on the park bench. Is that a crime?"

"Well, sir, it is when the park is closed." The man had raised his voice.

John turned around and there stood an imposingly tall policeman in uniform. He looked to see if the cop was holding a weapon, but noticed the Glock was still holstered.

John cleared his throat and stood. "Sorry, Officer. I live a few blocks up the street from here. I knew the man who was attacked here a couple days ago, and then I read in the newspaper this morning that he died. I'm paying my respects, if that makes any sense."

"Well, sir, I understand but I think it would be best if you went back home. I'd be glad to give you a lift."

"Thanks, Officer, but I think I'd prefer to walk, if that's okay. I need to clear my head. I never expected him to die."

"I will tell you that we've increased surveillance of the park since the incident."

"Good to hear but kinda late for Mr. Shipley."

The policeman frowned. "Unfortunately."

Slowly walking away, John noticed that the bushes had been marked off with yellow-and-black crime scene tape. He knew his favorite place in the park would never be the same.

Several blocks down the street, John saw two dark figures next to a late-model pickup truck on the street. He took a few more steps, then stopped, unsure if he should get any closer. He heard whispers.

"What's going on?" John said, raising his voice to get their attention.

"Huh?" A second later, he heard the sound of them running from the truck. One was wearing a dark skullcap and nearly knocked him down on the pavement with a forearm to his chest as he dashed by. John regained his balance and cautiously approached the passenger side of the truck. He saw where they had been trying to pry off the door handle. He quickly dialed nine-one-one, and within two minutes the officer he had encountered at the park pulled up in his cruiser with blue lights flashing.

John explained what he had witnessed. A minute later the owner of the black Dodge Ram 3500 truck, a bearded, overweight middle-aged man emerged from the house wearing baggy lounging pants that dragged on the ground, a T-shirt that revealed half of his bulging belly, and flip-flops.

"Are you fuckin' kiddin' me?" said the man, who identified himself as Virgil Roe to the policeman. "I just bought it two days ago. Now this shit! Damn!"

Virgil glared at John for a moment. "Who the fuck are you?"

"Now just hold it one minute," the officer said, stepping between John and Virgil. "This gentleman reported the crime."

"Oh, sorry, dude."

"Hey, I don't blame you," John said. "I'd be upset as well."

After the officer took information from him, John continued on the way to his house.

"Hey dude," Virgil said as John turned around. "Sorry 'bout what I said to ya. Thanks again."

"Anytime."

John picked up the pace when he thought he heard someone following him. He looked in all directions but there wasn't much to see as the early dawn light played tricks with his eyes. He glanced back and saw the police cruiser with its flashing lights still next to Virgil's vandalized vehicle. Several of Virgil's neighbors had turned the lights on in their houses, apparently curious to see what was going on.

He jogged the rest of the way home, leaving him a bit out of breath when he came in the front door. Sally was at the kitchen counter, reading the newspaper and drinking coffee.

"Where in the world have you been?" she asked. "I heard you pick up your clothes but didn't realize you were going out. I almost called the police."

"I'm sure you saw the story about Shipley on the front page," John said as he sat next to her. "I just had to get out of the house and think. I was at the park a few minutes until a policeman showed up. And on the way home, I saw someone trying to break into a pickup down the street. So that's what I've been up to this morning. I almost wish I had stayed in bed."

"You've got to be kidding me," she said with wide eyes. "Another break-in?"

"Believe it."

"That's so sad about Mr. Shipley. I've read where people who've had severe head injuries run the risk of having a stroke. I wonder how his wife is."

"No doubt she's devastated," John said. "I don't think she expected this, although she may have been warned about it. It looks like I may have to attend a funeral now."

Sally frowned.

"Oh, almost forgot, want to hear something funny?" John said.

"Something funny?"

He told her about seeing Allen leaving Betty's house as he was getting the paper.

"That's crazy."

"I suppose he's taken the Neighborhood Watch program to the personal level."

"Whatever."

Several hours later, as John was watching a news show on television, his cell phone rang.

"Mr. Ross?" the caller asked.

"Yes."

"I'm Bernard Shipley."

"I beg your pardon?"

"I'm sorry. I'm Bernie Shipley's son. My dad was assaulted in the park this week. I got your phone number from my mother. She told me that you found him, and you had also visited her at the hospital yesterday."

"Yes, I did," John said. "I'm very sorry about what happened to your father. My condolences to you and your mother."

"Thank you," Bernard said. "I wanted to tell you that my father did regain some degree of consciousness. He told police he was attacked by two young men. He said they had a gun and were aiming it at some of the ducks. My dad apparently said something to them, and then they attacked him. My guess is they struck him on the head with the gun and maybe kicked him a few times, considering the severity of the injuries.”

“No other leads?”

“The police plan to go examine the area again and see if they can locate a weapon, perhaps even use some sonar equipment in the pond.”

John told him about being at the park before dawn and seeing a police officer. The son thanked him again for his concern and informed him the funeral would be in a couple days.

After ending the call, John told Sally about the conversation. He picked up his phone and called Officer Washington and told her he would like to have some “Neighborhood Watch” signs to post at the perimeter entrances to the neighborhood. She told him there would be some for him to pick up at the front desk within an hour.

John headed over to Bert’s house and told him about posting the signs. They also arranged to set up a day and time for the organizational meeting at the church.

John told him about Shipley, the increased patrols at the park and the truck that was vandalized on the street. He didn’t mention Allen and Betty.

“I wish we had started this a long time ago,” Bert said. “Maybe none of this stuff would be happening now if we had acted sooner. Maybe we have to take some responsibility for what has happened.”

“Let’s not get carried away, Bert. I doubt if many people would have been interested. When things are quiet and seemingly normal, people grow complacent. It’s after they feel threatened that they are motivated to do something. I think that’s just human nature. Remember how folks were after nine-eleven? They were ready to do about anything.”

"You're right, John," Bert said. "I guess we'll just have to make the most of this situation to get people involved. Let them know this is our nine-eleven."

"Uh, Bert, let's keep nine-eleven out of this."

"But that can be a rallying call for us."

"Please, Bert, no nine-eleven."

"But..."

"That's an order."

Twenty-three

Two days later the newspaper reported the police had found a gun in the pond. They ran a check on the serial number and it was the one stolen from John's neighbor, Rufus Martin. It had been discharged five times, with one bullet remaining in the chamber.

"I guess Mr. Shipley was right about being assaulted at the park," Sally said when John told her the news.

"He was lucky they didn't put a bullet in him," he said, "although the vicious beating he took was probably worse than that. Some people behave like wild animals."

"Did the police find anything else?"

"They're going to run some fingerprint checks on the weapon. Maybe that'll provide a clue as to who killed Mr. Shipley. Of course, the police will have to connect the weapon to the crime. I can't imagine them finding any blood on the gun. That may be difficult since Mr. Shipley wasn't shot."

"All this gruesome stuff anymore," she said, shaking her head in disgust. "I hope things improve with the Neighborhood Watch."

"You sound like Bert. It sure won't hurt matters. Bert and I plan to nail up some signs on utility poles tomorrow. I hope it'll raise awareness."

"It's sure keeping you busy nowadays."

"I don't mind. It keeps me out of the rocking chair, and I think it adds some meaning or purpose to my life. I just don't want it to be my life."

"That's funny you say that," Sally said. "I was talking to Wilma the other day and she said the Neighborhood Watch has been sort of a blessing for Bert. She said he was getting so bored and negative all the time. She even said he wasn't ranting quite as much about his years as a teacher. That now he has perked up and apparently looks forward to hearing from you."

"I'll admit Bert has been a big help in getting this program started. He gets a little carried away at times but he has good intentions."

"She did tell me that Bert is a lot of talk at times."

"As if we didn't know that?"

"She meant that he sometimes goes into a shell. He gets so worked up about things then he withdraws."

"I'll have to see it to believe it."

"So today is Mr. Shipley's funeral?" Sally asked.

"Yep, at eleven o'clock. I guess I should be getting ready for it."

After a quick shower and shave, John put on a white shirt, navy blue sports coat and dark gray dress slacks. Sally was in the den when he was about to leave.

"How do I look?" he asked.

"You look nice but no tie? It is a funeral."

"I hate wearing ties anymore," he said. "But you think I should today?"

"It's up to you but I think it would be more proper and show a bit more respect if you did."

"Okay, I'll go see if I can find something in the closet."

John returned several minutes later wearing a yellow-and red-striped tie. "How do I look now?" he asked.

"Honey, don't you think you can find something not quite so loud? Maybe something more conservative, such as a dark solid one?"

"I guess," he said as he hurried back to the bedroom. He returned wearing a dark blue tie. "Now?"

"Much better," she said with an approving grin. "You look very handsome."

"If you say so," he said.

"Can't you take a compliment?" she said.

"Okay, thank you, sweetheart," he said. "How's that?"

"Much better."

The funeral was attended by less than a hundred people. John learned during the eulogy by an Army chaplain that Mr. Shipley had served thirty years in the Army including two tours in Vietnam and had been awarded a Purple Heart and Bronze Star. At the gravesite, Mr. Shipley was given a 21-gun salute by soldiers from the local Army Reserve unit.

Before leaving the gravesite, John offered his condolences to Mrs. Shipley and Bernard Jr.. The mother and son were both teary-eyed as they thanked him for attending the funeral. He made a point of telling them that he appreciated Mr. Shipley's service to the country. He wiped away a tear as he left the gravesite.

John removed his tie once he got into the car. Instead of going home, he stopped at the park. It was an unseasonably warm, breezy November afternoon. John proceeded to his favorite bench and sat. He looked over at the area where he could visualize Mr. Shipley barking commands about cleaning up after Whiskers. John couldn't help but smile to himself. He wished Whiskers were with him.

The area around the bushes no longer had crime-scene tape. John thought about Whiskers going to the spot and discovering

Mr. Shipley's body. He sat a few more minutes, then rose and walked to the bushes. He glanced around for a few seconds before going to his car in the park's parking lot. He was hoping there would be some other clue regarding Mr. Shipley's death but there was nothing to be found as police had scoured the area thoroughly.

Instead of driving home, against his better judgment, he stopped at McDonald's. Mel and Curtis were sitting at the usual table in the back. He went to the counter and ordered a large sweet tea and joined them.

"You're getting here kinda late," Curtis said as John approached the table. "Most of the gang left about an hour ago."

"I attended the funeral for the man who was attacked at the park," John said as he sat. "A nice, respectful service. Small crowd. Full military honors. So why are you two still here?"

"Nothing much else to do," Curtis said. "This is the highlight of the day for me. I guess that speaks volumes about my life."

"Millie's out shopping with our daughter so I thought I'd hang around here until I hear from them," Mel said. "As you know, it's always good for a few laughs."

"Solve any of the world's problems this morning?" John asked.

"Nah," Curtis said. "In fact, it got a little heated again. We try to stay away from politics and religion but sometimes one thing leads to another and the guys start popping off about all sorts of things."

"I hope it wasn't too serious," John said."

"The guys are too damn old to come to blows but some of them sure get pissed off and red-faced," Curtis said. "It's funny at times just to watch the guys go back and forth over things that don't mean diddly-squat."

"I try to stay clear of those things," Mel said. "Ain't worth getting mad over."

"Oh, bullshit, Melvin," Curtis said. "You're the instigator most of the time!"

"Just having fun," Mel said, rolling his shoulders. "They take it too seriously."

"The guys do seem to get over it and show back up in a couple of days," Curtis said. "They let off some steam. I don't guess there's too much harm in it."

"What was this one about or should I ask?" John said.

"Second Amendment," Curtis said. "Always a hot issue. And usually when Randy is here. In fact, he usually brings it up, along with his other extremist beliefs. We should make it off-limits. I almost wish Randy wouldn't show up because he's always spouting stuff like that. And I think some of the guys, like our esteemed friend Melvin here, egg him on a bit just to get a reaction. They know how to pull his trigger, pun intended."

"He was even talking about getting a tattoo with some sort of gun rights message, like having the Second Amendment tattooed on his chest," Mel said. "Crazy shit like that."

"To make things worse, Dan was here as well," Curtis said. "And you know what a nut he can be. Crazy as a fox at times. No respect for the president, liberals, or as he says, libtards. Damn, he's hot-headed."

"I hope he doesn't show up here with a gun," John said.

"Well, with the concealed weapon law, there's no doubt in my mind that he has one in his car," Curtis said.

"I wonder what joy these folks get in life," Mel said. "Always angry about something."

"Maybe that's their joy," John said.

"If so, it's pretty hollow," Curtis said.

"But that Second Amendment stuff really gets them going," Mel said.

"You know I'm starting up a Neighborhood Watch program," John said. "I'm concerned that it will be an issue as well with some of the homeowners."

"This may surprise you but I personally own a rifle," Curtis said. "I haven't used it in years because I don't hunt anymore. It's gathering dust above the mantle. There are times when I think about selling it, but then I think I might need it for some reason."

"Like a bear trying to break into your house?" Mel said with a chuckle.

"There you go again!"

"Maybe an invasion of illegal aliens?"

"Funny, Melvin," Curtis said. "Just keep it up. You're beginning to sound like Randy."

"Hey, believe it or not, but I have a Glock," Mel said. "I keep it next to my bed. Never used it, but it's kind of a comfort toy for me. I'm not sure if I could ever use it but it might scare the hell of somebody if they see me aiming it at them."

"It'd scare me if you weren't wearing your glasses," Curtis said.

"But they wouldn't know that," Mel said, removing his glasses and wiping the thick lenses on a napkin.

"Sally and I discussed purchasing a handgun but I just don't know. Even though our house was burglarized, we still have mixed feelings about getting one. Sally is against it. I'm not so sure."

"I see both sides," Curtis said. "It's the gun nuts and the crazies that worry me. I read where some idiots believe guns should be in schools for protection. Even in churches. Gimme a break. You'd think this was the Wild West."

"I personally think it's good to have one in the house," Mel said. "It sure makes me and Millie feel safer. It seems like some punks target older folks because they see us as vulnerable and defenseless."

"Oh well, it's something Sally and I will probably talk about again," John said. "No hurry."

"Just don't mention it when Randy and Dan are here," Curtis said. "They're too gung-ho about Second Amendment rights."

"I kinda figured that from talking to them about other things," John said. "They seem like nice guys until you get into politics and they go overboard with it."

"Nut jobs, both of 'em," Curtis said with a laugh. "Pure and simple. It'd be interesting to see background checks on them. I wouldn't put anything past them."

"I'm a conservative," Mel said, "but I hope I can respect others. I'd like to think I learned a few things in seventy-one years."

"Some folks carry some hateful thoughts from birth to the grave," Curtis said. "It's kind of a shame for people to be that way. It seems like an endless cycle that passes on from generation to generation."

"I agree with you," John said. "To be honest, it's kind of surprised me to hear what some of these guys think. I guess I had some preconceived notions about folks I've known for years, only to be shocked by what comes out of their mouths. They'd seldom utter some of the things in public or at the newspaper, but I suppose they get loose tongued here."

"I wish they'd just keep their damn thoughts to themselves," Curtis said. "I don't want to hear their shit. I wish they'd spew their crap on those who care about it. Better yet, just keep it to themselves."

Mel nodded. "Amen."

"If you ever hear any of that vitriol coming from me, knock me on the side of the head or throw something at me to shut me up," John said.

"With pleasure," Curtis said with a wink.

"Well, maybe not you, Curtis, after I saw what you did to that big guy the other day." John glanced over at Mel, who was about a half-foot shorter. "But you can."

"I'll promise not to shoot you," Mel said as he pointed a finger at him.

"Gee, thanks," John said. "I guess I'd better be going. Sally is probably wondering what's happened to me."

"I need to go as well," Curtis said. "I've got a few errands to run."

"Millie is probably at home now," Mel said. "If not, that means I get to watch what I want to on TV."

~ * ~

Sally and Whiskers were napping in the bedroom when John got home. He picked up the newspaper in the kitchen and headed to the den. A few moments later, Whiskers wandered in and rested on the floor next to him.

"So what's up, little fella?" John said as he reached down and stroked Whiskers' back. Whiskers turned over, and John rubbed his belly for a minute. "Doesn't take much to please you."

John turned to the obit page and saw the notice of a high school football coach he'd known for many years. After reading the funeral notice, John thought the coach had lived a productive life, influencing hundreds of students and running a clean program. He wouldn't be remembered like some big-time college or professional coach, but his impact would probably be greater on those lives he touched on the playing field.

John grabbed the lever on the recliner and leaned back as far as it would go. He closed his eyes and dozed off.

Twenty-four

"I think I'm going to take a trip," John said to Sally during breakfast. "You're welcome to go with me."

"Where?"

"Chicago."

"Oh, no, you haven't heard from Brody again, have you?" she asked.

"Not since the last time you heard from him. I've given it some thought and decided it'd be nice to pay a surprise visit."

"You really think you should? He might not like that."

"He might not like a visit from his parents?"

"Well, I'm not going," she said as her back stiffened. "I don't go to places uninvited. You know that."

"Suit yourself. I think it's the best way to get to the bottom of his problems. If he knew I was coming, he'd probably hide what's going on in his life. Or simply leave town for a few days."

"I'd probably do the same."

"Huh?"

"Because it's not any of our business."

"Not our business when he's always hitting us and his sister up for money?"

"I think there's a better way of going about it."

"Such as?" John said.

"We could wait until the next holiday when he and Chloe are here and have a family discussion. Thanksgiving and Christmas aren't that far off."

"You think that'd be best way?"

"Yes, I do, John," Sally said, with a touch of emotion in her voice. "Show him some respect."

"I'll think on it," John said.

"I hope you do." Sally smiled. "More coffee?"

"No, thanks. I'm going to get Whiskers and take a little walk around the neighborhood."

"Going on patrol?"

"Hah, hah," John said. "Very funny."

"I'm teasing," she said, giving him a peck on the cheek.

John hooked the leash on Whiskers' collar and grabbed a doggy bag. Whiskers was eager to leave the house, nearly pulling John for a block before finally slowing down next to a tree to lift his leg.

With an overcast sky and chilly breeze, John didn't want to be out too long since it was probably going to rain, or maybe even some snow showers. He knew Whiskers wouldn't like that either, since he wasn't keen on being wet.

"Let's get moving, little fella," John said as they rounded a corner in front of the park. They entered the park but stayed on the path instead of going to the bench next to the pond.

As they climbed over a small knob, John fell to the ground, pulling Whiskers with him, as a boy on a ten-speed bicycle barreling down the middle of the walk nearly struck them. John cradled Whiskers in his arms for a few seconds, making sure the area was clear before standing. The youngster had stopped and looked back at them as he straddled his bike.

"Get out of the way, old man," the boy shouted before raising his middle finger and riding on down the path.

"You watch it," John retorted, resisting the urge to return the gesture. The boy either ignored or didn't hear him as he sped away without looking back.

John squatted and petted Whiskers on the back and they proceeded on the path for five minutes before leaving the park. As they turned a corner and headed up the street toward John's house, Hank Summers was stepping off his front porch and going toward his work truck in the driveway.

"Off to work?" John asked.

"You know it," Hank said. "Must be nice to be retired."

"It has its advantages."

"Any more word about the robberies in the neighborhood?"

"Not really."

"Like I told you before, it's probably those illegal gangs from over the way."

"Illegal gangs?"

"That's what I call 'em now since they're made up of them illegals."

"Oh."

"Let me know if you hear anything."

"I'll let you know about the Neighborhood Watch as well."

"Whatever I can do."

"Have a great day," John said as he proceeded on to his house.

Sally had left a note on the kitchen counter, telling him she had an appointment for a mammogram and would be back by three o'clock. He put food in Whiskers' bowl, then headed to the bathroom for a quick shower and changed into some clean clothes.

He was sitting in the den immersed in a National Geographic special on volcanoes when Sally returned.

"How did it go?" he asked, watching the TV screen as she sat on the couch.

"Well, they're never comfortable but it was okay. Nothing like having your boobs squished. I don't have to have another one until next year unless they find something."

"I wouldn't worry about that," he said, turning down the volume.

"That's easy for you to say," she said. "They're not your boobs."

"You know what I mean."

"I'm just sensitive about it. I've had too many friends who didn't think a mammogram would show up anything. I won't feel comfortable about it until I hear from the doctor."

"I wasn't making light of it," he said. "Remember a long time ago when they thought there was something but it was only some fatty tissue?"

"And I was scared to death," she said.

"I know but it turned out to be nothing. That's what I meant when I said not to worry about it."

"Okay, honey," she said. "I think I understand."

"Oh, one other thing. I agree with you about Brody. It wouldn't be fair to just drop in on him, although it's very tempting. He's been known to do that to us."

"That's because we're the parents."

"Yes, I know," John said. "What goes for the child doesn't necessarily go for the parents unless there's some extreme reason for it, like an illness or accident. We're kinda there for convenience. Never mind that he's an adult child three years from turning forty."

"John, I don't disagree with you that there is some kind of problem with Brody. I want you to know that. We just need to approach it in another way."

"Yep. We'll figure something out, one way or another. And I'm still not writing off going up there for a visit."

"I've heard a lot of parents say they're always your child, regardless of age. It's a lifetime covenant."

"I don't know if I should laugh or cry," John said. "You know, I don't recall us being that way with our parents after we got married. Do you?"

"I don't think we were, but we were so wrapped up in each other we may have done it a few times. There were a couple of times when we had to ask for a loan."

"But we always paid them back. That's the big difference."

"I'm sure they didn't mind but I wouldn't be surprised if they had a similar conversation about us and how they were with their parents. We'll ask Mom when she visits."

"A generational thing?"

"Possibly. And I'm sure Chloe and Brody, if he ever has kids, will be saying the same thing."

"Even Brody?" John asked, raising his brows.

"Especially Brody. He has a selective memory."

"Yeah, you're probably right. And Chloe?"

"I think she's got a good head on her shoulders," Sally said. "She's generally been very expressive and honest with us, even when she told us she was a lesbian, and when she was going to marry Samantha and adopt a child."

"Took after her dad," John said.

"Yeah, right!" Sally looked up at the ceiling with a skeptical smirk.

"We've got our Neighborhood Watch meeting tomorrow night."

"You've haven't said much about it lately. Have you notified everybody?"

"Bert said he'd handle it so I'm counting on him."

"Anxious?"

"I wouldn't say that," John said. "But I'll be glad to finally get it up and running. Maybe some folks will feel better about the neighborhood."

"Are Preston and Margaret involved?"

"You know, I haven't been in touch with them. I hope Bert contacted them. He doesn't say much to me anymore, especially after putting up that privacy fence. Speaking of Margaret, I haven't seen her in a while."

"He's an odd person. They've lived here five years and we hardly know them."

"We've tried. I really think he's a pompous ass, the way the struts around like he's something special. I really don't care to know him anymore."

"I don't know if she's unfriendly or just shy. She'd sometimes smile or say 'hi" when I saw her at the grocery. But it's been a while since I've seen her, too. I hope there's nothing wrong and she's okay."

"I guess living with him makes her that way."

"Now John, you don't know that."

"Yeah, but it makes sense."

Sally took a deep breath and slowly exhaled. "If you say so."

Twenty-five

The Methodist Church's fellowship room was empty when John arrived ten minutes before the scheduled time for the Neighborhood Watch organizational meeting. He was surprised there wasn't a single person in the room other than the janitor, who had unlocked the door for him. John waited inside the door, wondering if he had gotten the date wrong.

When it was time to begin, Bert's car pulled into the parking lot. After a minute, Bert stepped out and meandered to the door with his hands stuffed in his pant pockets and his head lowered.

"Where's everybody?" John asked. "We're the only ones here."

Bert turned red-faced and looked away from John. "I messed up."

"Messed up? What do you mean?"

"I forgot to send out the meeting notice."

"You're kidding me," he said, louder than he wanted in a church building. "This is all we've talked about the past few weeks, and you forgot to notify anyone about it?"

John thought Bert might cry as his eyes welled up, his chin jutted out and he wouldn't look at him in the eyes.

"It just slipped my mind. I'm sorry, John," he whined.

"Slipped your mind?" John could feel his back stiffen and mouth tighten as if to prevent a verbal outburst. He felt like going to the back of the church property and screaming his frustration for everyone to hear.

"I just couldn't..."

"Couldn't what?"

"I don't know," Bert began squeezing his fingers in and out. "It won't happen again."

"I know it won't happen again because I'll handle it next time," John said. "Even the other officers aren't here. What's their excuse? You didn't tell them either?"

Bert wouldn't make eye contact.

"Let's go. I can't believe this happened. After all the planning and discussions we had about this. Unbelievable." John raised his hands and looked away.

"It's all my fault," Bert said.

"I know it's your fault. You don't need to remind me. I don't know what else to say. Let's drop it."

"Do you want me to get with the minister and reserve the room again?"

John wrapped his arms across his chest and took another deep breath. "Are you serious?"

"Let me try again."

"I don't know. Let me think about it. I'll have to check my calendar when I get home."

"Again, I apologize," Bert said meekly as they left the church building for the lighted parking lot. Bert's hands never left his pockets as he toddled with his head lowered.

Since his house was only five blocks away, John had walked in the cold evening air. As he headed across the parking lot, Bert shouted, "Do you need a ride home?"

"No." John picked up his pace as he left the church property. Bert passed him on the street, but if he looked over, John didn't know because he kept his eyes straight ahead. He was home in less than five minutes.

Sally was in the laundry room taking clothes out of the dryer and folding them when he got home.

"That was sure a quick meeting," she said. "I thought you'd be there for an hour or two."

"Meetings are generally very quick when no one shows up," John said as he sat at the kitchen bar.

"No one showed up? How come?" Sally stepped out to the kitchen, her head tilted and eyes narrowed.

"One of the fundamentals of holding a meeting is notifying people about the meeting. That was Bert's sole responsibility. He volunteered to do it. And he didn't," he said as his voice grew louder. "It's that simple."

"How do you know?"

"Because Bert told me. He was the only person there, not counting the janitor. I don't know why he even made the effort to show up."

"There must be a reason," Sally said with concern in her voice. "That's not like Bert."

"I couldn't believe it either." John planted his hands firmly on the counter.

"I hope you didn't say something to him."

John pounded his hands on the counter. "Say something? What in the hell are you talking about? Of course, I said something. It was his responsibility. I couldn't act as if nothing happened."

"Did you get angry with him?"

"What in the hell do you think? I tried not to but I'm sure he could sense that I was a tad upset. I'm still pissed. Can't you tell?"

Sally went over to John and massaged her fingers on his shoulders. "Don't get all worked up, honey. You'll get your blood pressure up."

"Fuck my blood pressure!"

Whiskers let out a couple of barks before John reached down and tapped him gently on the shoulders. "It's okay, buddy." He took a deep breath.

Silence flooded the room for a few seconds as he tried to regain his composure.

"I'll give Wilma a call tomorrow and see what happened," Sally said.

"You do that. In the meantime, I have to schedule another meeting. And this time I'll notify folks."

"Let me finish the laundry and we'll discuss it more. Can I get you anything?"

"A beer."

Sally took a bottle of beer from the refrigerator and set it in front of John.

"Thanks," he said. "I apologize for taking it out on you."

"That's okay, honey. I understand. Really. Now I have to finish the laundry. Are you going to be okay?"

"Take your time. I'm over it. I'm going to go read in the den." Whiskers followed him to his spot next to the rocker. John took a swig from the bottle and closed his eyes for a few seconds before glancing at Whiskers.

"Sorry if I upset you, too, little fella," John said as he tapped Whiskers on the rump.

After folding and putting the clothes away, Sally came into the den and sat on the couch. "I don't blame you at all for being upset, honey. I would be, too."

"You know, I guess it's just a matter of not wanting to get too involved in things," he said. "I want my life to be as stress-free as possible. I don't want get involved in things where I have to carry the load. I don't need that at this juncture of my life. I had enough of that at work. Is that asking too much?"

"But you don't want to stay at home and do nothing either."

"That's beside the point. I don't want to get stuck doing it all when I do something outside the home. Does that make any sense?"

"Oh, honey, give it time."

"I'll try," he said before finishing the beer and setting the bottle on the floor. "I suppose I was counting too much on others to pick up the slack. And maybe next time we'll have someone show up. That's what made me upset. It was Bert's fault it turned out that way. I guess I put too much trust in Bert. And I don't know why I did because I really don't know him outside of being a grumpy-ass neighbor."

"I'm sure he feels bad about it as well," Sally said.

"Enough about Bert," John said as he picked up the remote and turned on a channel televising a basketball game. He turned up the volume, a signal that he was through talking about it. Sally took a *People* magazine from the periodical holder and flipped through the pages. A few minutes later her cell phone rang in the kitchen.

"Where are you going?" John asked as she got up from the couch.

"To answer the phone."

"Oh, I didn't hear it."

She returned in fifteen minutes and sat back down on the couch. "That was Wilma."

"Oh, fuck," John said as he turned down the volume on the TV. "What's her damn excuse?"

"Now John..."

"Okay, what did she have to say?"

"She said Bert was very upset when he got home. That he was nearly in tears."

John leaned over the side of the rocker and looked at her. "Nearly in tears? He was practically in tears at the church. I figured he'd be bawling like a baby when he got home."

"He feels like he let you and everyone down."

"Well, to be honest, he did. He finally figured that out?"

"Now, John, please settle down."

"Okay." He put his head back against the cushioned headrest, closed his eyes and tried to listen.

"She said he got very nervous about making the calls, and kept putting if off until it was too late. He talked to a few people this morning but they said it was such short notice they weren't sure they could be there. He was hoping a few of them would. He almost didn't go."

"He got there at seven. Apparently, it was a last-minute decision on his part. So considerate of him."

"She said he's more talk than anything. He freezes up when asked to do things. She was worried it would be the case with this. She also mentioned his incontinence problem. She wanted to talk him out of it, but he seemed so gung-ho to help. So she apologized as well."

"I guess that explains it somewhat," John said, tipping the rocker back and forth with his feet.

"I hope you won't be too hard on him now," Sally said. "Some people just can't handle the pressure."

"Hey, it's only a volunteer job so I can't be too rough on him. Everything's okay. All is forgiven." He partially flashed a faint smile before turning up the TV volume again.

Sally sweetly smiled. "Good."

"Any more beer in the fridge?"

Twenty-six

"Hey stranger."

John looked around as he stood in line at the counter at Starbucks to order a cup of French vanilla cappuccino. He spotted Breck Rogers, the newspaper's chief photographer for many years and now the *de facto* head of the paper's alumni group, seated near the corner of the dining area.

John picked up his drink, went over and sat next to his old friend. "I see you're still snapping photos."

"I'll be doing that until they wheel me away," said Breck, who had a Nikon dSLR on the table. "Old photographers never die; they just fade away like an old print."

"Sounds like old sportswriters except that we get old, yellow and crumpled."

"You've probably been warned about me," Breck said with a grin.

"I wouldn't say warned," John said, "but your name has been mentioned, and not in a bad way."

"Have you been back to the newspaper?" asked Breck, a tall, wiry man with a snow-white full head of hair and a long ponytail. "Hasn't it been several months since you retired?"

"A few months. But to answer your question, nope," John said as he stirred his cappuccino. "Really no reason to. And I haven't heard hardly a word from them."

"That's about par for the course. As Clay Rawlings always says, 'Out of sight, out of mind.'"

"No problem for me. It's probably mutual. When I leave a place, I don't turn around. I try to look ahead and move forward with my life."

"But you haven't even heard from any of your colleagues?" Breck asked with furrowed brows.

"I've heard from my assistant but that's about it. Quite frankly, I didn't socialize much with any of them. I see Clay for a beer on occasion, but that's about it for me."

"I was going to ask you if you'd like to join the paper's alumni group," Breck said with a grin. "Interested?"

"I think you know the answer to that. But thanks for asking. I'm just not ready. Get back with me in a few years." John winked. "Just kidding."

"John, I must admit I'm surprised you didn't have that many friendships at the paper. You were well-liked and respected."

"Maybe that's the reason for it. They didn't really get to know me."

"I know better than that," Breck said. "You're one of the good guys."

"Well, most of the folks I socialized with were outside the paper. And for the most part, I've been a loner. I never liked all the gossip and newspaper talk. Honestly, it bores the crap out of me. I prefer being around others, not that there was anything wrong with my co-workers. They were a nice group of people. I just didn't care to spend my off-hours with those I saw at work practically every day. Outside of work I wanted other friends. You know, some variety."

"Makes sense," Breck said. "I was just curious."

"I know you photographers are a different breed of journalist."

"You're probably right about that. We tend to show up with our cameras at any and all events, whether we're working or not. You could say we're like ambulance chasers."

"You won't see that much in other journalists unless perhaps it's political reporters. They seem to thrive on politics at every level."

"And sports writers?"

"They mostly stayed glued to the TV."

"Interesting," Breck said.

"So how long have you been retired?"

Breck thought for a few seconds. "Let's see, it was fourteen years ago last August."

"You must have taken the big buyout."

"You've got that right. When that chain bought the paper, I knew things were going to change. I was in my late fifties, so it was a great opportunity for me. As you know, several of us got what they called golden parachutes."

"Wise decision on your part. Things did change, and for the worse, as you well know. It wasn't a horrible place when I left, but it wasn't the cozy place it used to be where most everyone took pride in the product. Now it's pride in the profit, especially from the powers-that-be. That's probably another reason I don't have any interest in the place."

"I've heard similar comments from some recent retirees and others who left for various and sundry reasons."

"You were there during the so-called glory years, when it was great to go to work every day and produce something that everyone would be proud of. Probably didn't get paid a lot but the experience was rich. I know that sounds a bit corny but I think it's the truth."

"I believe that was the case," Breck said. "We took a lot of pride in putting out the best product we could. A lot of teamwork, on every level of the paper. If you pardon my cliché, but the good old days."

"That's not to say the folks today aren't trying to put out a great product, but it's more like work than something you love to be doing," John said. "I think you know what I mean."

"Sure do," Breck said.

"Are you doing anything since you retired?"

"Phyllis and I were able to do some traveling before she developed some hip problems," he said. "I've done a little work with an English as a second language program at the learning center and help some with local theater group to occupy my time. I also do occasional freelance work for a few magazines. Even the newspaper calls me when they get short-handed. Other than that, it's doing stuff around the house and visiting the kids and grandkids. And, of course, the alumni group."

"Sounds like a fulfilling life."

"For the most part, I suppose. I don't have the energy to do a whole lot now so I'm slowing down. I just try to pace myself. How about you?"

"It's still kind of early but I got roped into Neighborhood Watch. I'm looking into some other things as time goes on. And I occasionally go to McDonald's and shoot the bull with some other old-timers from the paper. You need to drop by there. You might find some folks for your alumni group."

"I used to go there but those guys are a bunch of rowdies and free spirits like you," Breck with a chuckle. "And a few radicals. It wore on me after a while."

"They're a nice, unruly group, for the most part. But I know what you mean."

"Let me tell you, don't let too much time pass by or you'll find yourself out of energy and doing nothing," Breck said with his hand propped under his chin. "I've seen that with too many people. You gotta stay busy, mentally and physically."

"I hear ya," John said.

"And stay social. You lose friends and associates, and it's something you can't regain. I'd love to see you with the alumni group, but if that's not your thing, that's okay. Just find a circle of friends. Loners don't seem to last long as they grow older."

"Thanks for the advice."

Twenty-seven

Sally was weeping as she sat on the corner of the unmade bed, still in her gown and slippers when John returned home from the coffee shop.

"What's the matter, sweetie?" John asked softly as he walked up and placed his hand on her shoulder. She glanced up at him with puffy eyes and tear-stained cheeks.

"The doctor's office called," she said. "They want me to come back in for another mammogram and consultation. They think they found something on my left breast."

John sat next to her and held her in his arms, then kissed her softly on the temple. She rested her head against his neck for several seconds in the silence.

"When do you go back?"

She eased her head from his shoulder and sat up. "I have an appointment in the morning at nine."

"I'll go with you." He tenderly squeezed her hand.

"I'm so afraid about this." She wiped her nose with a tissue and looked at him with droopy eyes.

"I know you are. But let's not jump to any conclusions. Let's see what the doctor says."

Sally pursed her lips, then a weak smile came over her drawn face. "I will."

They looked down and saw Whiskers staring at them. He seemed to be upset with the news as he let out a few whines.

"Good boy," John said as he petted his head. "Mommy's going to be okay."

He reached down and picked up their furry family member, who let out two quick licks on Sally's cheek. She put his head between her two hands and kissed his forehead.

John set Whiskers on the floor and they went to the kitchen. Sally put some food in Whiskers' bowl as John sat at the counter.

"What do you want for lunch?" she asked.

"I'm not hungry. Maybe something later," he said.

"Me either." Sally sat next to him and rested her head on his shoulder for a few seconds.

"I think everything's going to be fine," he said.

"Me, too, but I'm preparing myself for the worst. I've been healthy for a long time. Maybe it's my time."

"Now don't say that."

"But you know it's true. We see it all the time in the people we know. There's no reason why I should be excluded. And don't forget that TIA episode you had."

"I just don't want anything to happen to you," he said, putting an arm around her slender waist. "I don't know what I'd do."

"Now don't write me off so soon," she said, laughing between tears and sniffles. "Even if it is cancer, that doesn't mean I'm going to die anytime soon. At least I hope not."

"I don't mean it that way," he said. "I just don't like anything happening to you or the kids."

"I understand. I feel the same way. Now let's change the subject."

"That's fine with me," John said.

"Are you going to get in touch with Bert soon?"

"Maybe later today or tomorrow. I don't want to put any more pressure on him. Or me. And I don't want to see a grown man cry. And that includes me as well."

"Now don't be saying those kinds of things," Sally said. "That's not like you."

"Just kidding."

"I can always help contact people."

"I appreciate that. I want to get the ball rolling on this."

John told her about talking to Breck Rogers at the coffee shop.

"He mentioned the paper's alumni group. I told him I wasn't interested right now. He seemed to understand."

"You probably need to get some distance between you and the paper," Sally said. "You might feel differently about it later on. Those people are your peers so you share a lot in common, just like I do with my retired teachers' group."

"Let me tell you something. You know there were some folks I simply tolerated when I was at the paper. And truth be told, they probably tolerated me as well. I don't miss them, and I'm sure they don't miss me. I don't want to be around those folks anymore. I've got choices I can make now and I don't want to be around them. Life's too short to be around people you don't care about. I don't want the negativity. I'd rather be around those I like. And to be honest, I'm having second thoughts about some of the folks I see at McDonald's. I get tired of listening to some of the hateful comments. If I want to hear that stuff, I'll just turn on the TV or listen to talk radio. Or call your brother."

"Now leave Brandon out of this. I can mention some of your relatives."

"Only kidding, sweetie."

"Sure you were."

"But getting back to the folks you don't care to be around."

"I don't blame you," she said. "I've discarded a few like that since I retired."

"I'm going to concentrate on doing things I want to do, like traveling, writing, and some volunteering."

"That's what I've tried to do," Sally said. "The main thing for me is not for it to become too time-consuming because there are other things I like to do and time to spend with you. I don't want it to become another job. It should be something like a hobby, something that brings a degree of pleasure."

"That's what I want. I sure as hell don't want it to be like a job. And Neighborhood Watch, while I think it's important, it isn't something I want to consume my time. It's not my end-of-life calling. At least I hope not."

"You might think about going over to the learning center and teaching English to immigrants. I've heard they have a big demand for instructors. With your background, you might find it rewarding. That's only a suggestion."

"That's something Breck and Curtis do. I'll give that some thought as well."

"Just find something satisfying."

"Yep, whatever floats your boat."

Twenty-eight

"Ready for a walk, little fella?" John said to Whiskers, who was at his feet within seconds. He connected the leash to the collar and remembered to grab a doggy bag. He couldn't help thinking about Bernie Shipley as he stashed it in his back pocket.

They were halfway across the front yard when Whiskers stopped and lifted his leg. "Boy, you really had to go," John said. "Take your time."

John glanced up and down the street. It was relatively quiet—not even Bert was anywhere to be seen unless he was behind one of his manicured shrubs. Preston came out of his house with a camera strapped around his neck holding a bag. He saw John and smiled smugly.

Moments later, John and Whiskers were breezing down the sidewalk toward the park, making brief stops along the way for Whiskers to sniff and leave his mark on trees, bushes, poles and other stationary objects. John learned early on that taking Whiskers for a walk was more of a stop-and-go experience. He allowed Whiskers to set the pace and use that time to relax and think.

And his thoughts along the way focused on Sally. Before he realized it, he was teary-eyed, thinking about the possibilities affecting her health. He wanted to remain positive and strong, especially around her, but when alone he could let go of his feelings. They had been married for so long he didn't know what his life would be like without her in it. He wasn't jumping to any conclusions, but he thought living without her would be unbearable. He took a deep breath and told himself to take matters one step at a time, kinda like Whiskers. And like he'd been telling her. Live in the present. But he knew what he was feeling was more than a sense of sadness.

When they reached the park, Whiskers knew where to go as he led them directly to their usual bench next to the pond. Ducks and geese were milling about on the banks, picking up whatever food scraps people had tossed their way.

John unleashed Whiskers, who ran toward the waterfowl. They initially seemed unfazed by his charge, then took to the water, flapping their wings and sending ripples across the pond. Whiskers appeared to take great pride in his bravado as he patrolled the banks, pacing back and forth, with the birds only several yards away and squawking to return to dry land.

John glanced to his right and saw two boys on skateboards whizzing along, a grating and humming grind on the asphalt path, forcing several people to make way for them as if they owned the walkway through the park. He tightened his jaw. So much for a quiet time.

John called to Whiskers, who scampered up to him, tongue wagging. "It's time to go home, little fella,"

After putting Whiskers on the leash. John stood for a few seconds and watched the waterfowl reclaim their territory.

As they went down the walk, John was pushed from behind and knocked to the ground by one of the skateboarders. He was on his hands and knees for a few seconds, stunned for a moment by the unexpected blow. Whiskers came to his side.

"Are you friggin' deaf, *old man*?" the boy said, laughing like a jackass.

John rose to his feet and dusted off his hands. "I beg your pardon?"

"You heard me." The pimple-faced boy was about John's height but lanky and probably about fifteen years old. He glared at John, although maintaining a safe distance. Wearing baggy jeans hanging low on his hips, and a soiled green sweatshirt, the boy wasn't intimidating.

"Do you talk that way to your parents, grandparents and other adults?" John asked, taking one step toward him.

"It's none of your friggin' business, *old man*."

"What did you say?"

When John took another step with his fist in a ball, the scruffy teen quickly jumped on his skateboard and began scooting away. "You can kiss my ass, *old man*," the boy snarled.

John didn't say another word as he glared at the childish assailant in disbelief. The boy grinned, flipped up his middle finger, and skated away.

"Unreal, Whiskers," John said, brushing the dirt off his pant knees. "Totally unreal." He wasn't sure if he ever wanted to return.

Leaving the park, he saw Bart's shiny red Camaro parked along the curb. He walked toward the car and noticed smoke drifting from the front windows. The closer he got, the more distinct the smell—marijuana.

Bart suddenly got out of the car and bounced up to John. Whiskers began barking.

"Hush, Whiskers!" John said as he picked up the dog who continued to growl.

"Hi, Mr. Ross," Bart said with a loopy smile. "What are you doing here?"

"Whiskers and I walk over here several times a week, over by the pond. It's real peaceful, for the most part. Until the past week."

"How so?"

"Almost got run over by kids on bicycles and skateboards."

"Man, they can be a pain."

"So what are you up to?"

"Just chillin'. Know what I mean?"

"I suppose so. I guess that's what I've been doing."

Bart let out a goofy laugh.

"Let's get going," came a voice from the car.

"Yeah, dude," Bart said. "Great seeing you, Mr. Ross. Need to run."

"Be careful."

As Bart returned to his car, John had to restrain Whiskers from trying to twist out of his arms.

Bart's friend Derrick, donning dark sunglasses, rolled up the passenger window and they left, screeching the tires when shifting gears. John didn't know who Bart was trying to impress.

~ * ~

Bert waved his hand for John to wait when he returned home twenty minutes later. John let Whiskers in the front door. Bert hurried up to him at the porch.

"I'm sorry I let you down with the meeting," Bert said. "There's no excuse for it. I simply let you down. I don't know what else to say…"

John raised the palm of hand. "No problem, Bert. Just forget about it. It's not the end of the world. We'll get another meeting scheduled and move on."

"I appreciate it. You don't know how much."

"What's been up with you lately?"

"What do you mean?"

"Nothing, Bert."

"To be honest, I haven't been up to anything since I botched that meeting."

"Just forget about that meeting. Okay? It's history."

"But you asked."

"I'm sorry," John said. "I thought perhaps you'd taken Wilma to dinner, made some home improvements, something like that."

"Like I said, John. Nothing since I screwed up the meeting."

"Okay, then, do you have any plans coming up?"

"Such as?"

"Nothing in particular."

"I'll let you know if I do."

"Thanks, Bert."

They stood in silence for ten seconds.

"What about you?"

"I got run over by a kid on a skateboard at the park," John said. "Knocked me to the ground. Kid didn't apologize or anything except cuss me and give me the finger."

"I haven't been to the park in a long time," Bert said. "Thanks for the warning. I'll be careful if I ever go there again."

"Kids are getting to be a bit unruly nowadays."

"I wouldn't know, since I stay around the house most of the time."

"I understand," John said. "Maybe I should do the same."

"You might think about it. It's a lot safer."

"Oh, well. You're probably right."

"Another reason I don't miss teaching. I couldn't wait to get away from the classroom soon enough."

"You've told me."

Bert's eyes suddenly widened. "Gotta go." He turned and scuttled back toward his house.

"Take care," John said, waving his hand. Bert didn't respond.

John let out a deep breath and ambled into the house. Whiskers was in the kitchen munching on food in his bowl while Sally was preparing a pizza to put in the oven.

"I saw you talking to Bert out front," she said as she put the pizza in the oven.

"I guess you could say that," John said. "I learned he hasn't done anything since the meeting."

"Wilma said he really felt bad about that."

"Yes, he told me several times."

"What's that scuff on your knee?"

"Oh this?" he said, pulling his pants from one of his knees. "I got knocked down at the park by a skateboarder. I guess you could say just another day at the park."

"An accident?"

"You could say that if old me not getting out of the friggin' way could be called an accident."

"Why did you say that?"

"That's what the skateboarder said to me."

"I hope you didn't hurt yourself."

"Maybe my pride a little bit," he said. "There's nothing like being called an old man several times and then having them give you the finger and cuss you. The little punk."

"Just be careful the next time you're there."

"That may be the last time."

"Oh, honey."

"You know, I hate to admit it but things were better there when Mr. Shipley was keeping an eye on things."

"Maybe someone will start doing that."

"Until then, the punks will take over."

"I hope not."

"I wish I were about ten years younger," John said, raising his hands. "I would have run after that scrawny punk, grabbed him by the ears, and dragged him to his parents."

"No, you wouldn't have," she said with a laugh. "You're the adult."

"Yeah, but it still pisses me off. I can't believe these kids don't show more respect toward others. It made me think about Mr. Shipley and the abuse he may have taken. Like I said, I don't have any plans to return in the near future."

"I wouldn't either. It doesn't seem safe anymore," she said.

"And I thought the police were going to increase patrols there after Mr. Shipley's death."

"They can do only so much."

"I guess kids on bicycles and skateboards don't rate high on the priority list, even if they are terrorizing others."

"Why don't you go to the den and settle down a bit?" Sally said. "Pizza will be ready in about fifteen minutes."

"Any beer in the fridge?"

Sally opened the door and handed him a can.

"Only domestic?"

"You buy the beer in the house."

"Let me know when the pizza's ready."

"I will," she said. "You just go and relax for a few minutes."

"I know. I don't want to get my blood pressure up."

"You're learning."

A few minutes later, there was a knock at the front door. Clay, in a suit and loosened tie, opened his arms when Sally opened the storm door.

"My goodness, what a surprise!" Sally said. Clay stepped inside and kissed her on the cheek. "To what do we owe this special visit?"

"Took off from work early and thought I'd drop by and see how my retiree buddy and his lovely wife are doing. I bet he's taking a nap."

"He's in the den," Sally said as she led him to the doorway. John had dozed off in the recliner, letting out an occasional snore.

"Didn't I tell you?" Clay said with a chuckle.

"I'll let you wake him up."

"Boy, some folks sure do lead an easy life of Riley," Clay said as he walked up to the recliner. John jerked his head, startled from his light nap. He eased the recliner to the upright position.

"Just resting my eyes."

"Bullshit." Clay let out a big laugh.

"I have pizza in the oven," Sally said from the kitchen. "I hope you can stay for a while. Want a beer?"

"Sure," Clay said. "A free afternoon. Nothing going on so decided to drop by."

Sally opened a can of beer and brought it to Clay. "Pizza'll be ready in about ten minutes."

"What brings you here?" John asked. "Slow news day?"

"Just wanted to see you. Is that a crime? Want me to leave?"

"Of course not, you crazy fool."

Clay took a swallow from his beer and grinned. "Remember how we talked about going to the Grand Canyon years ago and taking that hike in the gorge?"

"We discussed that many times but never took that proverbial plunge."

"I was wondering if you'd still like to do it. Maybe early spring. We could fly out to Phoenix and drive up to the canyon, maybe even spend a day or two at the lodge."

"You think we could handle it? We're not as young as we used to be."

"Hell, I know we're older but we're still in relatively good shape. Don't you think we could handle it?"

"I think we could," John said. "I guess there's only one way to find out. And that's by trying to do it."

Sally returned with the sliced pizza and paper plates. "You guys want another beer?"

"Yep," John said as they handed her their empty cans. "Guess what we're planning?"

"Let me guess," Sally said, putting a finger on her cheek. "Hiking the Grand Canyon?"

"How did you know?" John asked, tilting his head.

"I'm not exactly deaf, dear. I heard you discussing it. I think that'd be great. Just don't get lost."

"And overdo it."

"That, too."

Sally returned to the kitchen to eat her pizza, leaving the men in the den to talk.

"I've been thinking about some things a lot lately," Clay said. "Ever since you retired, I've come to realize that there's more to life than the newspaper. Since Marge and I divorced, I've also come to understand that my career was probably the biggest reason for it, as well as a few other things I'd prefer not to discuss here. I want to prioritize things in my life now."

"It's never too late," John said. "To be honest, I was probably the same way, but not to the same extent as you. Since I've retired, there's a lot that was going on that I wasn't even aware of. I realized I hardly knew my neighbors. It was like being a stranger in my neighborhood."

"I want to reconnect with my kids, too. I haven't been on the best of terms with Rob and Rona since Marge and I divorced four years ago."

"Maybe you can invite Rob to go with us?"

"That's a thought."

"It takes a while to get things in order, but better late than never."

"Well, I hope to do the same," Clay said. "I'm still considering early retirement if I can take care of some financial matters. There've been rumors about some more early retirement packages."

"I hope you can do it."

"Me, too. Life can get away from you if you don't watch out."

"Go ahead and start making plans for our trip out west," John said. "Let me know if I can do anything. I'm sure I've got more free time on my hands."

"I'll send you an email in the next week," Clay said with a smile. "Want to take Sally along? She's more than welcome."

"I'll ask her but I think she'd rather for it to be a guys' trip. She knows I need an escape once in a while."

They finished eating and chatted briefly about work and other happenings in their lives.

"I guess I should be going," Clay said as rose from the rocker. "I'm glad I stopped by. I'm looking forward to our trip."

"Same here, buddy."

"One thing I'm going to do is get a physical, just to make sure I'm up for it," Clay said. "Sure don't want to throw out a knee or something in the canyon."

"Good idea. I'll do the same. Get over that bug you were talking about a couple weeks ago?"

"A little bit," Clay said. "I think most of it comes from sitting on my ass most of the day attending meetings. That's another reason I want an active vacation. Get the blood circulating again."

"It certainly can't hurt."

After seeing Clay to the door, John went into the kitchen and sat with Sally.

"I'm glad he visited," Sally said. "It's always nice to see him."

"Same here," John said. "I suppose you heard most of the conversation. It sounds like he's wanting to get his life in order."

"Sure seems that way," she said.

"Do you want to go with us?'

"Nope," she said with a caring smile. "I want you guys to go out there and have some fun. Maybe you can invite Bert."

"Are you serious?"

"Nope," she said with a grin. "Just wanted to see your reaction."

"You've really become the comedienne since I retired."

"That's from living with you, dear."

Twenty-nine

The following morning, John drove Sally to the hospital to have the biopsy on her breast. She would know within an hour if it were cancerous or benign. John kissed her lightly on the mouth before the nurse led her through a swinging door to one of the prep rooms.

John tried to watch television but someone had it on a news channel espousing views that were far from fair and balanced, at least in his opinion. He glanced at several others in the waiting room, intently watching the program. He could feel his blood pressure rise so he walked to another part of the waiting area, out of sight and nearly out of earshot of the TV.

He thumbed through several magazines, mostly health-related and aimed toward women, as he tried to kill time. But he couldn't concentrate as he looked up every time someone came into the room, hoping it might be Sally.

An hour later, Sally was wheeled through the door. He had difficulty reading her face. She had been crying but she also wore a slight smile. John quickly stood and ambled over to her, his forehead furrowed, unsure what to expect.

"It was benign," she said. "Just some fatty tissue, like last time."

John bent down and hugged her, then lightly kissed her on the cheek. He held back tears because he wasn't one who cried in public. But he felt an inner tension flow from his body with the news. "Oh, dear, that's wonderful. Didn't I tell you everything would be okay?"

John walked out teary-eyed to get the car as the nurse took Sally to the front entrance. When John pulled up by the door, Sally rose from the wheelchair and stepped into the car.

"You okay?" John asked, reaching over and touching her hand.

"I'm fine, honey. A little sore but that's about it. I'm starving. Let's go get a bite to eat."

"Still up for breakfast?"

"I'd love an omelet."

John drove to Belle's, a small diner near the hospital, where they ordered breakfast and coffee.

"You know, I was expecting the worst," she said before taking a sip of her coffee. "I've known so many women who've had breast cancer. It's just so scary. I just knew it was my time."

"I'll admit I was concerned but kept hoping for the best." John gently squeezed her hand. "I wanted to remain positive for you."

Seconds later the waitress returned. John and Sally smiled tenderly at each other as she placed their food in front of them.

"We would've adjusted, just like we have to everything in our marriage," Sally said after the waitress went back to the counter. "And it's not necessarily a death sentence. I know many women who are cancer-free for many years after being diagnosed and having treatments."

"I know that," he said, "but when it happens to someone you love, your mind has all sorts of grim thoughts."

"That's sweet. I love you, too. It looks like you're going to have me for a long time." She blew him a soft kiss.

"I wouldn't want it any other way."

When they returned home, Whiskers barked a few times when they entered through the kitchen door. He ran right directly to Sally, almost as if he were happy with the news about her biopsy. She knelt on one knee and ran her fingers through his furry coat.

"Love you, too," she said.

They removed their light coats and draped them over the back of a chair. Sally poured some dry kibble in Whiskers' bowl while John led him outside to his favorite spot at the side of the house.

"I guess I'm going to make a few calls and send some emails to folks about the next Neighborhood Watch meeting," John said when he returned.

"Has Bert given you a day and time?"

"I guess that information would be helpful before I get in touch with anyone."

"You're getting as bad as Bert."

"Please!"

John dialed Bert's number but there wasn't an answer.

"That's odd," he said. "I could have sworn I saw his car in driveway when we drove past their house."

"I thought so, too. Maybe Bert and Wilma are out walking?"

"Perhaps," John said. "Maybe I should go ahead and call the church and set up the meeting."

"Why don't you want until we know something about Bert? I don't think you want to take a chance and hurt his feelings."

"Hurt his feelings?"

"Come on, you know how sensitive he is," Sally said. "Can you wait just a little longer? You need to give him another chance."

"I suppose so."

He retreated to the den and picked up the newspaper, going through his routine of looking at the front page and turning to the obituary page. It was a good day since he didn't recognize any of the names.

An hour later, John returned to the kitchen and dialed Bert's number again. Still no answer.

"I think I'm going to walk down to their house," John said. "Care to go with me?"

They put on the jackets they had left on the chair and put the leash on Whiskers to go with them.

Two minutes later they were out the door and turned left to Bert's house. His car was still parked in the driveway as they walked up to the front door. John rang the doorbell and knocked several times.

"They're not home," came a voice from the sidewalk. "Didn't you hear the ambulance a couple hours ago?"

"I'm sorry but we weren't home then," John said. "Ambulance for what?"

"Bert apparently suffered a heart attack," the neighbor said. "He was taken to medical center."

"Have you heard anything from Wilma?" Sally asked.

"Not a word. She said she'd call once she knows something."

John looked at Sally. "I think we'd better go to the hospital."

~ * ~

Bert had been moved to the intensive care unit when they arrived. Wilma was sitting in his room, next to his bed, her hands folded in her lap. She looked frightened, sitting there quietly with mouth drawn. Bert was sleeping. A heart monitor was beeping. He was hooked up to various medical monitors.

When Wilma saw them at the door, she hurried over with her arms out. Sally hugged her while John patted her back. A nurse came to the door and told John and Sally they could only stay for a few minutes.

"We overslept this morning," Wilma said as tears trickled down her plump cheeks. "Bert said he had to plan for your meeting at the church and quickly jumped out of bed. He took a few steps, then collapsed on the floor. He had trouble breathing so I called nine-one-one. The doctor believes he suffered a minor heart attack."

"I hope it wasn't because of the meeting," John said. "I know he's been a bit stressed about it." He knew that was an understatement.

"Oh, no," Wilma said. "The doctor said it was probably because he got out of bed too quickly, that it affected his blood pressure, or something like that. Bert's been having some chest pains lately. He thought it was some kind of angina attack the past week and wouldn't go see the doctor. They may have to put in a stent."

"I'm so sorry about all this," John said.

Bert slightly groaned but was still asleep. Sally walked over to him and squeezed his hand. Moments later the nurse returned and told them they would have to leave.

"Please let us know if we can do anything," Sally said, taking hold of both of Wilma's hands. She hugged her again.

"Don't you worry about anything," John said. "We'll keep a watch on the house."

"I appreciate that," Wilma said, wiping away the tears with the back of her hand. She opened her purse and removed the house keys. "Here, please take these with you. They open the front and side doors."

As they drove back home, John noticed several teens at the entrance to Bert's driveway. He slowed down and looked at them but they seemed oblivious to him, almost as if they were in a trance.

"I'm going to walk over to Bert's house," John said as they got out of the car. "I don't think those kids are doing anything, but I'm not going to take a chance."

John glanced at the teens when he crossed Bert's yard to the front porch. They stared at him as he unlocked the front door and slipped into the house. He checked each room to make sure there were no unwanted occupants and looked at the windows and side door to ensure they were locked.

When he stepped back outside five minutes later, the teens had dispersed. The neighbor came over and John gave him details about Bert's condition and asked him to keep an eye on the house.

"Do you know any of those kids who were here a few minutes ago?" John asked.

"I believe a few of them live down the street and a couple of the others another street over," the neighbor said. "They congregate around here several times a week. Sometimes they're at my driveway. I've never seen anything out of the ordinary with them. I think they're good kids."

"Well, I'm sure you know about the vandalism and break-ins we've had around here the past few months, even Bert's house, so it never hurts to play it safe."

"Oh, don't worry about that. And you can count on me with Neighborhood Watch. Bert's discussed it with me. By the way, my name's George Underwood."

"I'm John Ross. I hope to see you at one of the meetings. It's nice meeting you. By the way, have you noticed anything unusual in the neighborhood?"

"I can't say that I have. My wife and I both work so we don't see a lot other than a few teens here and there.

As John walked back to his house, he encountered Preston standing at the end of his driveway, holding a straw broom.

"How's everything, Preston?" John asked.

"About the same." Preston appeared distracted, looking up the street.

"I saw you with a camera the other day. I didn't know you were a shutterbug."

"Oh, it's just a hobby I took up some time ago. I play around with it once in a while when I get the chance. I'm not sure about the shutterbug label. Maybe a bit more serious about it than that."

John sensed he had insulted his neighbor and moved on to something else in trying to strike up a friendly conversation.

"I understand you're tutoring students, too."

"Huh?"

"I've noticed some teens at your house lately."

"Oh," John said, pursing his mouth. "Yes, I've been helping some young people with English and some other subjects."

"Once a teacher, always a teacher?"

"I suppose you could say that."

"How's Margaret? I haven't seen her in a while."

"She's doing well, thank you. She's currently visiting her sister in Oklahoma on an extended visit, then they're going on a cruise to Alaska."

"I've always wanted to do that."

"Listen, John, I need to be going. I'm expecting a call from Margaret and I need to get back in house."

"Okay, it was nice chatting with you."

"It's mutual," Preston said with a mannered smile, turning to return to his house holding the broom. "Have a nice day."

Sally was talking on the phone at the kitchen bar when John entered through the garage door. He took a soda from the refrigerator and retreated to the den to see if anything was on TV. A few minutes later Sally came in and sat on the couch.

"That was Brody," she said.

"Good news or bad news?" John said, looking upward.

"Hah!"

"Okay, what is it?"

"He's short on cash again and rent is due in a few days. He wants to know if we could spare him twelve hundred dollars."

John didn't reply. He took a few deep breaths because he could feel his temperature rising and didn't want it to reach a boiling point. Or, as Sally would say, get his blood pressure up. He clenched his jaw.

"Did you hear me?"

"Oh, I heard you all right," he said. "How in the hell do you come up short on rent? I wish he would explain that. Did you ask him?"

"He said he had an unexpected medical expense."

"Medical expense? Doesn't he have health insurance?"

"Maybe he hasn't reached his deductible."

"If you want to believe that, Sally," John said, sitting up on the edge of the rocker. "So what did you tell him?"

"I told him I'd have to discuss it with you."

"I'm sure he was excited about that. When does he need the money?"

"He just said in a couple of days."

"Do you think I should pay a visit?"

"I don't know, honey," Sally said with a wary expression. "I don't know what to think anymore."

"Me either."

"So what are we going to do?"

"Give me the check book."

"Are you sure?"

"Yes, I'm sure," John said. "This is the last time."

Thirty

Two weeks later, Clay asked John to meet him at Bailey's Pub. Clay arrived first and ordered a pitcher of beer. He found a semi-quiet place at a table in the rear corner away from the U-shaped bar, jukebox and tiny kitchen. Only about ten patrons were in the place, most of them old regulars sitting around the bar. They were probably retired or out of work.

"This place brings back memories," John said. "It's hardly changed since we used to come here after work. Even some of the same UK memorabilia on the walls."

"I always liked it here." Clay wore a pinstriped suit sans tie, casual for him at midweek. "Nice clientele for the most part. Blue collar to a few white collar. Still do karaoke?"

"As I remember, you were the karaoke fool."

"It's been ages since I did that. I don't think I'd have the nerve to do it again, even with too much to drink."

"Same here."

After the waitress brought their pitcher and frosted mugs, John poured equal amounts with minimal foam on top of each mug.

Clay lifted his mug and offered a toast. "Here's to our long friendship." John raised his mug, tapped it against Clay's.

"Mmmm," John said, taking a sip. "I know why I liked this place so much. So what's going on? Been working on the Grand Canyon trip?"

"Sorta."

"I've been waiting to hear from you. If you've sent an email, it slipped by me. You know I'm not the most tech savvy."

"I haven't." Clay pursed his lips tightly.

"So what's up? Something wrong? Can't make the trip?"

"I want to discuss something else with you if you've got the time."

"Hey, look at me," John said, looking down at his jeans and purple Henley shirt. "I've got all the time in the world. Remember, I'm a member of the pajama club. So what's up, buddy?" His smile left his face when he sensed Clay was getting into something serious.

"Kinda personal."

"Personal?"

"We've known each other for a long time. I've always considered you my best friend."

"Thanks," John said. "I've felt the same toward you. So what is it? Nothing too serious, I hope."

"It's kinda difficult to talk about."

"The easiest way is just to let it out," John said with a concerned look. "That's what Sally tells me all the time."

"I've got the big C. I haven't told many folks, not even my ex or children."

"Cancer? Are you serious?"

"Pretty fuckin' serious." Clay took a big swallow from his mug and paused from a few seconds, looking down at the black tabletop. "Remember that physical we talked about? Well, about week ago I had a colonoscopy and they discovered some masses. I have stage-four cancer. It's spread to part of my liver. I'm going to have surgery in three days."

"Three days?" John paused and took a sip from his mug. "I don't know what to say."

"That's how I felt when the doctor told me the biopsy results, although not quite that mild. More like fuck me."

"Damn. What can I do?"

"I don't suppose there's much you can do unless you know of a cure for cancer. I just had to tell someone. I must admit I'm both stunned and even a little afraid. I've hardly ever been sick a day in my life. You know that. And now this shit. I guess I'm a poster boy for what can happen by putting off a colonoscopy. I should have had one three years ago. If I had, maybe we would be here talking about the big trip instead of this."

"Well, you know I'll do anything I can. Just ask."

"Would you mind being at the hospital when I have the surgery?"

"Sure, but aren't you going to tell your family?"

"I guess I will, but I wanted to make sure there would be someone there. I'm not on the best of terms with them since Marge and I split. I don't have any relatives living close by. My brother lives in San Francisco and my sister's in Miami. And I'm not that close to anyone at the newspaper."

"I think you have more friends than you realize."

"Maybe, but I just want to make sure everything is taken care of. I don't want to start a lot of talk or commotion at the paper. I've already given the doctor and hospital my advance directive, in case there are any problems or complications during the surgery."

"That's a smart thing to do."

"Can you think of anything else?"

"I assume you have a will."

"I updated that after the divorce."

"Clay," John said, "you need to tell your children. Today. They're adults and they can handle it. Regardless of the situation, they deserve to be told. I'm sure they'll tell Marge."

"You're right. I'll do that."

"And you know you can count on me."

Clay reached over and gripped John's hand. "I know. Ain't life a fuckin' bitch?"

After finishing their mugs, they weren't in the mood for more beer, leaving the pitcher half full.

Clay was grim-faced as he waved when they went to their cars. As he reflected on their conversation while driving home, John thought Clay seemed physically weak and pale. A feeling of emptiness spread over him thinking about Clay's condition, much like he felt after Sally's biopsy. He knew Clay's situation was graver. John almost pulled his SUV over to the side of the road as he could sense tears welling in his eyes.

~ * ~

A few minutes after he got home, John put on a sweatshirt to take a walk to help clear his head. Sally had left a note on the refrigerator that she had gone to the supermarket. He left Whiskers whining at the front door.

"Sorry, little fella," he said. "I need some alone time."

John stepped out on the porch and saw Bert clearing off his driveway with a blower and immediately veered to his right. He felt the muscles in his arms and shoulders tensing as he rushed down the sidewalk as if he were late for an appointment. If there were neighbors in their yards, he didn't see them. Everything was like a blur as he was totally focused on Clay's condition.

Sally pulled into the driveway as John was barreling up the street toward the house. She motioned to him with her hand and took one sack of groceries and went through the garage door to the kitchen. He grabbed a bag and a gallon of milk, slammed the trunk shut and went inside. He set the milk in the refrigerator and placed the groceries on the counter without saying a word. As Sally put away the items in the cabinets, she glanced at John sitting at the counter, lost in thought.

"What's up? Run into Bert on your walk?" she asked with a grin.

"Hardly."

His face was buried in his hands. She stopped what she was doing and walked over to him, running a hand over his hair.

"What is it, honey? You look like you've lost a friend."

"I don't know," he said, looking up at her. "Maybe, but I hope not."

"What do you mean?"

"I met Clay this afternoon at Bailey's."

"What brought that on? Change of heart about your trip?"

"I wish."

"What is it then?"

"Cancer."

"Cancer? Who has cancer?"

"Clay's been diagnosed with stage-four colon cancer."

"Oh, my god." Color drained from her face and her mouth opened as she sat across from him.

"He asked me to go the hospital with him on Thursday. That's when he has the surgery."

"How's his family taking it?"

"Would you believe he hasn't told them?"

"You can't be serious, John. He needs to tell them."

"I know but he says he hasn't been on good terms with his children since he divorced Marge."

"But they need to know."

"That's what I told him. I think he was going over to tell them after we left Bailey's."

"I pray everything goes well. He needs all the support he can get now."

"When's the next blood drive?" John asked.

"Next week."

"I think I may go donate."

"Really?"

"With Clay going to have surgery, maybe I can do my part to help someone. I need to do something."

"Let's go out to eat a little later."

"That's not a bad idea."

"Let me get cleaned up."

"Okay," John said. "No hurry. I need to change clothes as well."

An hour later they drove over to O'Malley's neighborhood Irish pub. It wasn't crowded when they arrived since it was a little before happy hour. They found a booth near the entrance. The waitress offered happy hour prices on drinks so they both ordered a Guinness draft and an appetizer of fried zucchini and cheese sticks.

"It really bothers me about Clay," John said. "I've known him for more than twenty years."

"It makes me sad as well," Sally said. "It's just so unexpected."

"I know I've said this before but this growing older stuff really sucks. You have friends get sick, others die, and you start having physical ailments. And like Bert, maybe some physical and mental issues."

"I think Bert has had mental issues for quite a while," Sally said. "I don't think we recognized them until recently."

"You're probably right. But still, I find it depressing to see this happening. At the time you should really start enjoying life, shit begins to hit the fan. Pardon my French."

"You need to accept it."

"I accept it but I don't have to like it."

Thirty-one

John was leaning back in the recliner reading the newspaper when the cell phone rang. Sally turned down the volume on the TV.

"Can you be at the hospital at six a.m.?" Clay asked, sounding more like setting up a meeting to discuss a story than major surgery.

"Of course I'll be there," John said as he rose up and laid the paper on the floor. "What about your family?"

"I told the kids," he said. "I assume they'll be there as well but you never know."

"And Marge?"

"I guess the kids told her. I didn't see any reason for me to do that. And quite frankly, I'd rather for her not to be there. I have enough on my mind without having to deal with her."

"That's your call."

"I did have a good talk with the kids," Clay said. "I took your suggestion and even mentioned the Grand Canyon trip to Rob. He seemed interested. Now I've got to get through this damn surgery."

"How about Rona?"

"There's something she wants to tell me after the surgery."

"Any idea?"

"She's been dating this young man for quite some time now so I'll venture a guess that she's engaged. I'll let her surprise me."

"That's something to look forward to after you come out of surgery."

"Anyway, the doc says the surgery shouldn't last more than two hours unless there are complications."

"Let's hope that doesn't happen. By the way, do you want me to take you to the hospital?"

"I'm good."

"Well, you know I'll take you home if you need me to."

"Sure, but we can talk about that later."

"No problem. See you at the hospital."

After ending the call, Sally asked, "How's he doing?"

"Seems to be handling it very well. Sounds upbeat. And he did tell his kids but not Marge."

"I think he should have done that."

"Done what?"

"Told Marge."

"They're not on good terms. And you know the kids probably told her. They'll keep her posted, if she wants to know."

"I sure hope they did. I know I wouldn't want to find out after the fact."

"I suppose so," John said.

"Why do you say that?"

"Because they're divorced, honey. They've gone their separate ways. It's been four years. They're no longer in love. Not even friends. It's as simple as that."

"But don't you think she'd like to know?"

"Maybe. I don't have a clue. You'd have to ask her."

"Under similar circumstances, wouldn't you want to know about me?"

"Honey, what difference does it make?" John said. "That's strictly hypothetical. Everybody's marriage, separation and divorce, is different. If it makes you feel better, then yes, I'd want to know."

"I'm sorry I asked," Sally said with a hurt expression.

"It would depend on the circumstances. If we had a bitter divorce, then perhaps I wouldn't want to know. But this is silly because we aren't divorced, separated or anything like that."

"And still in love with each other?"

"Yes, sweetheart," John said, reaching over and patting the top of her hand. "You know that. That's never going to change."

Sally smiled and the conversation turned to her garden club activities. John half-heartedly listened, and smiled on occasion but didn't say a word.

Thirty-two

The alarm sounded at four a.m., jarring John out of a deep sleep before he realized he had to be at the hospital at six to be with Clay. He eased out of bed, rubbed his eyes and went to the kitchen. Sally had already set the timer on the coffee maker, and the carafe was already full. As he took a cup from the cabinet, he felt something lick his ankle. He quickly jumped back before looking down and seeing Whiskers.

"You scared me for a second, little fella," John said, reaching down to pet Whiskers on the head. Whiskers went to the door and tapped it twice with his paw. John opened the door and stepped outside while Whiskers padded about twenty feet away in the darkness. Thirty seconds later he returned and followed John into the house. Sally was in the kitchen, wearing a light blue chenille robe, preparing a bowl of food for the dog.

"Are you okay, honey?" Sally asked as John stood with his arm around her shoulders.

"I'll be glad when it's all over. I've been dreading this day. I'm just wanting Clay to get through it and then get on with the rest of his life."

"You know it's going to take a while for him to recover."

"A long time, with chemo and whatever. This is a life-changing event. I hope he's up for it. I'm not so sure I'd be."

"People make adjustments in their lives."

They quickly drank their coffee, got dressed, and departed for the short drive to the hospital. When they arrived at five-fifty, Clay was sitting up in his bed in a white gown, waiting for a nurse to take him down to the surgery unit. Sally gave him a light hug and kissed him on the cheek.

"Everything good?" John asked with a tight smile, tapping him on the shoulder. "Anything you need us to do?"

"Just be there with my kids," he said.

"Will do."

"I thought they'd be here. At least that's what they told me." Clay pressed his lips in a straight line.

"Maybe they overslept," John said, trying to make light of the situation. "You know how they can be."

"Yeah, probably so."

"Anything else you need me to do?"

"You can hang around a bit after I return to my room, if that's not asking too much."

"Of course it's not too much," John said. "We'll stay as long as needed."

"Thanks, friend."

"Anything else?"

"Can I get a rain check on our trip to Grand Canyon? I may not feel up to it for a while." Clay's eyes were suddenly teary as he bit his lower lip.

"Hey, whenever you're ready, that's when we'll head out west. Until then, just get through this surgery and get well. We've got all the time in the world."

"I wish."

Two nurses and an aide entered the room, lowered the head of the bed, and wheeled Clay out. John and Sally smiled as Clay looked at them with sad eyes and pursed lips on the way out. He didn't look like the brash, confident editor who ran the newsroom, as his hair wasn't neatly combed back, there was a day's growth of a beard, and a pallid appearance.

"Let's go to the waiting room," Sally said as John followed her down the hall. Several other people were there, some asleep on the chairs and others in quiet conversations. A moment later two twenty-somethings, a man and woman, entered the room and looked around.

"Mr. Ross?" the man said, lifting a forefinger to get John's attention. "I don't know if you remember me but I'm Clay Rawlings' son, Rob. This is my sister, Rona." John introduced them to Sally and they shook hands.

"How's my dad?" Rob asked. "I'm sorry we're late but my car wouldn't start. I had to call AAA to get a jump."

"He seemed to be okay," John said. "We spoke to him just before you got here. I thought he was rather calm, considering the situation."

"That's good," Rona said. "I feel awful that we're late."

"Why don't we go to the surgery unit and see if they'll let you see him before the surgery?" Sally said.

"You think they'll let us?"

"They might if we tell them what happened."

They hurried out of the waiting room and to the surgery section. John recognized one of the nurses who had been in Clay's room and waved her over to them. Sally explained to her what happened to Rob's car. The nurse disappeared to another room and came back within thirty seconds.

"The doctor said only a minute," she said. "They're about to administer some drugs for pain and anesthesia to put him to sleep. They need to keep everything on schedule."

Rob and Rona followed her into the room. John could see them next to their father, then Rona bending over and kissing Clay on the cheek and Rob patting him on the forearm. When they left the room, both had tears in their eyes. Sally thanked the nurse for allowing the brief visit, and they returned to the waiting area.

"Your dad told me the entire procedure, including prep and recovery, will last about four hours," John said. "Why don't we go to the cafeteria and eat breakfast, or at least get some coffee?"

They followed the black arrows on the gray walls that led them to the cafeteria. It had just opened at six o'clock, and they were the first customers. They each got coffee, which John paid for at the cashier, as the others went to a table.

"Do you expect your mom to show up?" John asked.

"I doubt it," Rona said. "They don't speak anymore."

"Has your dad spoken to you about the surgery?"

"Would you believe he only told us about it three days ago," Rob said. "He said he didn't want to worry us."

"That sounds like your dad," John said.

"But he explained it to us and about the advance directive," said Rona, who pressed two fingers against her mouth and fought back tears.

"That's good," John said. "Sally and I have them as well."

While sitting there, John and Sally learned that Rob was working on his doctorate in classical literature while Rona was involved in an internship program at a newspaper in the South.

"You should know better," John kidded Rona. "Or your dad should have raised you better."

"Probably so," she said, smiling. "But I always enjoyed being at the newspaper and I like to report on things. I can see myself working for several years before moving on to PR or something."

After getting refills of coffee, they walked to the waiting room. Several people were watching TV news, while others were glancing through newspapers and old magazines, or simply talking to each other. John led them to four seats in the corner.

"I sure hope it doesn't take Dad too long to recover from the surgery," Rob said. "He told me that he'd like for us to take a trip somewhere. We haven't done much of that since my parents took us to Disney World when we were children."

"It may take him a while to feel up to doing that," John said, "but that's sure something he'll look forward to. He's mentioned Grand Canyon."

"That would be great," Rob said. "Now we'll have to drag him out of the newspaper."

"He told me a few weeks ago that he wanted to change some things in his life. I think maybe you and Rona had something to do with that."

"Dad promised to visit me once he gets better," Rona said. "He knows one of the editors at the newspaper where I work."

"He can't get away from the newspaper business, can he?" John said. "I guess once it gets in your blood, it never leaves you."

"How about you?" Rob asked.

"Me?"

"Is it still in your blood?"

"A little bit, I suppose. I have coffee with a few old-timers every week or so and it's nice talking to them. But really, once I left the newspaper, I decided to do different things. The only problem is that I'm not sure what they are."

After a while, they didn't say much as they waited for someone to return and tell them that Clay had recovered from the surgery. John's thoughts were on Clay and he was sure it was the same with the others. They watched CNN Headline News on the flat screen TV mounted on the wall but grew tired of seeing the same news stories recycled every thirty minutes. John couldn't help glancing at his watch every few minutes as the minutes dragged by. Rob got up several times and paced back and forth in the hallway. Rona occasionally would send text messages on her smart phone.

Rona looked at Sally and said, "I plan to tell Dad I'm engaged. My fiancé gave me a ring last weekend. I decided to hold off telling

Dad until after his surgery. I didn't want too much on his mind, especially when it comes to wedding plans."

"I'm sure he wouldn't have minded," Sally said. "But that's understandable. I assume he knows your fiancé."

"They met a year or so ago. Michael was a year ahead of me in college. He's now working at the Atlanta paper."

"Well, that's wonderful," Sally said. "I hope we get an invitation to the wedding."

Rona grinned. "Of course."

She beamed as she held up hand to show Sally the engagement ring.

"It's beautiful," Sally said, holding Rona's fingers and leaning to get a closer look.

"It's been longer than four hours," Rob said as he returned to the room. "I hope everything's going okay."

"He's probably in recovery now," John said.

"I just want him to get through this surgery. Everything was so unexpected. I'll feel better about it once I see him in his room."

John saw a nurse enter and look around the room. She finally made eye contact with them and came over to Rob.

"You're the Clay Rawlings family. Right?" she said softly.

"Yes ma'am. I'm his son, and Rona here is his daughter," he said, tilting his head toward his sister. "And Mr. and Mrs. John Ross are his best friends."

"Please come with me down the hall to our post-op room," the nurse said. "Dr. Bingham will be there in a few minutes."

They followed the nurse to a small, pale-yellow room, with blinds closed on the hallway window. They sat at a table and didn't say a word. Dr. Bingham tapped on the door and came in. He wasn't smiling.

He hesitated for a moment, then said, "I'm sorry, but your father didn't survive the surgery." Rona began to cry while Rob was speechless. Sally looked at John and lowered her head into her hands.

"Mr. Rawlings came through the surgery all right but threw several clots in recovery that caused a coronary thrombosis, or heart attack," Dr. Bingham said. "We tried to revive him but he never recovered from it. I'm sorry. We did everything we could do to save him."

Rob put his arm around Rona to console her as they both wept. John gently patted Sally's back. John had trouble comprehending what the doctor had said to them. Trembling slightly, he took several deep breaths to regain his composure.

Sally walked over and wrapped her arms around Rona. John did the same to Rob. The doctor watched silently, then quietly left the room. The nurse remained standing at the door, solemn and silent.

"I can't believe he's gone," Rona said between loud sobs. Sally took tissues from a container on the table and handed them to her. "I wasn't able to tell him about my engagement. There are so many things I wasn't able to tell him."

"He loved you and Rob very much," Sally said quietly as she gently patted her on the back. "I'm sure he realized there was something special between you and Michael."

After sitting in the room for several minutes, and emotionally spent, they got up to leave. The nurse handed several forms to Rob and said they needed to be completed and returned to the hospital by the next day.

"Can we see him?" Rob asked.

The nurse studied him for a moment, then left. She returned several minutes later.

"Please come with me." She led them to a room off from the surgical area. Clay's body was under a white sheet. She opened the sheet, revealing Clay's head. There was a calmness about him. Rona and Rob each gently touched his forehead. John and Sally stood several feet from the table, holding hands and gazing at their departed friend.

"We need to go now," the nurse said as she pulled the sheet back over Clay's head a minute later.

Nothing was said as John and Sally walked Clay's children down the busy corridor to the elevator, and then to Rob's car in the parking lot. John was emotionally and physically drained and he was sure the others felt the same.

"Please call on us anytime," John said after Rob lowered the car window. "Let us know what we can do."

A sad smile spread over Rob's youthful face, then he slowly drove away. John and Sally walked to his SUV, his arm around her shoulders to comfort her and to provide some support for him.

"I still can't believe it," John said as tears filled his eyes. "I just never expected anything like this." He began to sob as he opened the passenger door.

"Oh, honey," Sally said, wiping away tears from her cheeks. "How could anyone expect this?"

"I thought it was a relatively safe surgery. This is so unreal. I feel so empty."

"We all do."

When they got home, they were greeted at the door by Whiskers, who quickly ran to the side of the yard as they waited next to the garage door. The dog scampered back and followed them into the house.

Sally opened a small box of dog treats and put one in Whiskers' mouth. "Good boy."

"Do you want something to eat?" Sally asked as she removed her coat.

"No," John said. "I'm not hungry for anything. Maybe later."

"I'm the same way."

"Why don't we go take a nap? We've been up since four. I know I could use a little sleep. I'm exhausted, and I'm sure you are as well."

They removed only their shoes and got under the bedspread. Sally rested her head on John's shoulders. Whiskers climbed into his bed, and before very long, they had drifted off to sleep.

Thirty-three

There was a large turnout for Clay's funeral. While he didn't have many close friends, he knew a lot of people. Some came out of respect for him and his family, and probably a few who simply wanted to be seen, especially local politicians and other powers-that-be in the community. The pews were full in the Unitarian Church he rarely attended and his open casket drew attention for all to see in front of the pulpit—Clay lying in a dark blue suit and white shirt with a dark rose in the lapel, hair combed neatly back, and eyes and mouth closed tightly. An assortment of large and medium flower arrangements on wire easels lined the walls on each side.

John stared at the casket almost in disbelief, remembering only a few days earlier they were talking about the future. He tried to think good and pleasant thoughts of the times they spent together to keep from crying, but those memories brought tears as well.

Rob and Rona had asked him to deliver the eulogy but he declined, telling them it was too emotional to speak before an audience and he feared he would break down. They told him they understood and got *The Post-Chronicle* publisher Irwin McGill to give the final tribute to their father.

McGill's remarks were mostly impersonal, highlighting Clay's career with a cursory mention of his devotion to his family, which wasn't surprising to those who really knew the newspaper editor because they would say he was married to the profession. Family wasn't a priority. John appreciated the publisher focusing on Clay's leadership and numerous awards but felt somewhat guilty that he didn't have the strength to speak about his close friend. He knew if the roles had been reversed, Clay would have entertained the mourners with embellished praise about his life and career. But again, Clay enjoyed being the center of attention and John didn't like being in the limelight.

John was ready to leave with the family for the cemetery after the service, but the event turned into more of a mini-reunion of old friends and colleagues. He wanted to be with Rob and Rona as Clay's body was lowered to its final resting place. Sally ended up tugging John away from everyone and back to their car to follow the long procession down Main Street to the Lexington Cemetery.

"I hope I didn't come across as rude," she said as they headed to his SUV. "I had to get you out of there."

"I really don't care," John said. "I know those folks didn't mean anything by it but we had to get away. Some folks seem to think it's a social outing. I appreciate you stepping in and rescuing me."

"Did you see Marge in the church?" Sally said of Clay's former wife.

"No, I didn't. If she was, she must have been seated near the rear or the balcony because I didn't see her anywhere near the children."

"That really surprises me if she didn't attend. Although they had their problems the past few years, at least she could have been there out of respect and support for their kids."

"I'm sure she had her reasons if she did, and she discussed it with Rob and Rona."

"I certainly hope so."

When John and Sally arrived at the cemetery, the sun was shining brightly in spite of a breezy coolness in the late fall air. They waited a few minutes on the winding road before getting out of their vehicle and following the pallbearers to the gravesite. A small green tent had been erected that reserved a place for family and relatives to sit on folding chairs in front of the casket for the final words by the minister. John and Sally were offered seats, but they declined so older friends could sit. The minister's words were brief yet consoling before he read several verses, from Romans 14:7-9:

"For none of us lives to himself, and none of us dies to himself. For if we live, we live to the Lord, and if we die, we die to the Lord. So then, whether we live or whether we die, we are the Lord's. For to this end Christ died and lived again, that he might be Lord both of the dead and of the living."

When John and Sally offered final condolences to Rob and Rona, they noticed Marge standing solemnly off to the side, wearing a plain black dress. They hadn't seen her in several years, and almost didn't recognize her. She had gained weight and her hair was cut short near her ears. Her hair had previously been dark brown, but now there was a dark red tint to it.

"Marge?" Sally asked softly as she stepped toward her.

"Hi Sally," Marge said with a faint smile. "I'm glad you were able to be here. And thank you and John for being with the kids at the hospital."

Sally hugged her as John walked over to them and hugged her as well.

"I'm so sorry," he said, his hands on her shoulders. "I can't imagine how difficult this must be for you and the children."

"It's much for harder for them." Marge got teary-eyed. "Clay and I hadn't spoken to each other in quite a while, which I'm sure you know. But it still hurts to have him gone."

"You produced two wonderful children," Sally said. "I'm sure you're very proud of them."

"They were there for me after Clay and I divorced," she said. "It was a difficult time for all of us. But I felt I should be here for them."

"I'm so glad we got to see you," Sally said, gently holding Marge's fingers. "Please don't be such a stranger. We thought of you as much as we did of Clay."

"I appreciate that," she said, stepping away to use a damp and crumpled tissue to wipe tears trickling down her cheeks.

"Let's get together soon for lunch."

Marge nodded without saying a word.

Sally hugged her once more before she and John headed back to their vehicle. John looked back and saw Marge with Rob and Rona, arms around each other.

"I'm glad she showed up," John said. "That has to mean a lot to the kids."

"I would think it would help some with closure," Sally said.

"For all of them."

As they drove away from the wooded cemetery, John glanced at some of the tombstones, monuments and markers that spread on for acres and acres.

"It makes you realize how fragile life is when you go to a funeral," he said. "I never imagined I'd be attending Clay's funeral. It was more like Clay attending mine."

"Life's so unpredictable," she said.

"I couldn't get over Marge. I don't think I would have recognized her if I had seen her somewhere else."

"She used to be so petite."

"Now she's chubby. And her hair."

"I thought her hair looked nice. That's fashionable now," Sally said. "I imagine she gained weight after the divorce. I don't recall her that way when they were together."

"Maybe she had and we just didn't notice."

"Regardless, it was nice to see her. She's still very attractive. I do hope we can get together for lunch."

"You may have to get in touch with her first."

"I didn't get her phone number."

"I can get it from Rob or Rona," John said. "I have their phone numbers and email addresses."

"Speaking of lunch, I'm getting a bit hungry. Do you mind if we get a bite to eat before we go home?"

"I was going to suggest that."

John stopped at an Italian restaurant near their home. They got a carafe of red wine to accompany their garden salads and baked spaghetti.

"I'm so glad our children won't have to deal with what Clay's did," John said.

"What do you mean?"

"Split family. A mom and dad who don't get along. Things like that. It must be difficult for children, regardless of their ages. Probably everyone was involved, trying to placate everybody, which is next to impossible. People taking sides. You know what I mean?"

"We have a good relationship with Brody and Chloe. At least I hope we do," Sally said. "But you never know what can happen years from now. They could have a falling out."

"You think so?"

"I said could, not would. Chloe's got a good head on her shoulders but Brody can be something else. Would you have ever guessed that Clay and Marge would have divorced?"

"Well, to be honest, it didn't surprise me that much."

John poured more wine into Sally's glass, then poured some for himself. The waiter returned with their salads.

"So why did you say that?" Sally asked before taking a small bite.

"Say what?" John said.

"About Clay and Marge, that you weren't surprised they got divorced."

"Clay was a big flirt around town. Quite the urbane guy. You know how some women act around those they see in positions of power. Some are drawn to it. After a while Clay couldn't handle all the temptations. At least that's what I was told. And I believe it probably happened, just from what I observed, but not with gals in the newsroom. I think he kind of drew the line there."

"Why didn't you say anything?"

"What was I to say? It was none of my business."

"I mean to me."

"I never gave it much thought," John said, taking a sip of wine. "And I didn't think you'd care one way or another. It was just gossip and rumors. I never ask you about your friends."

"You never ask because I generally tell you everything. And secondly, you don't know all my friends. You guys must have a secret code of honor when it comes to doing and telling things you shouldn't be doing."

"I don't know about that," he said with a chuckle. "I just don't think most of us care one way or another. It goes on all the time. As long as it didn't affect my job or my family, it was none of my business."

"I can see that in some way."

"And don't you think women are a bit more gossipy?"

"Maybe," she said with a grin. "We're more open about things. Our feelings."

"That's the difference between the sexes."

"Did he ever mention names?"

"Of course not," John said. "He wasn't crude about it."

"That's good to hear."

Their entrées arrived and they took their time eating. More customers came in, slowly filling the restaurant and gradually raising the noise level to the point that it was getting difficult to hear the traditional Italian instrumentals playing in the background.

John poured some more wine, emptying the carafe, after he finished eating. He watched Sally as she took her time with her food.

"Room for dessert?" he asked.

"No, I don't think so," she said. "I'm getting full."

After she finished, they paid the bill and headed home.

"I wonder what Whiskers has been up to?" John said.

"I hope he hasn't been up to no good," Sally said with a quick laugh. "We've been gone for quite a while."

"I guess we'll see once we get there."

Whiskers let out a small bark when they turned the doorknob. When the door opened, he dashed to his favorite spot in the backyard. John watched him while Sally went into the house.

"No accidents," she said when they returned. "He holds it well."

John looked at the telephone. "And no messages."

Sally went to the bedroom and changed into something more comfortable while John fed Whiskers. While the dog was eating, he went to the bedroom and put on some casual slacks, a red University of Louisville sweatshirt, and his walking shoes.

"Are you looking to get shot on your walk wearing that?" Sally asked.

"I'll take my chances," he said with a laugh.

"I think I'll watch TV while you're gone."

"Ready?" he said to Whiskers, holding the leash at the front door. Whiskers bounced over to him and took off down the street in the direction of Bert's house. John knew it would be difficult to change Whiskers' course.

Fortunately, Bert wasn't anywhere to be seen. John briskly picked up the pace and got as far past Bert's house as he could just in case Bert bobbled his head from behind something he had been tending to in the yard.

But two blocks farther down, after turning the corner, there were Bert and Wilma, decked out in matching University of Kentucky blue sweatshirts and blue jeans, apparently on their way back home from taking a walk.

"Good afternoon, folks," John said with a smile.

"Hi John," Wilma said. "We've been seeing you take walks for so long I told Bert we should do the same. It's such good exercise. And the doctor said it's good for his heart."

"I don't know about that," Bert said, raising his eyebrows.

"I agree with Wilma," John said. "It's good for you. Good for the heart. Fresh air. Relieves stress."

"Have you thought about the pollution in the air and all that you're exposed to?"

"The benefits outweigh the negatives," John said, who didn't want to argue the point with his neighbor. "And I don't think the air pollution in our little neighborhood can be that detrimental to one's health."

"Bert always wants to make excuses," Wilma said. "Don't pay him no mind."

"Oh, hush," Bert said, nudging her with his elbow. "What's with the sweatshirt, John?"

"You don't like it?" John asked with a grin.

"Loserville?"

"Now, Bert, you know better than that."

"That's what I've heard some of the UK fans say."

"Oh well, I need to be going if I'm going to get back before it gets dark," John said. "I'll see you guys later."

"Sure," Bert said.

"Oh, by the way, let's get working on the Neighborhood Watch organizational meeting. Call the Methodist church and see when we can have the community room."

"Really?" Bert's eyes brightened. "You want me to do that?"

"We need to get moving on it. Let me know if you have any problems."

"I'm on it," Bert said. Wilma glanced at him with a wide smile.

Thirty-four

"I wonder how Rob, Rona and Marge are doing?" Sally asked as they watched TV in the den two weeks after Clay's funeral.

"I've thought about them as well," John said, turning down the volume. "They have each other for support. I'm sure they're doing well."

"It's never easy to lose a parent, especially when it's so unexpected."

"I still miss my parents," John said. "It's hard to believe Dad was only sixty-three and Mom was sixty-two. They seemed so old at the time. And now we're at that age, even a couple years older."

"I wonder how our kids will be when we die?"

"Well, one of us will die one of these days," John said. "I would hope they could deal with it. We've been a close family so I can't see why anything would change. We have our advance directives, our will which evenly divides the estate, and so on. We even have our burial plots. So it shouldn't be that difficult for them, aside from the emotional aspects."

"You're right. I could never imagine Brody and Chloe getting into some kind of squabble."

"Anything can happen," John said. "We haven't heard from Brody in a few weeks so I assume he's getting his life back in order, knock on wood. I guess that twelve hundred dollars covered him for a while and he's not living on the street as a homeless person. I hope."

"Better watch what you say about Brody."

"I hope I didn't jinx us."

"We'll just turn off our cell phones for a few days."

"You know, I don't believe Sam would interfere with Chloe."

"Sam's been good for Chloe. I had some doubts in the beginning but they've become a supportive couple and good parents to Whitney."

"So how are you going to handle it when I die?" John said.

"Oh, I'll give it a few weeks then go to one of those online dating services for mature adults," Sally said with a laugh.

"Hah, hah."

"Of course, I'm going to be devastated," she added. "We've spent most of our lives together. How will you be if I go first?"

"What's that website address?"

"Funny, funny," she said, throwing a pillow at him.

"I don't know about you, but I'm not in the mood to talk about it now," John said. "It's so close after Clay's passing. There'll be a time and place when we can discuss it. At least we've done all the paperwork. That's the important thing right now."

"And don't forget about our European vacation."

"I almost forgot about that. Let's start planning on that."

"Yes, and focus on living rather than dying."

"Let's go to bed," John said.

"But it's only around eight-thirty," Sally said.

"I didn't say to go to sleep."

"Oh."

John took her hand and led her to the bedroom while Whiskers hopped into his bed. A few minutes later they were out of their clothes and snuggled under the sheets. About fifteen minutes later, after a few giggles and kisses, they fell asleep in each other's arms.

Thirty-five

Bert delivered on setting up the Neighborhood Watch organizational meeting at the Methodist church. More than seventy-five people showed up, even though it was a bone-chilling night. John had picked up materials from Officer Washington at the police department and distributed them to the eager attendees.

"Great job," John said to Bert after they turned off the lights and were ready to go home. "The turnout exceeded my expectations. You put a lot of work into it."

"Wilma gave me a hand. We dropped off flyers at the homes and made calls to a lot of other folks."

"I really appreciate it. But next time, don't feel you have to do it all. This is a neighborhood effort so we need to get more people involved."

"I just wanted to make up for flubbing it last time."

"As I told you then, that's history," John said. "I think we're off to a great start. Now we just have to keep people motivated and looking out for their neighbors."

They got into their cars and returned to their homes. As Bert was walked to the front porch, he noticed a dim light flickering from inside his neighbor George Underwood's house. George had told him the day before that he and his wife wouldn't be able to attend the Neighborhood Watch meeting because of a prior commitment where he worked in Nicholasville.

Bert quietly opened the door to his house, turned off the overhead light and tip-toed to a side window facing the Underwoods' home, pulling back the side of the curtain to see what was going on.

Wilma came into the dark living room. "What are you doing, Bert?"

"Shush!" he said, turning around and placing a finger to his mouth. "I think someone's in George's house." She crept next to him and peeked out the window.

"What are we going to do?" she whispered.

"Maybe I should call John."

"Why don't you call nine-one-one first, then call John?"

Bert took his cell phone from his belt holder and punched in the number. He quietly gave the dispatcher the information on what he thought was going on at his neighbor's house. After ending the call, he called John and gave him the details.

"Just hold tight until the police arrive," John said. "Don't do anything drastic. I'll be down there in a few minutes."

"Will do."

Within minutes a police cruiser pulled up in front of the Underwoods' house. As the officer approached, the inside of the house went dark. Bert watched attentively as the officer went to the front porch, then he walked toward the side of the house.

"What are you doing, Bert?" Wilma asked. "Stay here."

"I'm going to make sure whoever is in there doesn't leave the back way."

"Bert, get back here!"

Bert was out the back door and standing in the middle of the yard when someone bolted out of Underwoods' home and soared over the fence. As he dashed toward the rear of the property, Bert dove at the intruder's legs and pulled him down like a linebacker taking down a tailback. The man began kicking his legs and punching his arms in all directions, trying to break free. Bert refused to let go, clutching the waistline on the burglar's jeans. Moments later, the officer jumped over the fence, and shone his flashlight on the two men grappling in the grass.

"Hold it right there," the officer said as he removed a Glock from the holster. Bert released the man as he rolled over on his back with his hands raised. A few seconds later, the backyard floodlight came on as Wilma stepped out onto the back deck.

"Are you all right, Bert?"

"Yes, dear," he said as he gingerly stood up. Blood ran down his neck and his face was smudged with soil from the altercation. The police turned the intruder over on his stomach and placed handcuffs behind his back. He then called for backup.

John hurried over to Bert's house, with Whiskers slipping out the front door and racing along in his tracks. He noticed a dark figure wearing a skull cap climbing out of a rear side window. When the person's feet hit the ground, John wrapped his arms around his waist, flung him down, and straddled him. Whiskers snarled, inches away from the man's head.

A second cruiser pulled up in front of Underwoods' house. As the officer was making his way to Bert's yard, he heard the tussle on the opposite side of the house. The burglar broke free from John's weakening grasp, only to run directly in front of the policeman's pulled Glock. John followed, slightly hunkered with blood flowing from his injured mouth and scratched forehead.

The street lit up as neighbors streamed out of their houses and dogs began barking as the officers placed the prowlers under arrest and guided them to the back seats of the cruisers with the blue lights pulsating from the rear windows.

John hobbled over to the cruisers, curious to see who was inside. He didn't recognize the intruder Bert had subdued. When he looked inside at the other, it was Bart Summers, wearing a dark skull cap and blood flowing out of each nostril. Whiskers growled and lurched at him as John held the pup back in his arms.

After the police finished questioning Bert and John, they took the young men to the police station to be booked. John learned that the other person was Bart's friend, Derrick, who had always worn dark sunglasses. Hank Summers followed the cruiser, keeping his hands on the steering wheel and apparently avoiding any eye contact with his neighbors. John wondered if Hank considered Bart and Derrick to be illegals. He smiled as he watched the vehicles disappear in the darkness.

Sally rushed over to John and hugged him while Wilma rested her head on Bert's chest. Several neighbors came over and asked what had happened.

Bert was about to say something when John interrupted.

"Folks, this is Neighborhood Watch at work," he said. "And it took the courage of Bert Reliford to make it happen. He saw someone in a neighbor's house and called nine-one-one. Bert is a hero."

Bert was at a loss for words as he blushed and a shy smile emerged on his bruised and swollen face. Wilma kissed him on the cheek. One neighbor began to clap, then another until everyone was applauding the new neighborhood hero.

John handed Whiskers to Sally as they walked across the street to their home. He looked at Preston's house and noticed a light shining in the living room. He wondered why Preston hadn't made an appearance during all the commotion.

Thirty-six

Sally returned from the grocery where she had picked up several items after hearing the TV meteorologist warn that snow was in the forecast in the central Kentucky area.

"I can't believe you did that," John said as she put the items away in the kitchen.

"Better safe than sorry," she said.

"But they're only calling for one or two inches," he said. "How often do we get that much snow in November?"

"Whether we get that much is beside the point. I did it for you."

"Me?"

"Yes, we're about out of those things."

"Well, as long as you did it for me, that's fine," he said.

"I saw Preston while I was there. I thought that was odd."

"Maybe Margaret is still with her sister in Oklahoma?"

"Could be," she said with a slight shrug.

"Did he speak?"

"Nah, only that fake smile."

Whiskers began barking, running from his bed to the front door.

"What in the world is up with him?" Sally asked.

"Let me check." John went to the front window and looked outside. Several police vehicles and a mid-size truck marked with an FBI logo on its side were parked in front of Preston's house. Three officers stood in front of the residence blocking the sidewalk and driveway while others carried boxes inside.

Without putting on a coat, John rushed out to the edge of his yard next to Preston's house, while others came out of their homes to see what was going on. It didn't take long for television news crews and a reporter and photographer from the newspaper to appear at the apparent crime scene.

Minutes later, Preston was escorted to a police cruiser, his hands cuffed behind his back. He kept his head lowered and eyes squinted as if trying to disappear from the cameras.

"What's going on?" John asked one of the reporters.

"Porn bust. Apparently, this guy is allegedly involved in child porn."

"You've got to be kidding me," John said. "He's a retired university professor."

"What do you know about him?" the reporter asked.

"Oh, nothing much, other than him being an educator." John winced about even saying anything to a reporter. "I barely know him."

After Preston was whisked away in a police cruiser, an FBI spokesman came out to the end of the driveway and handed out a brief news release about the arrest. The release didn't say much other than it being an ongoing investigation, and the spokesman offered little additional information. John used the opportunity to sneak back to his house and away from the reporters. He told Sally what was going on and not to answer the door.

Watching from the living room window, John noticed several neighbors being interviewed on camera, no doubt being asked what they knew about Preston and if they ever suspected any criminal activity.

"Are you surprised?" Sally asked.

"Hell yes!" John said. "Who wouldn't be? I never suspected anything like this. I guess that tutoring he was providing was simply a ruse."

"It's hard to believe. He's always acted so proper."

"You know, looking back, I guess it was odd because I saw some kids go into his house. A few weeks ago, I saw him with a camera. But that's about it."

"I wonder if Margaret's involved?" Sally asked.

"I don't have a clue. I guess we'll find out later."

John couldn't resist wanting to know more. He picked up his cell phone and called Eric Walsh at the newspaper to see if he knew anything about the bust.

"Not much," said Eric, who had just returned from a budget meeting. "Apparently there are several folks involved from around town."

"How about his wife?"

"From what I could gather, she left him several months ago. I believe she filed for divorce."

John thanked him for the information and apologized for calling to see what happened.

"I understand," Eric said. "I'd probably do the same thing. I'm sure you'll get more details in tomorrow's paper."

~ * ~

John was up early the next morning, eagerly looking forward to reading about Preston's problems in the local newspaper. When he peered out the front door, six inches of snow lay on the ground and no newspaper was to be found.

After pouring a cup of coffee, he retreated to the study to see if the story had been posted on the newspaper's website. As luck would have it, the website was down for maintenance.

"Have you thought about turning on the television?" Sally asked, standing in the doorway in her robe.

"Uh, forgot about that," John said as he headed to the den. He turned on the TV, but every local channel was reporting on the weather. Then came a report of school closings. John tapped his foot on the floor, waiting for the news coverage.

"I told you it was going to snow," Sally said with a giggle as she ambled to the kitchen to get a cup of coffee.

"Thanks for reminding me." John threw up his arms when the station began listing closings or delayed openings at government buildings, university classes, church functions, and practically everything under the snow-filled clouds.

After several minutes, the morning anchor provided details on Preston's arrest, noting it also involved a lawyer, local official, and a high school teacher. The reporter said the sting investigation had been going on for several months and more arrests were likely in the coming days.

"Man, that's hard to believe," John said as he turned down the volume when the meteorologist came back on the screen. "It only goes to show that you don't have a clue about who's involved in that kind of stuff."

"I hope it's nobody else in our neighborhood," Sally said.

"I've never seen anyone else around his house other than some kids. I remember seeing one of the boys who helped me move that box that time when I injured my back. I believe his name was Trace. I wonder if he was a victim?"

"I wouldn't be surprised. What other reason would he be at Preston's house?"

"Makes me sick."

Thirty-seven

Five days later, after the snow melted and vanished from the landscape, John received a call from *The Post-Chronicle's* human resources office, asking him to drop by to sign some paperwork relating to his retirement benefits.

John parked in a visitor's space in the front parking lot rather than the one for employees in the rear. When he walked into the building, there was a paper at the front desk for him to sign in. Since he had seldom come in that way, the security and employees didn't recognize him. They called for a person in human resources to come down and get him. He was given a temporary badge to wear.

Cammie, an HR representative, was there within a minute and took John to their department on the second floor. He was taken to a small office where the person opened a folder, and following a brief explanation of the contents, John signed the requested paperwork.

"Is it okay if I drop by the newsroom and say hi to a few folks?" John asked. "This is my first time back since I left a few months ago."

"Oh, I don't know," she said, with furrowed brows and pursed lips. "We're not supposed to let people wander about the building."

"I don't plan to wander. I worked here for nearly thirty years. I was the sports editor. I just wanted to see some friends before I left. But if that's a problem, so be it."

"I'll be right back," Cammie said with a programmed smile as she got up from her desk and left the room.

Less than a minute later, she returned with the same smile plastered on her face.

"My boss said it would be okay," she said. "Do you know where the newsroom is?"

"Unless they've moved in the past few months, I should be fine."

Cammie led him to the elevator. "Just be sure and turn in your badge at the front desk when you leave, Mr. Ross. Have a nice day."

"Thanks, and the same to you." John got on the elevator and pushed the button to the fourth floor.

As he stepped out, he noticed a few reporters busy at their workstations, either talking on phones or typing on computers. He saw his old office with Eric Walsh's nameplate on the outside panel.

John knocked on the door and peeked inside. Eric was reading copy on his monitor. "What do you want?" he said without turning around.

"Just paying a short visit," John said.

Eric turned around in his chair, surprised and slightly red-faced, then got up and shook John's hand.

"Sorry, I was so wrapped up in editing a story," Eric said. "It's great to see you. How are things?"

"Can't complain," John said, who then explained why he was at the newspaper.

"I've got a budget meeting coming up in a few minutes."

"No problem. I just want to say 'hi' and see how things are going."

"Pretty good, I hope."

"Well, the section looks good," John said with a smile. "You're doing a great job."

"Thanks, John," Eric said, glancing at his watch. "I need to get to the meeting. Give me a call the next time you're around and we can do lunch."

"I'll do that. By the way, who's the new editor?"

"Bonnie Rosenberg. She doesn't start until next week. She's from one of the sister papers out west. Need to run." Eric grabbed a clipboard and hurried to the budget meeting.

John walked through the newsroom and spoke to several copyeditors and reporters. Most of the editors were clustered in the budget meeting. He was back at the elevator in less than fifteen minutes.

"What are you doing here?"

John looked to his left and saw Fred Akers sitting in a wheelchair with an oxygen tube running to his nose. He barely recognized him.

"Doing some paperwork for the HR folks," John said as he walked over and tapped his shoulder. "You?"

"Still working."

"Are you serious?"

"Got a few more months to put in before I can fully retire with all my benefits."

"So why the wheelchair and oxygen?"

"COPD. I'm sure you've heard about it."

"Yep."

"That must be some neighborhood you live in," Fred said. "I worked on that story about the porn prof."

"It's been interesting. Anything else coming up about it?"

"This'll be hot off the presses in the morning so don't peep a word to anyone, but it was his wife who blew the whistle on him."

"You've got my word."

"She notified the FBI and it took them a few months to investigate and find those other pervs."

"Thanks for the info, Fred," John said. "Where are you headed now?"

"Smoke break out front."

John couldn't suppress a laugh. "Take care."

"Oh, I will," Eric said as he turned and wheeled himself to the front entrance.

John turned in his badge at the front desk and went to his SUV. One thing struck him as being odd was that not a single person mentioned Clay Rawlings, a man who had spent more than twenty years of his life at the newspaper.

"Clay was right. Out of sight, out of mind," he said before pulling out of the parking space.

Thirty-eight

John was in the process of helping Sally go through some items in the bedroom closet to be given to charities when the doorbell rang. Whiskers roused from his mid-morning nap and barked three times before John shushed him to be quiet.

"I wonder who that can be," said Sally, who was sitting on the floor sorting through some old clothes.

"I guess we'll find out," John said, as he got up from the side of the bed and left the room.

"Mr. Ross?" the man said when John opened the front door. "I'm not sure if you remember me. Bernie Shipley's son."

"Oh, yes," John said with a warm smile. "Please come in. Have a seat on the couch."

"I hope you don't mind me dropping by," Bernard said as he sat down with his hands at his side.

"No problem." John closed the door and sat on the accent chair. "How's your mother?"

"She's doing well, thank you. It was a difficult period for us but she's getting her life back in order."

"That's great. I think of your dad every time I go to the park."

"The reason I'm here is that I heard from a police detective yesterday that there has been a break in my dad's case."

"Really?" John said as he eased to the front edge of the chair. "What have they found?"

"They did find fingerprints on the gun that was found in the pond."

"I wasn't aware they could do that."

"Under the right circumstances, they can. It also helped that the gun was retrieved so soon after my dad's assault."

"So have they traced it?"

"That's the reason I'm here," Bernard said, opening his eyes wider. "Do you know a Derrick Ruter?"

"Derrick?" John squinted as he pondered the name. "I'm not sure. Let me think on it some more."

"There was a gun theft from a car in your neighborhood a while back. Do you know Rufus Martin?"

"Of course, Rufus lives down the street. In fact, I was the person who reported it to the police."

"The police dusted for fingerprints on the glove compartment that night and discovered a few days ago that the prints matched the ones found on the gun."

"So who is this Derrick?"

"Well, there was another break-in at one of your neighbors, I believe a Mr. Underwood, a week or so ago. One of the burglars was Derrick Ruter."

"Oh, damn!" John stood and raised his hands in the air. "Of course, I know who he is. I was over there that evening at George Underwood's house. He's a friend of Bart Summers, who was also arrested that night. Bart lives down the street... Hank Summers' son."

"That's what the police have right now."

"Do they know who assaulted your dad with the gun?"

"Police say the men have been pointing fingers at each other during interrogations."

"So at least they know they were involved?"

"My guess is they'll both be charged with my dad's murder, regardless of who struck him in the head with the gun."

"That's still hard to believe," John said with a sigh. "We've known the Summers boy since he was in grade school. My wife was his teacher."

"Oh, there's one more thing," Bernard said. "Apparently Bart and Derrick have been involved in other break-ins in this area."

"That probably includes my house," John said, taking a deep breath and slowly exhaling.

Bernard rose from the couch. "Again, I apologize for dropping by uninvited but I thought you'd like to know."

John took two steps toward him and shook his hand. "I appreciate it very much."

After Bernard left, Sally came to the doorway. "I heard what he told you. It's just hard to believe."

"I know," John said. "I guess you really never know your neighbors. First, there was Preston and now Bart Summers."

They went to the kitchen and John sat at the counter while Sally poured two cups of coffee. She brought the coffee over and sat across from him. Whiskers padded into the room and went to his water bowl.

"Now I know why Whiskers got so excited every time he was around Bart," John said.

"I don't understand."

"If Bart and his lowlife buddy robbed our house, then it was Bart who nearly killed Whiskers. Since then, every time we've come in contact with Bart on our walks, and even at the break-in at George Underwood's house, Whiskers would go ballistic when he saw him."

Whiskers looked up at him when he heard his name, then started nibbling on a rawhide bone.

"I didn't realize that," Sally said, shaking her head in disbelief. "That's so awful. Poor Whiskers."

Whiskers glanced up again.

~ * ~

The next day, Bart Summers and Derrick Ruter were charged with murder in the death of Bernard Shipley. During interrogation, Derrick told police that Bart had been the one who viciously pistol-whipped Mr. Shipley and that he took the weapon from him and tossed it into the pond. Bart's attorney entered a not guilty plea during the arraignment.

Three days after the court appearance, while on his daily walk with Whiskers, John noticed a "For Sale" in the front yard of Hank Summers' house. Two weeks later it was sold.

~ * ~

Bert and Wilma were sitting in the kitchen eating breakfast when John knocked on their side door at six-thirty. Wilma hurried from the table and opened the door to let John in.

"Coffee still hot?" John asked as he stepped inside.

"Have a seat," Bert said as he spread grape jelly on a slice of toast. "Wilma, get our friend some coffee."

John sat at the same table, holding a binder. "I need your help on a project."

"Neighborhood Watch?" Bert asked, taking a bite of the toast.

"Sort of," John said as Wilma carefully set the coffee in front of him along with containers of creamer and sugar. She returned to her seat across from Bert and nibbled on a piece of bacon.

"What is it?"

"A petition." John opened the binder. "I need your assistance gathering signatures from the neighborhood. Can you help?"

"Of course we can," Wilma said before Bert could reply.

"What's it for?" Bert glanced at her with a furrowed brow.

"Remember Bernard Shipley, the guy who died from an assault at the park a few months ago?"

"Sure do," Bert said. "The Army veteran. Hank Summers' boy and some other guy were involved in it. So what do you want to petition? Death penalty or something?"

John took a sip of his coffee and cleared his throat. "This is to rename Garden Ridge Park to Bernard Shipley Memorial Park. The old man took a lot of pride in the park and tried to keep it safe and clean for everyone. I'd like to gather as many signatures as possible and submit it to the city council."

"Count me in," Bert said with a smile. He took the binder from John and opened it. "Give me a pen, Wilma."

Wilma got up, went to the drawer and took out a pen and handed it to her husband. He pushed back his plate and signed the petition, then gave it to Wilma for her to sign.

"That's a start," John said with a grin.

"We'll get on it later this morning," Bert said as he wiped his hands with a napkin. Wilma reached over and knocked away a few breadcrumbs from the corner of his mouth. He gave her an irritated expression. John sensed that was a good cue for him to leave.

"Thanks again," John said as he pushed his chair back. "Drop it by the house in the next few days."

John noticed a "For Sale" sign in front of Preston's house as he walked across the street. Preston's trial would be coming up in a few months if there weren't a plea bargain in the works. He wouldn't be surprised.

Looking down the street, John saw Georgina in front of her house wearing her bright yellow bonnet and blue overalls. He was curious to see what she was doing since the flowers had disappeared after the freak snowfall and the trees along the streets had shed nearly all their leaves.

"Mornin', Georgina," he said as he walked closer to her. She turned on her stool and smiled.

"Hi, Mr. Ross," she said. "Another beautiful day."

John felt a chilly breeze against his face and looked up at the gray sky. "Beautiful day?"

"Oh, yes," she said as her green eyes sparkled from the tiny crow's feet wrinkles. "Every day when I open my eyes and get out of bed is a beautiful day."

"I suppose so," John said, stroking the beard on his chin. "What are you planting?"

"Tulip bulbs."

"For next spring?"

"It's something I can do today to make my future beautiful as well."

John smiled. *Well said*, he thought.

Meet Michael Embry

Michael Embry is the author of seven novels, three nonfiction sports books, and a short-story collection. He spent more than 30 years in the news media as a sportswriter, news reporter and editor, working at two newspapers, a national news service, and a magazine, and nearly six years as a public information officer in state government. He is listed in *Who's Who in America*.

Embry lives in Frankfort, Ky., with his wife, Mary, and two chorkie dogs, Bailey and Belle. Among his interests are travel, hiking, writing, reading, music, and family activities, especially those involving his three granddaughters—Lily, Lola and Ellie.

Other Works from the Pen of Michael Embry

Shooting Star - Jesse Christopher finds that it's not easy being the new kid in school, no matter how well you play basketball. When discovered shooting hoops at a school playground by a high school coach, Jesse seems to be the missing piece to the puzzle for a team that aspires to win the Kentucky state championship.

But Jesse faces an array of problems in his new environment as he tries to make friends in the classroom and become part of the school's close-knit basketball team. Can Jesse overcome the obstacles and lead his team to a state high school basketball title?

A Confidential Man - Sports columnist Chase Elliott has earned a reputation around the newsroom of being a person that others can confide their deepest problems. What happens when someone goes over the line? And what if a fellow worker dies from mysterious circumstances?

Elliott tries to deal with all the rumors and innuendos circulating around the newsroom while coming to terms with his own sense of trustworthiness and high ethical standards. Can he discover the truth without betraying confidences?

Foolish Is the Heart - Brandon Wilkes is a 45-year-old sports columnist who has never settled down to the point of marriage. At first it was his career that caused him to go the bachelor route. He became a respected and successful sportswriter. As he grew older, he seemed content to be single the remainder of his life. That's not to say that he didn't have relationships or that women didn't pursue him. He just didn't want to make a permanent commitment to a woman.

He was content with the way things had been in his life. Going to work, meeting friends at the local pub and covering various sports events for Kentucky Sports Weekly. His easy-going lifestyle undergoes changes as some big events happen in his personal and professional life. Brandon tries to come to terms with the direction his life is heading and trying to deal with those things he believes to be important.

A Long Highway - Micah Stewart is in the throes of a mid-life crisis. He's bored with his job as a sportswriter. While he maintains a good relationship with his ex-wife and children, he feels unfulfilled in many areas of his life.

A random act of violence in the workplace forces Micah to hit the road in search of meaning to his life. Will he find enlightenment? Can he find happiness again? Can he find contentment at the end of the long highway?

The Touch - Blake Williams is a widower trying to raise three children. He has been careful to open his heart to another woman, fearful of the pain he might suffer again. His attention is focused on providing a loving home for his kids.

Carla Reeves is involved in an abusive relationship. She doesn't know who to turn to for advice. She meets Blake by chance on several occasions and the relationship evolves into much than casual interest in each other.

The Bully List - Dealing with bullies isn't an easy thing to do. My parents tell me to ignore or avoid them. But it seems if you ignore them, it gets under their skin and they want to bully you even more. And that makes it's even harder to avoid them. Does that make sense?

My teachers seem to be too busy with other things when it comes to bullies. I guess they have so many students they can't be bothered by it all. They say they want to treat everybody the same.

I think I understand that but it doesn't always work out so well. I even wonder if some of the teachers aren't scared of bullies.

I'm not the only one who gets bullied. I have some friends who have to deal with bullies, too. Sometimes we hang out together in hopes that the bullies will leave us alone. It works most of the time unless there are some bullies together.

Dear reader,

I hope you've enjoyed reading this tale of the problems one man
faced when retirement knocked on his door.

Your opinion is valuable to other
readers like you,
who may be looking for books like mine.

Please consider taking a few minutes to post a review, however
brief,
on the site where you purchased this book
or on the Wings ePress web page.

You may also want to visit my author page
at the Wings' website, where you can find
all the other books in my series.

Thank you!

Michael Embry

Visit Our Website

*For The Full Inventory
Of Quality Books:*

<u>*Wings ePress, Inc*</u>

*Quality trade paperbacks and downloads
in multiple formats,
in genres ranging from light romantic comedy to general
fiction and horror.
Wings has something for every reader's taste.
Visit the website, then bookmark it.*
We add new titles each month!

*Wings ePress, Inc.
3000 N. Rock Road
Newton, KS 67114*